TREWLEY AND STONE MYSTERIES
BY SARAH J. MASON

Murder in the Maze
The village of Redingote anticipated the usual misbehavior during the annual summer fête. But no one expected murder . . .

Frozen Stiff
The new management consultant at Tesbury's grocery chain has annoyed a lot of people with his meddling. Now he's made someone angry enough to commit murder . . .

Corpse in the Kitchen
She was baking bread—until an unknown party turned the staff of life into the stuff of death . . . and choked her with a wad of raw dough. Now the heat is on Trewley and Stone . . .

Dying Breath
Dr. Holbrook was a brilliant scientist—until somebody made him the guinea pig for an experiment in murder . . .

MORE MYSTERIES FROM THE
BERKLEY PUBLISHING GROUP . . .

THE HERON CARVIC MISS SEETON MYSTERIES: Retired art teacher Miss Seeton steps in where Scotland Yard stumbles. "A most beguiling protagonist!"
—New York Times

by Heron Carvic

MISS SEETON SINGS

MISS SEETON DRAWS THE LINE

WITCH MISS SEETON

PICTURE MISS SEETON

ODDS ON MISS SEETON

by Hampton Charles

ADVANTAGE MISS SEETON

MISS SEETON AT THE HELM

MISS SEETON, BY APPOINTMENT

by Hamilton Crane

HANDS UP, MISS SEETON

MISS SEETON CRACKS THE CASE

MISS SEETON PAINTS THE TOWN

MISS SEETON BY MOONLIGHT

MISS SEETON ROCKS THE CRADLE

MISS SEETON GOES TO BAT

MISS SEETON PLANTS SUSPICION

STARRING MISS SEETON

MISS SEETON UNDERCOVER

SISTERS IN CRIME: Criminally entertaining short stories from the top women of mystery and suspense. "Excellent!"
—Newsweek

edited by Marilyn Wallace

SISTERS IN CRIME

SISTERS IN CRIME 2

SISTERS IN CRIME 3

SISTERS IN CRIME 4

SISTERS IN CRIME 5

KATE SHUGAK MYSTERIES: A former D.A. solves crimes in the far Alaska north . . .

by Dana Stabenow

A COLD DAY FOR MURDER

DEAD IN THE WATER

A FATAL THAW

A COLD-BLOODED BUSINESS

DOG LOVERS' MYSTERIES STARRING HOLLY WINTER: With her Alaskan malamute Rowdy, Holly dogs the trails of dangerous criminals. "A gifted and original writer."
—Carolyn G. Hart

by Susan Conant

A NEW LEASH ON DEATH

DEAD AND DOGGONE

A BITE OF DEATH

PAWS BEFORE DYING

MELISSA CRAIG MYSTERIES: She writes mystery novels—and investigates crimes when life mirrors art. "Splendidly lively."
—Publishing News

by Betty Rowlands

A LITTLE GENTLE SLEUTHING

FINISHING TOUCH

TREWLEY AND STONE MYSTERIES: Even the coziest English villages have criminal secrets . . . but fortunately, they also have Detectives Trewley and Stone to dig them up!

by Sarah J. Mason

MURDER IN THE MAZE

FROZEN STIFF

CORPSE IN THE KITCHEN

DYING BREATH

DYING BREATH

Sarah J. Mason

BERKLEY PRIME CRIME, NEW YORK

This book is a Berkley Prime Crime original edition,
and has never been previously published.

DYING BREATH

A Berkley Prime Crime Book / published by arrangement with
the author

PRINTING HISTORY
Berkley Prime Crime edition / June 1994

ISBN: 0-425-14245-0

Berkley Prime Crime Books are published by
The Berkley Publishing Group,
200 Madison Avenue, New York, NY 10016.
The name BERKLEY PRIME CRIME and the BERKLEY PRIME CRIME
design are trademarks of Berkley Publishing Corporation.

PRINTED IN THE UNITED STATES OF AMERICA

10 9 8 7 6 5 4 3 2 1

THIS BOOK IS FOR W.G.W.,
MY FAVOURITE METALLURGIST

One

It was the first week in November, and the first morning of winter. Cat-footed fog, icy cold, had crept during the night from its autumnal lair to enfold the sleeping town of Allingham in a chilly embrace. Even dawn had failed to repel the silent intruder, which swirled still about trees and walls, and drifted into quiet side streets, and slowly spiralled upwards to where the sun hung heavy in a pewter sky, too feeble to melt the icy patches on roofs and roads.

Hearty cotton-wool puffs periodic along one particular road punctuated the progress of Mrs. Mint on her bicycle. She kept her head down, watchful for potholes and frozen puddles; she wore her hat pinned farther back than usual. Its cherries bobbed in rhythm with her energetic pedalling, and a cheerful clanking kept time at her handlebars, from which depended a capacious pink linen bag bulging with anonymous and mysterious shapes.

Whining along in her wake the milk-float, accompanied by its own, more resonant clankings, was bound to catch the attention of Mrs. Mint. Or so its driver thought: but her mind was evidently much abstracted—almost as much as that of the milkman—for she suddenly pulled out towards the middle of the road, making to turn right, without either looking behind her or giving any signal.

"Hell!" The milkman jerked his thoughts from the buxom blonde awaiting him, and his steering wheel sharply to the left. "Bugger!" He skidded in a nervous parabola around the erratic cyclist, crunchingly close to the cars parked alongside the kerb, and came—saved at the final moment by a providential pothole—shuddering to a halt. "Oy, you!" And he climbed from his cab to give Mrs. Mint a selection of his views on her birth, ancestry, and moral character.

"You blanking old basket! Why cantcher watch where the bloody hell yer going? You could've bin killed—blind as a bat and twice as daft!"

Mrs. Mint had dismounted, to manoeuvre herself behind the frame of her heavy bicycle, from where she felt sufficiently safe to retaliate. "Watch where I'm going? I like that—it's *you* as oughter be watching, coming up so fast that way, setting me all off balance. You're a downright menace! They oughter take your licence off of you before you kill someone, they really ought!"

"And they oughter take yer bike off of you, *and* getcher eyes tested, *and* teach you how to signal proper . . ."

They squabbled uselessly for a while, but it was far too cold to stand hurling insults for long. Warmed by the lively little exchange, they parted, glowing and glowering—Mrs. Mint in a half-trot, pushing her bike towards the nearby house where she "obliged" three days a week; her adversary back to his float, towards an obliging lady of quite a different sort.

Mrs. Mint leaned her bicycle against the garden wall, and shut the gate, which was always temperamental, firmly behind her—let the milkman open it again for himself, with his hands full of bottles! With a toss of her head to set her cherries all a-bounce, she trotted up the front path and climbed the few steps to the porch, where she bent automatically to lift the third flowerpot from the left.

She reached beneath it, and frowned. "That's funny."

She fumbled again, and again retrieved an empty hand. Her black eyes darted along the row, counting out loud. No, third from the left all right, same as usual . . .

Only it wasn't usual for the key not to be there.

She beat a sharp tattoo on the knocker. No reply. She tried the handle, then rattled the door with a bony shoulder—nothing moved. She clicked her tongue, shook a puzzled head, then darted down to raise the eight flowerpots one by one, peering carefully underneath each in turn.

Still nothing. Tutting at the aggressively cheerful sound of the milkman's distant whistle, she knocked once more— waited—rang the bell—waited; then hurried down the steps, along the gravel path at the side of the house, and round to the kitchen door.

She tried the handle. This door, too, was locked. She thumped with an insistent fist—and still had no reply.

"He's never skipped! Not owing me two days' money, he can't have," she muttered, as she peeped on tiptoe through the kitchen window. "No," as she made out the neat array of crockery on the dresser. "No, he's just forgot to leave the key for me, that's what—and me coming all the way here in this weather, too! I'll make sure as I'm paid for my time, whether I went inside the place or no—and he'd better not try telling me he can't afford it, or else!"

But a frown creased her forehead as she returned to the front of the house. It was rare—it was unheard-of—for Dr. Holbrook to forget to leave his key. In the four years she'd been doing for him, ever since his wife, poor soul, had passed on, not once could she remember such a thing happening. There the key was, and there, she'd been led by the doctor to understand, it would always be.

The sound of a sharp dispute, shrill voice and baritone snarl, came from the house next-door-but-one. Mrs. Mint, scenting scandal, stretched herself up to peer over the intervening hedges, and caught the glaring eye of the milkman as he stamped back down the path. In a bustle of embarrassment, she turned away, rapping and ringing again at the doctor's unyielding door . . .

And was staring, helpless and perplexed, about her, when she was hailed from the neighbouring garden.

"Got trouble too, have yer?" The milkman spoke in tones of glum sympathy: the husband of his buxom blonde had worked overtime this week, and she'd been able to settle her bill in cash. "What's up? Locked yer aht, has he?"

The earlier disagreement was clearly forgotten. "Always leaves me the key, he does," fretted Mrs. Mint. "Not once has he missed—not till today, first time ever—and how I'm supposed to get in to do my work I just don't know!"

"Leave a note?" The milkman screwed up his eyes against the foggy glare to peer into Dr. Holbrook's porch. "No message or nothing—yer sure?"

"Would I be standing here like a dummy if there was?" Mrs. Mint was careful to avoid the reply direct: she could neither read nor write beyond her own name, and, while her employer knew this for purely practical reasons, there was certainly no need for anyone else to be told. "So I ask you—what am I to do now? Go back home, I suppose, and miss my morning's work, and it's not right, when I need the money—and with him being so careful like he is, I'm going to have a real hard job making him pay for my time today, I know." Mrs. Mint contrived to wring her hands. "Oh, it's a wicked world! I thought he'd treat me better than this, the old skinflint!"

By now the milkman had deserted his post and hurried up the path to join her. "Look," he said, "there could be summat wrong—the curtains're still shut, see? We're told to watch aht on our rounds for that sort of thing, old folk living by theirselves not taking in bottles and stuff—two last winter, I saved, with hypothermia."

"So they are, and all." Mrs. Mint stared at the blank-eyed look of the downstairs rooms. "Fancy me not noticing! So you reckon he could be ill, do you?"

The milkman shrugged. "Could be—after all, it was the first real cold night of the year, weren't it? And proper brass monkey weather, too. Maybe he's bin took bad, fell over in the dark and lying inside now half froze to death. How did he seem yesterday—off-colour at all? Sickening for anything?"

"You know I only work every other day, for goodness' sake. Monday, Wednesday and Friday's my days, so, with seeing how yesterday was Thursday . . ."

"All right, Ma. Point taken. But . . ." The expert gazed thoughtfully at the front step. "The milk's gone from yesterday, so he can't've bin took bad then—and there's no empties out for today. So, if he *is* ill, it'll be just for the one night . . ."

"And what if he is?" demanded Mrs. Mint, happy now for the decision-making to rest in more capable hands.

The milkman frowned. "Best thing then's for us to get in there and find out, poor old basket."

"Oh? And just how," scoffed Mrs. Mint, "are we going to do that, may I ask? With no key, and the kitchen door likely bolted from the inside, as well!"

With a wink, the milkman laid a finger along the side of his nose. "Oh, you learn a fair number of useful things in my job. Just keep them beady eyes of yours shut a moment, will yer, if yer the sort as shocks easy . . ." And from his pocket he produced a slim but sturdy penknife, which he extended with one flick of his thumbnail. "Lucky this lock ain't a Chubb," he muttered, to Mrs. Mint's horror, as he poked the steel blade into the keyhole, fiddled, pressed and strained for a while—until, with a triumphant grunt, he pushed the front door ajar.

"Clever stuff, eh? If you know whatcher doing, that is. These old locks, a kid could break into every house in this road—just a knife or a hairpin or summat like that . . ."

He was chattering nervously, and Mrs. Mint was paying him closer attention than he deserved, as they both hesitated, staring at each other doubtfully. It was Mrs. Mint who, in the end, broke the awkward silence.

"Knowing what I know now," she said with a sniff, as she gathered her big pink bag into her protective clutches, "I'd say you ain't never to be trusted no more with nothing! But—well, come on in. Might as well, only watch out if—"

"Pheewooooch!" The milkman, who had taken one step inside, jumped back, cannoning into Mrs. Mint where she still hovered on the doorstep. "Gas!"

"It's a leak!" Mrs. Mint, sniffing again, began to cough. "A leak—he'll be dead in his bed, poor man, and us the ones to find him! Whatever shall we do?"

"Try the kitchen," he suggested, swinging the door to and fro on its hinges. "Get up a draught, see? Clear summer this stink—get the back door open. How about gas fires, cookers, that sorter thing?"

"Cooking's all electric," coughed Mrs. Mint, clinging to her bag as the only safe thing in this topsy-turvy world. "But there's gas fires all over the house—not that he ever uses more'n the downstairs, so far as I know. You'd think he'd feel the cold with being so thin, but he never."

"You go and open the back door, Ma," said the milkman, still swinging. "I'll check the rooms along the hall—we can look upstairs later—and I'll get them windows open as I go along. Right?"

Mrs. Mint scurried towards the kitchen, then stopped. "Oh! Come quick—it's awful strong here, by the study!" She pointed a wavering finger, and coughed once more.

"Don't waste time talking. Let's get it open!" As he spoke, the milkman bypassed several half-open doors to rush straight to the end of the hall. He tried the handle. It was locked. "His study, you say?"

"Oh dear, yes—poor Dr. Holbrook!"

"He likely to be inside?"

"Worked in there every night—regular as clockwork, he is . . ." Mrs. Mint seemed unable to decide whether to speak of her employer in the past or present tense. She gave an unhappy sniff, and coughed hackingly.

"Oy—Holbrook! Dr. Holbrook—you in there? Are you all right?"

But to the milkman's frantic shouts there came no answer from behind the study door.

He shook his head. "Better break in, I'm afraid. Can't say I like the looker this—he's had all night, from the smell. . . . Here, you go on and get that other door open, will yer? And then get yerself aht in the fresh air—I'll deal with this lot—"

"What? With all the poor doctor's papers inside?" She failed to grasp that he had, for once, her best interests at heart. "Worth a fortune, they are—and me not to be here keeping an eye on you? Get away!"

"Then *you* get away," he said, as with one cool look he estimated how much effort it would take. "Stand right back—now, then!" And, with a quick run and a mighty heave of his shoulder, he worked off some of his frustration in a stalwart assault on Dr. Holbrook's study door.

At the third crashing blow, it buckled; at the fourth, it gave way completely. A powerful wave of gas emerged as the milkman, on top of the door, tumbled into the room: and Mrs. Mint peered cautiously past him.

The curtains were closed; the desk lamp still burned; but, though the gas fire was hissing loudly, it sported no flickering flame. The study was its normal, shadowy, studiously cluttered self . . .

Apart from the slumped, spare, white-haired form seated in front of the desk—a form whose forehead drooped forward on scattered papers, whose hands hung swollen at its sides.

"It's him!" screeched the cleaning lady, dropping her pink bag to clasp her hands in anguish. "Dr. Holbrook—Dr. Holbrook!" Oblivious of the clattering tools of her trade, she rushed across to shake him by the shoulder. The milkman, more realistic, held his breath, picked himself up from the floor, and ran to turn off the gas fire and deal with the windows.

Mrs. Mint, meanwhile, opened her mouth to scream again . . . and found out, the hard way, that rooms filled with gas contain no oxygen. As the milkman hurried from the first window to the second, she fell heavily into his arms.

It was true that he'd been expecting some close female companionship that milk-round payday morning—but he had never dreamed of anything like this. . . .

TWO

ALLINGHAM ALLOYS, ON the High Road Industrial Estate, was as yet unaware of the recent loss of one of its top employees. Life for the living continued as usual: late arrivals, fog-delayed and irritable, hurried past the security man on the main gate with none of the normal cheerful backchat. When the latecomers reached their designated territory, more punctual persons mocked their tardy colleagues, passing pointed comments on starting the weekend a day early, on lacking the foresight to keep the battery warm; but a little of such friendly insult can go a very long way.

One who almost always went too far with his backchat was Bob Heath. With the incurable vanity of youth, this lanky young lout, just past his twentieth birthday, saw himself as the Casanova of the Research and Development Department, and therefore spent as little time as possible in the pursuit of his appointed laboratory duties, and as much as could be contrived in pursuit of various female members of staff.

His unwelcome attentions were currently directed towards (some might even say against) Julia Springs, secretary to Dr. Kirton, the departmental head. Miss Springs, a crisp, efficient thirty-year-old of stunning good looks, was recently divorced, and therefore (for the moment, at least) resolutely antimale. Yet Bob had decided, contrary to all common sense, that it was for him and for him alone to modify her views.

"Morning, doll!" He sucked his teeth, and winked. His quarry gritted her teeth, and ignored the greeting. "Had time to think it over yet, have you?"

Julia made herself busy about her desk in what anyone else would have recognised as a dismissive manner, but Bob Heath would not be so easily dismissed. "I said," leaning on her desk at an unnecessary angle, "how about it, then?" And he leered hopefully at what he could see of her discreet cleavage.

"I'm busy," said Julia, without looking up. "Kindly go away and let me get on with my work."

"I'm busy too—but never too busy to spare some time for you, darling, so how about you returning the compliment, eh? Spare some time for me this evening, maybe?"

"Maybe not. Definitely not. Never, in fact." Julia at last looked up, and fixed her obstinate admirer with a withering glare. "I told you yesterday—I have told you often—and I do not wish to keep having to tell you. Will you kindly understand that I have absolutely no intention of ever going out with you. I repeat—not ever!"

"You don't mean that—you're just playing hard to get, 'cos you know you're missing a treat, with me. That's the trouble with you frigid types, you take too long to let go and have yourselves a bit of fun." He sucked his teeth and winked again. "Just you ask anyone, and they'll tell you—go on, give yourself a good time, like a sensible girl!"

"You will not, Heath, address me as *girl*." Julia's tone would have shrivelled a salamander. "Indeed, you will not address me at all, unless you can do so with courtesy—and only then on matters pertaining to work. Since nothing you have said so far this morning has been remotely concerned with work, you will kindly get off my desk this instant and for pity's sake *go away*!"

Her final words brought several curious heads up from their desks to turn in her direction. Julia blushed at having acquired an audience, while Bob, delighted to have roused her, smirked; but the look in her eye made him take discretion as the better part, and he slipped from the desk, leaving grubby marks on the edge where his hands had gripped it.

"So long for now, doll," he told her in a stage whisper. "But I know you'll miss me really—you can't fool me! No use trying to pretend, so don't you worry your lovely head about it, I'll be back. I won't keep you waiting long!"

"I can wait," muttered Julia viciously after his retreating yet jaunty back. "I can wait forever!" And, silently— unfairly—cursing all men, instead of limiting her curses to tall, thin, self-deluding youths, she settled to some thera-peutic typing, wishing for once that she had a manual rather than an electronic machine, so that she could vent much of her wrath by banging the carriage back and forth in style.

The clatter of her cathartic keys mingled with other sounds of industry in the open plan office. Pencils scratched on paper, desks were kicked in frenzies of creative thought, gusty sighs accompanied the tearing of fruitless notes into wastepaper-basket-sized shreds. Telephones rang, to be either answered or ignored; messages were taken and delivered. Across the waist-high partitions, from work station to work station, voices called in banter or in gloom; formulas were confirmed, theories rejected; and, from their desks, scientists came wandering down the main corridor, despairing of inspiration and desperate for coffee.

To these passersby, gentlemen all—there were no lady metallurgists in Allingham Alloys—Julia nodded, and smiled polite greeting. After six weeks with R&D she knew not only the faces to fit the names, but the habits, too. Mr. Tilbury (impossible to think of him as Oscar) could survive only half an hour without a cup of coffee, and would serenade the machine quietly as it gurgled about its busi-ness. Stephen Brown clicked his teeth with a pencil as he worked, and kept extra sugar in his desk to augment the automatically dispensed "black, sweet" he drank at nine-twenty on the dot. Dr. Fishwick always chose drinking chocolate, and brought cheesy biscuits from home to dunk in it—a concept from which Miss Springs, shuddering, shrank in some revulsion. Dr. Holbrook took tea, but poured a stiff whisky in it when he believed nobody was watching . . .

Dr. Holbrook. As the haphazard promenade passed her desk, Julia realised that the tall, white-haired figure of the chief metallurgist had not yet joined it. Normally, he was so punctual that a watch might be set by his movements: she'd come to rely on his first machineward foray of the working day as warning that it was time for her to prepare the early-elevenses tray for Dr. Kirton, who (on account of his privileged position) was alone of the department so honored. It wasn't like Dr. Holbrook to be late—and now (she clicked her tongue) so would the tray be, for the first time since she'd come to work here. She frowned at the reflection this must cast on her efficiency, checking her wristwatch with an irritated sigh.

"Why so glum, doll? Cheer yourself up—say you'll come out with me tonight!" Her tormentor, a cardboard box in his arms, was with her once more. "There's a whole lot of fun just waiting for you, if you'd only give yourself a chance to find out."

Julia took a deep breath. "Once and for all, I—don't do that!"

But she spoke too late. With a thud, Bob deposited his box on top of the papers from which Julia had been copying, and perched himself on the other corner of her desk, ready for a further bout of chatting-up.

"Go away!" snarled Miss Springs. "Take your rubbish with you, and get out of my sight this minute! Oh!" She had tried to push the box off the desk, but it was unexpectedly heavy: her hand rebounded, jarring every nerve in her forearm. "Oh . . ."

Shaking her wrist and blinking, she suppressed another curse, while at the same time wondering just what could weigh so much in so small a box. Bob, observing her curiosity, chuckled.

"Dr. Holbrook's samples, these are. Top secret, mind—

but I'll stretch a point for you, darling, seeing as how you're my favourite girl. Go on—take a look. I won't tell a soul."

"I have no wish to take a look, thank you," said Julia stiffly. "I have no wish even to *see* the samples—or you. I suggest you take them and yourself away from here and get on at once with—with whatever you're supposed to be doing with them, before Dr. Holbrook arrives and finds—"

"What?" For the first time, Bob Heath's aggressive nonchalance wobbled. "You mean . . . the old boy's not in yet? Wonder if—if he's stopped off anywhere on the way?"

"If he has, I fail to see that it can possibly be anything to do with you. Moreover, if I knew, I would hardly discuss Dr. Holbrook's affairs with someone who has no business knowing them. Since your only connection with him is to carry out the work on his metallographic samples, I would strongly suggest that you do so. Now."

"No hurry," he assured her: but the assurance sounded, somehow, slightly forced. "No hurry—I've only got to polish and etch 'em, and that won't take long—but he's a funny bloke, old Holbrook. Got it in regular for me, he has—wouldn't even chip in for my wedding present, the mean old cuss." His eyes gleamed. "Ever tell you, did I, how I had to get married, straight from school? Means I got talent—experience. Girls like that. There's more life in us young ones as've bin around a bit than ever you'll get in yer old codgers with paunches and a mortgage, you know."

"I neither know," said Julia, "nor care. And—oh," as the telephone chirruped beside her. "Good. . . . Dr. Kirton's office," she said into the receiver. "Oh—yes, Mr. Woolverstone. . . . The very minute he's off the telephone, Mr. Woolverstone." With a bang, she rang off, and drew in a deep, dangerous breath before turning back to Bob, who hadn't moved one inch from his uninvited perch during her brief exchange with the managing director of Allingham Alloys. "Now, listen to me, Heath, and listen carefully, because this is the last time I intend to say this. It is not shyness. It is not modesty. It is not that I am playing hard to get—it is simply that I want nothing whatsoever to do with you, and I fail to see why you cannot get that one fact straight in your stupid, silly, conceited thick skull!"

"Oh, you don't mean that, doll. You're just saying it because you don't want to seem too keen, do you? But you can't fool Bob Heath—"

"I should very much like," interposed Julia through clenched teeth, "to *murder* Bob Heath!"

"Ahem." The discreet interruption came from behind her. Dr. Kirton had emerged, unnoticed, from his office, and his quiet presence was sufficiently commanding to silence both combatants. Julia jumped, and flushed; Bob hopped promptly from her desk, and fumbled for his box of samples.

"Miss Springs," began Dr. Kirton, eyeing Bob with disfavour, "I wonder if you have seen Dr. Holbrook this morning?"

"Just on my way to do his samples," mumbled Mr. Heath, vanishing towards the preparation room before questions could be asked of him. "Heavy, this box . . ."

Relieved to see him go, Julia was able to concentrate on the more pressing problem. "Dr. Holbrook? No—it's odd, I was just thinking that he hasn't come along yet for his cup of tea."

"I keep ringing his desk," fretted Dr. Kirton, "but he doesn't reply—though that, of course, means nothing. If he should happen to be having one of his, ah, sensitive mornings, there's every chance he'd simply refuse to touch the thing—but I keep having Mr. Woolverstone after me to talk with him as soon as possible, because Holbrook, you know, is really the only person who thoroughly understands the new process—and Mr. Woolverstone wants me to persuade him to put something more definite down on paper. Oh, dear—it's all very awkward. Very."

"Mr. Woolverstone," said Julia, smiling, "just rang *me*, I'm afraid. He said he couldn't get through on your phone, and would I ask you to call him as soon as you'd cleared the line."

Dr. Kirton sighed. "About Holbrook yet again, I suppose. Oh dear, it's too bad. Really, Mr. Woolverstone can't expect me to keep Basil Holbrook, of all people, in my pocket—and I can't think why there's suddenly so much fussing about the Squib, anyway." He brightened. "I think I might just pop along to his desk to check he's not come in—and, if he hasn't, then there's not much more I can do until he does."

Julia pushed back her chair. "I'll check his desk, if you like, to save you the bother. And perhaps you could try ringing him at home while I'm doing it—I'm sure you have a note of his number somewhere, because I don't think I have."

"Dear me, no, Miss Springs." Kirton looked shocked at the very suggestion. "It's clear you've never heard the story, but—poor Holbrook isn't on the telephone. It holds . . . memories for him, you see. He had it taken out—three, four years ago, after he lost his wife. An accident—she was hurrying to answer the phone when she tripped, and fell down the stairs—it gave the poor chap a dreadful phobia about using the instrument ever again. It was only with the greatest difficulty that we could persuade him to use the interoffice phones—and there are his, ah, bad days, you know, when he won't even do that. And if today should be one of those days . . ."

He sighed, and patted her shoulder. "Thank you, but it would be better if I went to check, my dear. Holbrook is—is a touchy fellow, and you are, if I may say so, a personable young lady. We don't," with a wry smile, "want to set his blood pressure boiling—and, now I think of it, a judicious amount of exercise will do me no harm, I fancy. Every little helps, when you're as unfit as I've been told I am!"

He hurried off with a smile, but when he came back it was with a downcast look and a baffled expression. "Oh dear—I can't think what I'm going to say to keep Mr. Woolverstone quiet. Has he been in touch again?"

"Just a moment or so ago . . ." Julia studied her flustered boss in some concern. Could she remember where he kept his emergency angina tablets? She still paled at the memory of his previous attack, exaggerated by a hangover from the Metallurgical Society annual dinner the night before: she would infinitely prefer not to go through anything like that ever again.

". . . though I think I stalled him—for a while," she concluded, in as reassuring a tone as she could manage. Really, poor Dr. Kirton was looking more harassed by the minute. "In case he rings again, why not switch all your calls through to me?" She smiled. "I promise I won't let him nag you until you've had a bit of a rest—it really can't be good for you to go worrying yourself this way. And it certainly won't help to make Dr. Holbrook turn up any faster, now will it?"

"No," he said, with a sigh, and a smile of his own. "No—you're right, it won't—and if you could keep Mr. Woolverstone off my back until Holbrook comes in, it would be a great kindness, Miss Springs."

But not even the efficient Julia Springs could be kind enough to keep the peace for Dr. Kirton until Dr. Holbrook came to work . . .

For nobody is immortal.

Three

As THE AIR began, slowly, to freshen, Mrs. Mint emerged from her faint. She dragged herself out of the chair on which the milkman (who preferred to hold more voluptuous females in his arms) had dumped her with a muttered "Bloody hell!" and, drawn by a horrid fascination, tottered across the room to examine the silent form of her employer.

She soon saw that this man was an opportunity not to be missed. With a thrilling scream, Mrs. Mint clasped her hands again, and proclaimed:

"Oh, he's cold—he's so cold, and he don't move an inch! He's gassed himself—he's dead! *Dead!*"

But when there came no suitable response, she realised that she had been balked of her audience. She scowled, and tottered onwards, still pale, to find out what her fellow intruder—with far less right than herself to be on the premises—might be about.

The milkman had been opening more windows. "We oughter get help," he said, as soon as he saw her. "Police, I reckon—ambulance'd be no use to him, poor old basket. Where's the phone?"

Sadly, Mrs. Mint shook her head. "Didn't have none."

"How about next door, then?"

"I'd've thought," she retorted, "that if anyone oughter know what's in the houses hereabouts, it's you, with being so familiar with their owners as you are!"

"Stow it, Ma." This was no time to indulge in their usual sniping. "Be okay if I leave you on yer own, will it? Or woodjer rather go insteader me?"

Mrs. Mint had the illiterate's fear of involving herself too closely with Authority. "I'll be fine. Not as if I'll be exactly on my own, is it?" She pointed a gnarled finger towards the open study door, and the grim tableau beyond. "You go—only do make haste," she added, uneasy now the moment was upon her.

"Well—all right, if yer sure . . ." And the milkman hurried away, leaving Mrs. Mint, her pink bag of cleaning equipment forgotten where it fell, to check quickly through each room in turn, lest in the course of the milkman's aerifying activities any small items of value had found their way into his pockets.

It was disappointing that nothing, as far as she could tell, was missing; but she brightened when, with the hearty clump of official boots behind him, her helpful adversary rematerialised, reassuringly soon, in the company of a young police constable.

"Bitter luck—flagged him down as he was driving past," said the milkman, much relieved.

PC Benson's face wore a thoughtful look as his eyes flicked from Mrs. Mint down the hall, and thence back to the milkman. He seemed in no hurry to examine the contents of the study: rather, he switched his attention again to Mrs. Mint, giving her his most soothing smile.

"Must have been a great shock for you," he said. "For both of you," turning to the milkman. "Good job you could let me know as soon as you did."

"Yes, well," said the milkman, "I'll be off then, shall I?" He was suddenly eager to abandon his role as Man of the Moment: he'd just remembered that the ravishing redhead four doors down was due to settle her account this week.

"If you wouldn't mind waiting, sir—just for a minute or two, that's all." PC Benson was courteous, but firm. "We can take a proper statement later, at your convenience, but until I've had a look inside . . ."

He looked. He inhaled. He spluttered. "Woof! It's gas, all right!"

"Toldjer it was," muttered the milkman, as Mrs. Mint

squealed a warning and Benson stepped gingerly across the threshold. "Gas it is, and plenty of it. Nothing anyone can do for him in there, believe me!"

Benson waved his arms. "If you'd both like to wait outside, while I examine the scene . . ." And he began to make his way warily along the passage, although any clues—if, indeed, clues were needed at all—would have been obliterated through the well-meaning efforts of the dead man's would-be rescuers.

Mrs. Mint and the milkman, for once united, glanced at each other; and silently followed him along the hall.

Benson bent over the body, and, after a moment's hesitation, felt for a pulse—first on the wrist, then, shaking his head, on the cold, clammy neck. With a gentle tug, he slowly raised the corpse's tumbled head. The milkman gasped; Mrs. Mint squealed again, and clutched him for fear she might fall.

But Benson ignored them—as did the open eyes of the swollen-visaged, blue-faced Basil Holbrook, deceased. He stared into infinity with unfocussed gaze, his mouth twisted in a sardonic grin. He was, beyond any doubt, dead.

Benson set Holbrook's head carefully back on the desk, taking care not to disturb the papers on which he seemed to have been working when disaster overtook him.

"*Asymptotic relationships in conductivity and hydrogen diffusion for amorphous ferro-alloys*," he read aloud, stumbling over every second syllable. "Blimey, what a jaw-cracker! This Chattisham character who wrote it probably *bored* the poor old chap to death! Looks as if this was the last thing he was reading before . . ."

He scanned the other papers, searching for some written evidence. There was no note—no obvious note, at any rate: suicide could not be a foregone conclusion. There was an empty whisky bottle by the side of the desk, hidden from first sight by the wastepaper basket, which was empty. Accident, then, the most likely answer: an old-fashioned gas fire, an elderly man, a chilly night . . .

"Was the fire still on when you got into the house?" he enquired, turning, and leading his shaken audience back out into the fresh air.

The milkman nodded. "Hissing like mad, it was."

"All that poison," moaned Mrs. Mint. "And poor Dr. Holbrook breathing it in all night, the nasty stuff! Never did hold with that North Sea gas, I didn't, and you can see I was right."

PC Benson ignored this. "Which of you two turned off that fire?"

"Me," admitted the milkman.

"And opened the windows?"

"Well, that's right, I did—but look, she"—jerking a thumb in the direction of Mrs. Mint—"can tell yer everything you wanter know. Can't I get on now?"

"Sorry, sir, not just yet." Benson watched him wriggle for a moment, then asked: "Were the windows all fastened— maybe locked, even?"

The milkman wriggled some more. "Uh—yes, they was. Leastways, I think so."

"And the doors?"

The milkman turned purple. Mrs. Mint cackled.

"Tight as a drum, the lot of 'em—ever so particular with his study, was Dr. Holbrook, always extra careful on account of them secret papers and his special work kept hid in there. Hardly never let me in to dust, he didn't—shut the door and turned the key every minute he could, he did!"

She was so obviously gloating for the milkman's coming discomfiture that Benson, at first puzzled, suddenly nodded, smiled, and said:

"I see, sir, thank you. Yes. So, apart from that, you didn't touch anything else—neither of you?"

An indignant duet of denial was his reply: upon which theme the milkman, more eager than ever to be away, chose to enlarge.

"Look here, son—I'm late enough now as it is—and I get no end of stick from everyone when I'm late . . ."

Relenting—having noted his name, address, and round number—Benson permitted the milkman to depart, with the farewell warning: "We'll be in touch later, mind. But only about the inquest," he added kindly, as the milkman reddened again.

"I'm not losing no money over this little lot," grumbled the lock-picker, thankfully making his escape. "Time off in the middle of the week to appear at some flaming inquest— you gotter be joking!"

"Lose money?" cried Mrs. Mint in protest, as his words rang an ominous bell. "And what does he think's going to happen to me, then—with Dr. Holbrook still owing me for all my time this week—*and* for today as well!"

She glared at PC Benson, who thought furiously. "Well," he said at last, "I reckon the best thing for you to do'd be to get in touch with his solicitors."

This advice did not comfort her. "Solicitors? I don't know nothing about solicitors," she cried. "Tried to keep myself respectable, I have, and never bin mixed up with this kind of thing before—but there, who's to take my word for anything? Who's to say now as I was really here them days?"

Benson, baffled, shook his head. "The solicitors'll be your best bet," he insisted, with what he hoped was a reassuring smile. "They'll see you right—they've their reputations to keep up. They won't want to see you cheated. . . ."

At which Mrs. Mint lost something of her anxious look, and tentatively returned the smile: and Benson was emboldened to ask for more information. Did she by any chance know who Dr. Holbrook's solicitors were?

The anxious look returned. "No, I don't—I mind my own business, so I do—and always have done, too!"

"But I never meant . . . I only thought," babbled Benson, "with you working here, I mean—just maybe, when you picked up his post from the mat, you might've noticed any names printed on the envelopes. I wasn't suggesting . . ."

He paused, smiling diplomatically—and infectiously.

Mrs. Mint, after a thoughtful moment, smiled back. Police Constable Benson was a pleasant, good-looking young man, with a kindly face . . .

And Mrs. Mint was encouraged to make her great confession. "Well, to tell the truth, dear—and I can see you're not the sort to gossip, so you won't let this go no further—well, even if I wasn't the sort to keep my nose out of other folks's business, which o'course I am—well, I—you see, I can't neither read nor write, saving my own name. So if there was a hundred letters to come from solicitors, I'd not be able to tell you who they was, dear."

Benson blushed. "Oh . . . Yes, I see. Yes, of course— but we'll be able to find out some other way, I expect, so never mind. His employers, probably. Worked for Allingham Alloys off the High Road, didn't he?"

"He did—poor soul," she added, with a sorry sniff. "And regular as clockwork, three days a week, I worked for him—and what I want to know is—"

He couldn't bear to hear wailing yet again for her lost wages. "Talking of letting know," he broke in, "we'd best let them know what's happened—his firm, I mean. But there's the station to be told first, of course. Where's the phone?"

She forgot her private woes in the larger catastrophe. "Oh, he wouldn't have the phone, on account of how he said it killed his poor wife—besides," with a grimace, "it'd cost too much. Always careful with his money, was Dr. Holbrook. And lucky to get me," she added, "for what little he paid. Believe you me—"

"I believe you." Once again, Benson abruptly stemmed the flow of lamentation and complaint. "I'll radio from the car, I think. . . ."

"No need for that, dear." Mrs. Mint caught him by the arm, gesturing towards the study. "Ever so clever with his hands, the doctor was, as well as careful with his money— there's a radio in there he built himself, being a scientist and good at electrical things. Mended the Hoover when they said in the shop it was done for—rigged up a dishwasher out of nobbut a few bits and pieces, too. Real proud, he was, of saving money that way. Got all the latest gadgets—colour telly, video, even one o' them computers—and I dunno as he paid more than a tenner for the lot!''

This inducement, however, failed to persuade PC Benson to return to the late doctor's study to make use of his custom-built radio transmitter. And so, with a still-chattering Mrs. Mint at his side, he went back to his car to report the accident. . . .

But—*was* it really an accident?

It is a truth universally acknowledged that, when you are in a hurry, whatever you have to do takes at least twice as long as you might otherwise reasonably expect—even taking into full account this universal truth.

An interesting application of the above theory might have been observed on this particular morning, when Philip Whatfield, having once discovered his flat tyre, found that it was past ten o'clock when he at last greeted the Allingham Alloys security man and hurried thankfully from the bicycle shed to the Research and Development Department.

Philip was a tall, thin, stooped figure, who merged with a high degree of success into the background. He hid from the world's general gaze behind tinted spectacles, thick-lensed and owlish, and hunched his shoulders to make himself seem less noticeable than his height would otherwise have made him. As he passed by the desk of Julia Springs, he affected an air of even more intense anonymity than usual, trusting that in this way she might be persuaded to overlook his tardy arrival.

Julia looked up as his shambling shadow fell across her desk. For one grim moment, she feared it was Bob Heath come back to infuriate her: but when she recognised the awkward form of the shy Mr. Whatfield, her glacial frown instantly faded to a welcoming smile. How embarrassed the poor man seemed at her noticing him! Didn't he realise that several other people had been late this morning? Nobody could blame him for not anticipating the bad weather.

"Good morning, Mr. Whatfield—if you can call it that, with such thick fog. You look frozen. I expect you'll be glad of a hot cup of something before you start work."

Shielded by his spectacles, Philip brought himself to blink once or twice before replying, almost calmly, to her salutation. "Why, er—yes. If the machine is working, I suppose . . ."

He shrugged, shook his head, then realised that he'd lost track of exactly where the sentence had been going. He took a deep breath, goggled at her, and blinked again. "It—it certainly is a very cold day," he brought out: which was true, but not the conclusion he believed he'd originally intended to reach. Julia's smile had confused him. He was not accustomed to close association with attractive young women, or at least not since his youth nearly a quarter of a century before.

Philip's overpowering diffidence made all who had dealings with him exert themselves to put him at his ease. This they invariably did by treating him with extra kindliness in almost every circumstance, since they were made more uncomfortable by his lack of social address than he himself seemed to be. He was obviously a Great Brain: like all boffins, he needed careful handling. Julia felt far sorrier for him than for anyone else in R&D, partly from her own embarrassment, partly from fellow feeling: Philip was almost as new to the company as she. He had joined Allingham Alloys at the beginning of September, two weeks before Miss Springs, yet he still seemed as ill at ease as if it were his first week instead of his third month. . . .

"If I were you," she now suggested, "I should have a cup of coffee this minute. Or something to warm you up, anyway—you look frozen." She smiled. Philip coughed, and ran a nervous finger around the open neck of his shirt: alone of the R&D scientists, Mr. Whatfield could never bring himself to wear a tie. "You certainly aren't the last one in this morning," she added, meaning to cheer him up, as he checked his watch with an unhappy glance, and sighed. "Dr. Holbrook for one," she went on, "still hasn't turned up—and he doesn't ride a bike, the way you do. A car isn't nearly as cold and unpleasant, in weather like this."

Philip shuddered, then forced a smile as she regarded him with some curiosity. "Oh," he said, deliberately casual. "Oh . . . You say Holbrook isn't in yet? How—how very odd, for a man so—so set in his ways." His mouth twisted sideways in what Julia took for another smile. "Almost an automaton, the good doctor," said Philip. Julia couldn't be sure whether he was sneering, or not. "Regular as clock-work, in fact. Utterly cold-blooded . . ."

"It's cold, all right," returned Julia. "Which is why," she went on, as Philip shivered, "everyone ought to come to work by car, when the weather's so bad. After all, you can switch the heating on—and then there'd be no need at all for you to be so horribly blue when you arrive."

"Me?" Philip blanched. "Me, drive a car? Never! To be cooped up in a ghastly smelly metal box on wheels—shut in from the fresh air, no exercise . . ." He grimaced in what she took to be an attempt at a grin. "When bicycles are so easy—no parking problems, low running costs . . ."

Julia, scorning a grin, nevertheless smiled back, ready to share a little joke. "It's surprising that Dr. Holbrook doesn't ride a bike all year round, isn't it? Knowing how, um, economical he can be. You might try suggesting it to him next spring, when the weather's a little better. . . ."

She was struggling now to keep the conversation going, as so often happened when people talked with Philip Whatfield: but she was surprised when something in her final words seemed to rouse him to a reply rather more coherent, and certainly more pertinent, than she might otherwise have expected.

"I dare say," he ventured, once more running his finger round the open collar of his shirt, "that you may have realised . . . Holbrook and I . . . we aren't exactly the—the best of friends?"

Julia bent her head in a gentle nod. The mutual antagonism hadn't escaped her notice, but she had considered it none of her business to comment on the matter unless asked to do so.

Philip gave his nervous little cough. "Yes, well . . . Yesterday, you know, in the afternoon—perhaps half an hour or so before we finished—he actually came along to my work station . . . a general discussion, that was all, a chat—but he was sneezing, snuffling into a handkerchief—and he kept on and on until I could have screamed—but I was just wondering—wondering whether he might have been starting a spot of flu, perhaps. . . ."

He blinked at her, waved his hands with one helpless gesture, and swallowed twice. Julia, groping for an interpretation, hazarded a guess.

"You mean he might have decided to dose himself up before he went to bed last night, and then overslept? That's a good point. Now you remind me, I heard him coughing a bit in the late afternoon, too. It must be the answer—I'll mention it to Dr. Kirton. He's been most anxious to know the moment we hear anything."

She pushed back her chair, and made to rise. She could easily have rung through on the internal phone, but this did not seem to have occurred to her: now that his habitual silence had been broken, Whatfield, like all shy people, seemed unable to bring the conversation to any comfortable finish.

"I do hope," he babbled, "that he hasn't—that is, he took away some notes to check over—not mine, you see, and I'd rather expected to be sending them back soon—he was only supposed to read them through and give me his opinion. If I have to wait—or to go over to his house . . . well, it could be—inconvenient, to say the least." And once more he fumbled with the collar of his shirt.

Julia was trying not to lose patience. "Dr. Holbrook," she

enunciated carefully, "has been with this firm for some years, hasn't he? And he's one of the leading researchers—a genius, they tell me. It seems to me perfectly reasonable that a sick, elderly man should have a lapse of mem—"

"Genius?" Philip goggled at her. "Basil Holbrook—a genius? Why, I—"

The telephone rang on Julia's desk. Immediately, she turned away to answer it. "Dr. Kirton's office. . . . No, I'm sorry, he hasn't, but"—she glanced at Philip, and smiled a faint apology for her abruptness—"someone has reminded me that he seemed to be starting a cold yesterday. It could well have developed into something more serious overnight—I expect we'll hear something of the sort from him once he's able to arrange for a message to be sent—"

The telephone interrupted with an insistent squeak. Miss Springs tried not to sigh. "Very well, Mr. Woolverstone, I will inform Dr. Kirton. . . . Yes, at once. Not at all. . . . Good-bye."

Even through the thick camouflage of his spectacles, Philip's contempt was plain. He jerked an irritable head towards the telephone. "So *he's* fussing over Holbrook's sniffles as well—Woolverstone?" He thrust his hands into his trouser pockets, and scowled. "Prima donnas . . ."

"I must see Dr. Kirton," said Julia, again conveniently forgetting the interoffice phone. She nodded to Philip, left her desk, hurried to the office door, tapped on it, and passed within to her boss, leaving Mr. Whatfield to watch as she closed the door behind her. He shuddered yet again, long and slowly, then shook his head, took a deep breath, and turned away to his own place of work, muttering, *"Genius? Ha!"* to himself over and over. It seemed to afford him some comfort.

Behind that closed door, Miss Springs was expounding the influenza theory to Dr. Kirton.

". . . which is what I told Mr. Woolverstone," she concluded. "But he still wants us to let him know the minute any message arrives—he even hinted that, if someone could be spared to go round to the house to find out for certain, he wouldn't object. It really does sound rather urgent. . . ."

Kirton sighed. "Oh, dear, if Holbrook has been dosing himself up with—with anything—for the flu, that is . . ."

He had no need to look so embarrassed: Basil Holbrook's fondness for the bottle was an open secret, its concomitant problems well understood. Urgent messenger or not, Allingham Alloys shouldn't expect to make any sense out of the scientist's messages until Monday, at the earliest . . .

But Dr. Kirton would have sighed even more deeply had he known that it would be Doomsday, at the earliest, before any message could possibly come from Dr. Holbrook.

──────── Four ────────

"IF ANYONE," REMARKED Detective Superintendent Trewley, as the police car made its way towards the premises of Allingham Alloys, "knows how he liked his drink, it'll be you, young Benson." He paused, and scowled. "I shouldn't think it's something you're likely to forget in a hurry."

Benson, at the wheel, nodded. "You can say that again, sir." Both men could recall, in vivid detail, the occasion a few years ago when PC Benson, newly arrived in Allingham, had spotted Basil Holbrook weaving home on his bicycle, and had administered a friendly caution concerning the perils of drinking and driving. His words had infuriated the cyclist, a man with a highly developed sense of grievance even in the ordinary way; the resultant uproar had forever coloured PC Benson's view of the Allshire force, when Trewley took the entire blame, very publicly, upon himself. The trouble (he had said) was that they'd all become far too used to seeing the silly old fool around the place in that condition, and hadn't thought to do anything about it: it had taken Benson to remind them of their duty, and if he, Holbrook, imagined that he, Trewley, was going to give the lad the rollicking he'd asked for, he'd got another think coming.

No rebuke had been administered to Probationary Constable Benson: his record had remained unblemished; and Holbrook had neither forgotten nor forgiven what he saw as an insult—though he had switched, during the winter at least, to a car, in which he hoped his erratic physical control might pass unnoticed.

"It sounds," remarked the third occupant of the car, "as if

he drank it straight from the bottle this time, if Benson's right about the empty one on the floor, and no glass. Probably," she added, primly, "trying to feel the effect faster—and goodness knows how much he'll have had to take to feel it, the state his liver must have been in." Detective Sergeant Stone, Trewley's inevitable sidekick, was a lapsed medical student—the sight of blood, she'd discovered, disturbed her almost as much as did a thunderstorm—who held strong views about moderation in all things.

Trewley and Stone made an unlikely, though undoubtedly successful, team. The superintendent was a big, burly man in late middle age, with a wrinkled face which reminded some of a bloodhound, some of a bulldog. Out of earshot, he was referred to by his colleagues—though never by Stone, a petite brunette with a black belt in judo—as the Plainclothes Prune.

It was unusual for the pair to be involved so early in the investigation of what appeared to be a routine accident: but Trewley was in hiding from Desk Sergeant Pleate, Terror of the Station and Champion of the Lost Property Cupboard. Pleate had recently reopened (for the umpteenth time) hostilities with his nominal superior over the statutory period for which stray items handed in by the public should be stored before disposal. The sergeant thought three months the minimum, the superintendent insisted one was enough—and neither was prepared to accept Sergeant Stone's suggested compromise of two months. There was, they both told her individually—and repeatedly—a Principle at stake.

Apart from the perennial problem of the Lost Property, there was also the matter of the floods. The first severe night of winter had caught the police—as it had the weather forecasters—unawares. In their wake, the frosts had brought burst pipes. One of these, to Sergeant Pleate's distress, had been too late discovered in the station basement, merrily inundating the cells in anticipation of the drunks and petty offenders always expected to brighten an Allingham Friday night.

"Every plumber in town," grumbled Desk Sergeant Pleate, "is out on call. I even tried the Water Board!"

"And what," demanded Trewley, with little hope of good news, "did they say?"

"They seemed to think it was funny." It was clear that Pleate did not share this view. "Said that in a building this old, it was all bound to be *copper* piping—and then they laughed, the fools. Said if anyone ought to be able to fix it for themselves, it was a police station, and there was no need to go bothering them."

"Very helpful." Trewley's snarl was that of a bulldog whose bone had been unexpectedly exchanged for a mess of pottage. "Didn't you tell 'em it was an emergency?"

Sergeant Pleate sighed. "So's everywhere in town, they said—and to try sawing it off and hammering it flat, and they might be around Monday. Monday! I ask you—what with the weekend ahead—all the Guy Fawkes parties, and the noise, and the drunks—"

"—and the Fire Brigade calls, and the speeding, and the traffic—"

"—and with gangs of yobs sending rockets through old folks's windows," concluded Pleate, "there won't be a spare handyman in town come the start of next week—and us with a cellar full of villains all getting their feet wet, just waiting to get out and write to their member of parliament about it. . . ." He paused. Having induced in his superior a more or less sympathetic frame of mind, this could be the time to strike.

"Not to mention," he meanly added, "that there's more than a foot of water in the Lost Property cupboard. We'll have to shift everything upstairs to that room you know I've said more than once'd be just right for three months, not wanting to waste any space if it's being used anyway . . ."

Which argument being regarded by the harassed Trewley as taking distinctly unfair advantage, he straightaway fled the scene. He was still letting off steam to Stone about Pleate's Machiavellian tactics when, providentially, PC Benson returned, requesting the presence of Sergeant Stone at the scene of the recent occurrence. Benson's arrival seemed to Trewley like the last-minute cavalry rescue so popular in film and fiction: its possibilities were endless. He had therefore attached himself to the party with threats of demotion (for Stone) and violence (for Benson) if either of them dared inform Pleate of his whereabouts. . . .

"Dunno about feel the effects, Sarge," said Benson now. "I shouldn't think he could've felt anything. I mean, if he didn't even smell that gas . . ."

"Perhaps the leak only started after he'd passed out."

"Perhaps," said Trewley, light-headed with having made good his escape, "he was poisoned, not gassed—and then someone took away the glass so as not to leave any traces. What's the betting the postmortem won't show any, either?"

He was generally so quick to pounce on her for flaws in forensic logic that Stone could not allow this to pass without comment. "Then why draw attention to a possible poisoning by removing the glass—if he used one? Surely, sir, it would be better to leave it near him. Everybody knew about his drinking problem, after all. I bet Benson's right, and he drank it straight from the bottle. . . ."

Trewley, who enjoyed his pint of beer whenever his wife hadn't put him on another diet, pulled a face. The idea of neat alcohol, so early in the morning, made him feel more gloomy than ever. "All right, then—if it wasn't poison, it was suicide. Right now, I know just how the poor beggar must have felt."

Stone resolved to be bracing. "It's probably an accident, after all. All the doors and windows were shut fast, Benson, weren't they?"

"Yes, Sarge—according to the milkman and the cleaning lady, anyway. And he was the sort of bloke who'd lock himself in, being a scientist—you know, keeping his work secret and that. Mind you," with feeling, "I still reckon the poor old perisher died of boredom. That paper I saw, honest, I couldn't understand a word of it—and that was just the title."

Trewley rumbled suddenly with laughter. "Can't say we've had many of them, over the years. Boring people to death, I mean. It'll be one for the books, if you're right. Still, between the three of us we've covered the lot—suicide, accident, murder. What does his cleaning lady think about it all?"

Benson hesitated. "Well, sir, she talked an awful lot, all right, but not much that'd be that useful from our point of view. I mean, mostly she kept on about how careful he was with his money—like it was typical of him to die at the end of the week, so he wouldn't have to cough up for the two days she'd already worked. . . ."

Stone gurgled with mirth. "I've heard of economy," she remarked, "but this is ridiculous!"

Trewley snorted at her side. "I'm never surprised, the things some folk'll do—not to mention the things they'll say about other folk behind their backs—and nor should you be either, Sergeant—nor you, Constable. A good copper knows it takes all sorts—and besides, some of the chat can come in useful, sometimes."

"Dunno about that this time, sir," said Benson cheerfully. "This Mrs. Mint, she was full of moans and groans half the time about his being dead, but mostly she kept rabbiting on about her three days' wages. Do you know, he only paid her one pound and fifty pence an hour?"

"Slave labour," snapped Stone, who held strong opinions on the subject of housework.

Trewley chuckled. "Best have a word with the cleaning ladies' trade union, then, if there is such a thing—though I somehow doubt if there'd be a legal minimum for charring. And even if there is, he probably wouldn't have paid it." The chuckle had gone, and the tone was one of resigned disapproval. "Some folk'll do anything to fiddle a few extra bob—like sneaking stuff through customs, or getting round the Value Added Tax by paying cash for odd jobs around the house. . . ."

Odd jobs reminded him of Pleate, and the absence of—among other odd-job men—plumbers. He shuddered.

"Anyone this mean with his money," said Stone, bracing as before, "won't have paid someone else to do odd jobs if there was the slightest chance he could do them himself."

"That's what Mrs. Mint said he did," Benson confirmed. "These boffins, you'd expect 'em to be, well, a bit head-in-the-clouds and no common sense, but according to her he was pretty good with his hands. Must've saved himself a bomb, the amount things cost nowadays. No need to worry about fiddling the VAT at all."

Trewley muttered of falling standards, and moral fibre, choosing to ignore completely his own lack of moral fibre in the matter of Sergeant Pleate.

Stone thought it safer to change the subject. "So what else did Mrs. Mint have to say, Benson? This secret work of his—might it be important enough for anyone to have wanted to murder him for it, after all?"

"Shouldn't think she could tell you any better than me, Sarge, if that report he was reading's typical of the man. He must've been a pretty bright bloke, I do know that—like he hadn't got a telephone, he'd got some sort of phobia with thinking it made his wife fall downstairs, so Mrs. Mint said, but he'd built a couple of radios, a ham one as well as the ordinary sort—and a television, and a computer, too. All from spare parts, she said."

"Does that," demanded Trewley, "prove he was a clever bloke, or a stingy one? Or both," he added, before Stone could say it.

"He watched the pennies, sir, no question. A bit on the deaf side, she said he was, but he wouldn't buy a new doorbell, he took a broken alarm clock to bits and made himself some sort of contraption with an old tin tray—above the door, it is, and when she showed me I'd have

sworn it was one of those infernal machines the mad
scientists have in the comics, sir."

Trewley was minded to scoff at this flight of fancy, but
Stone said quickly:

"That ties in with his being so parsimonious, of course.
You have to pay extra for one of those louder bells, I
think—and I know the Telecom people don't like you to
mess about with their equipment yourself."

"He was that all right, Sarge." Not for worlds would
Benson admit his inability to pronounce *parsimonious* with
any confidence. "When he lost his door key at work, and
didn't have the right gear to cut himself a spare, he wouldn't
pay to have one made, he just never took it out with him
anymore, in case he lost it. Used to lock the door and put the
key under one of the flowerpots in the porch, so Mrs. Mint'd
be able to get in to clean after he'd gone to work—only she
had to put it back, of course, before she went home at night,
for him to get back in."

"Typical!" Trewley rolled despairing eyes, and groaned.
"Thousands of pounds we spend on crime prevention—and
what does the silly old devil do but leave his only key, every
blasted day, under a flowerpot the whole damned town's
bound to know about, by now. Talk about *mad* scientists!"

Benson was indignant on Mrs. Mint's behalf. "She only
went on Monday and Wednesday and Friday, sir. . . ."

This artless comment did not comfort the superintendent.
"The same bloody flowerpot each time, of course?"

"Er—yes, sir. I'm afraid so. The, er, the third from the
left, Mrs. Mint said."

"Oh, my God!" Trewley was starting to turn purple; and
Stone, ever mindful of her chief's blood pressure, said:

"If Holbrook was deaf—and drunk—and if, through
some accident the fire went out . . . well, it's quite probable he would have noticed nothing when it happened. And
if there wasn't a note, it's unlikely to have been suicide—
and yet, I can't help thinking . . . Benson, what sort of fire
is it?"

"Dunno, Sarge. Pinched from a museum, by the look of it—the whole central heating could've done with scrapping and starting again. Except it would've cost him, of course, so he wouldn't have."

"Good!" Stone's eyes sparkled. "I did wonder. . . . So is it possible the fire was tampered with from outside the room? If he was always locking himself in . . . Are there any taps, say, in the hall that someone could sneak in and turn off?"

Benson flipped the indicator, and slowed for the turning to Allingham Alloys. "Don't think so, Sarge, at least I didn't notice . . . But then I was in a bit of a hurry, if you take my meaning. I'd sort of planned to leave the proper checks till later."

Neither he nor Stone allowed themselves even to glance at the superintendent, whose insistence on accompanying his sergeant had overturned the usual routine. Trewley had argued with Benson's identification of Dr. Holbrook was more then enough for him: a brilliant scientist, mysteriously dead, deserved top brass treatment even in death. While the Scene of Crime Officer, the forensic team, police doctor Watson and the ambulance people did their stuff back at the house, it was up to no less than a superintendent to advise the dead man's employers that there had been a tragedy.

And if such advising meant that he had to leave the police station for a while . . . that was just too bad.

Besides (he now reasoned, in silent self-justification), suppose there was something more in this than the accident it so obviously was. Who better than to want to kill one of the boffins than another boffin? The sooner he could spring the news of Holbrook's death on the suspects—before anyone from outside had time to let them know—the better. He'd get a good look at the slightest reaction—pick up on the very least hint of guilty behaviour . . .

He wondered whether Pleate would swallow it.

He feared not. He sighed.

"It would be quite a feather in our caps, sir," said his

sergeant, somehow divining the reason for his unease. "One of the classics. A nice, ingenious murder mystery—a great brain cut off in his prime by a method unknown even to medical science—wouldn't it be splendid!"

PC Benson said nothing. He remembered the locked and bolted, broken-down door; the testimonies from Mrs. Mint and the milkman to fastened windows and access otherwise undamaged; the absence of any obvious interference. The super might try to explain it away to Sergeant Pleate as murder—but Benson didn't think he'd succeed. Thinking about it, he was sure, now, that Dr. Holbrook's death was an accident, and no crime at all . . .

He'd be interested to see if he was right.

Five

THE RESEARCHERS AND developers of Allingham Alloys pursued their various tasks as yet untroubled by intimations of mortality. The hum of scientific worker bees filled the open plan hive. Visitations to the coffee machine continued, more frequent now as the morning drew on; Julia Springs had just taken in Dr. Kirton's personal tray, and was settling herself to enjoy her own, impeccable cup.

The telephone rang. She set down her coffee and picked up a pencil with one hand, lifting the receiver to her ear with the other: she was a picture of the perfect secretary.

"Dr. Kirton's office. . . . Visitors? In reception, I see. . . . If you could send them along to our entrance lobby, I'll meet them there. . . . Thank you. Good-bye."

Philip Whatfield, chancing to come from the area of the coffee machine, was fortunate enough to follow the undulations of Julia's trim hips as she hurried gracefully down the central aisle of the Research area towards the double swing doors at the end. With his own "office" lying almost at the edge of the area, he anticipated a long and pleasant walk back to it; and was disturbed to find his pleasure suddenly, and rudely, interrupted.

Bob Heath came swaggering from his lair, clutching a large glass bottle in one hand, and with a smirk on his face which did nothing to improve his sharp, sly features. Some instinct for mischief must have smoked him out at this particular moment. He gestured behind the oblivious Julia to her silent shadow, and sneered:

"This bloke bothering you, darling?"

Julia ignored him and walked on, neither tossing her head

nor turning round. Mr. Whatfield was far less intrepid. His footsteps stuttered; he flushed with mingled embarrassment and irritation. Bob Heath sniggered, and spoke as if in reply to some prurient remark from the older man.

"Ho, yes, couldn't agree more—a lovely little mover! Real style, she's got, a classy number all right—and looks as good as she moves, too!"

At the sight of this coarse hobbledehoy smacking his lips over the elegant Julia, Philip's gentlemanly fury was almost audible, but he managed to restrain himself. He knew the risks inherent in allowing his feelings to get the better of him; and duly returned in a grim silence to his desk, with the gloating chuckles of Bob Heath floating after him. Then the laboratory assistant, his ear half-cocked for the double doors' clatter heralding the return of Miss Springs, settled himself to his neglected duties.

The glass bottle was labelled *Picric Acid Solution*, and contained a bright yellow fluid. He set the bottle beside him on his workbench, reached for the box containing Dr. Holbrook's samples, switched on his hot plate, and wondered which size of beaker he should use . . .

". . . have to wait a short while, until he's less busy." Julia's clear voice followed immediately on the clunk of the double doors: she must be bringing the visitors back. Bob at once stopped what little he'd been doing, and moved across for a better view.

"Sorry, but we really would like to see him as soon as possible," came the reply from the taller of her two companions: a big, burly, world-weary man, with a knowing look in his eye.

Julia's reply was lost on the eavesdropper. A conscience far less guilty than that of Bob Heath must have identified the man as a policeman: that look, the young man could have sworn, had been very suspicious as it fell upon him. . . . And Bob was so disturbed by that suspicious look that he entirely failed either to appreciate Stone's quiet, dark good looks, or to wonder at her presence. His eyes were fastened on the disappearing form of Trewley, and his face turned slowly pale.

Miss Springs tapped on the door bearing Dr. Kirton's name, then entered, leaving the two detectives waiting outside, gazing about them with some curiosity.

"The privilege of rank, sir," whispered Stone, with a chuckle. "See how the big boss gets his own private den? While the lesser mortals have to pig it in the open."

Trewley shuddered. "*Open* isn't the word, girl—it's no more than a bloody great goldfish bowl! Privileges of rank be damned, it's no more than—than common sense, I'd have thought. Good grief, there's no privacy at all—and how can they possibly concentrate with that row from everyone talking at once, and the phones ringing?"

"I believe," she murmured, "the theory behind it is for the boffins to feel free to wander around talking to one another without the artificial constraints of office walls, or doors, or other barriers to communication—no hindrance to their potential brilliance, you see. A huge Exchange and Mart of brainwaves—a gigantic Think Tank for the benefit of everyone, all at once."

"Umph." Trewley rubbed his chin, and stared. "Really?"

"Really." Then she grinned. "That is, according to a copy of *Office Planning for the Future* I was stuck reading at the dentist's once."

"Thought it was something they might've taught you at medical school," he muttered, with some relief. "Glad to know they're still turning out doctors with their heads screwed on the right way after all."

"You could hardly have open plan surgeries, sir—any more than you could have open plan in our line of work. Not much chance of getting a confession out of anyone if everybody could hear it, is there? Only think what it would do for the villains' street cred if their friends knew they were grassing!"

"Don't joke, girl." Trewley frowned. "On the other hand, with open plan maybe we wouldn't have so many people claiming police brutality, if everybody could see how very gently we were doing the interviews . . . or then again," with a sigh, "we'd probably have even more, because they'd all get together to say they'd seen us beating some bloke up—and how could we deny it? If they made sure they got their stories right . . ."

"And I think, sir," said Stone, after a gloomy pause, "that it reduces heating and lighting bills, and other overhead expenses. You can see at once if everyone's gone home, so one switch deals with the lot, like a—a warehouse. . . ."

"And I suppose," said Trewley, glaring about him at the innocent work stations, "talking of warehouses, they'll claim it as industrial use—*and* they'll get lower rates, and taxes, and—and I don't know what else. Any more than I know how a man could ever call his soul his own, in a horrible hole like this. . . ."

Stone nodded towards the still-closed door. "I bet Dr. Kirton can. The one man in the whole department who's safe from prying eyes!"

The door received the full benefit of a bulldog glare. "That young woman's been a long time in there with him. I'd like to know—"

He spluttered into silence, as the door opened and Miss Springs appeared. "I'm so sorry," she said, "that you've had to wait. Dr. Kirton was busy on the telephone."

She spoke with a touch of less than her usual courtesy, and Trewley wondered whether she'd overheard his final remark, and whether he ought to apologize.

It was not so much towards Trewley as against Mr. Woolverstone that Julia's irritation was directed. During her brief absence from her post, the managing director had once again buttonholed poor Dr. Kirton and began to plague him: too much of this sort of pressure and he'd be, she feared, in line for another of his attacks . . . and whatever news of Dr. Holbrook it was that the police said they brought, Julia fervently wished they would deliver it without delay.

Having ushered them into the office and closed the door,

she settled to her typing, working off on the keys some of her wrath against the managing director of Allingham Alloys. The fast, flowing rhythm soothed her; she reached the bottom of one immaculate page, and wound it out, intending to replace it with a blank.

And the blank face of Bob Heath met her astonished eyes. He was standing, silent, before her; staring, the very picture of guilt, at Dr. Kirton's closed door. As he felt her gaze light angrily upon him, Bob turned his attention, with some difficulty, to Julia; but his normally ebullient manner was forgotten as he addressed her—for the first time she could recall—in subdued tones.

"Uh, that bloke," he began, nodding towards Dr. Kirton's door. "To . . . uh, to see Dr. Kirton, was he?"

Julia gave him a long, hard look. "Since he and his—his colleague are in Dr. Kirton's office with him at this moment, Heath, I believe you may take it that their business was with him, yes. Not with you, nor with anyone else."

He loomed closer, and lowered his voice. "A big bloke, weren't he? A policeman, right?"

His nearness unnerved her, though she was determined not to show it. "If he is, what is that to do with you?" And she noticed how his hands repeatedly clenched and knotted under the stress of some strong emotion. "Why," she demanded, "should the arrival of two detectives on the premises be any business of yours?"

"Two?" He rocked back on his heels, stunned. "Two detectives? The fuzz! Coming here . . . Did they say why?"

Julia sighed. "I repeat, Heath, it is no business of yours—or of mine—or, indeed, of anyone other than Dr. Kirton and Dr. Holbrook, and if—"

The yelp with which he interrupted her sent all heads turning in their direction. "Holbrook—I knew it!" He tried, too late, to cover it with a cough; and fell to choking. Julia, annoyed by the slip of the tongue to which he had driven her, watched him struggle, not sure whether or not she should be alarmed, but certain she should be justifiably annoyed that she had allowed him to startle her out of her professional secretarial persona.

She drew a deep breath. "It is nobody's business," she said, "except that of the principals. Nobody's business but theirs—so kindly leave me to mine—and be off about your own! There can surely be no need for you to persist in wasting everyone's time this way."

"Time!" His echo of her words was hollow, despairing. "Time's what I could be getting plenty enough of, soon . . ."

And then, recollecting himself, he shrugged his shoulders in a forlorn imitation of his customary insouciance—turned on his heel—and stalked silently away.

Dr. Kirton was apologising for the telephonic persistence of his managing director.

"To have kept you hanging on this way . . . Miss Springs has been marvellous . . . Every five minutes it seems he's after me, and it *would* happen again when someone was waiting outside . . ."

Trewley cleared his throat, and rubbed his chin. "Well, never mind, Dr. Kirton. Bad news can always do with waiting, can't it? Because I'm sorry to say we've called on a—a rather upsetting errand."

Dr. Kirton sat forward on his chair, mentally bracing himself: a detective superintendent was unlikely to interrupt him at work over any trivial matter. "Then kindly do not delay in discharging your errand, Mr. Trewley. I feel, if you will excuse me, that bad news is best imparted as quickly as possible, when there is nothing one can do about it anyway. . . ."

The final phrase had a slight upward intonation, as if the scientist did not quite dare to enquire whether something could, in fact, be done about whatever bad news the visitors brought.

Trewley nodded. "Fair enough, sir. We've come to tell

you that Dr. Basil Holbrook was found dead at his home earlier this morning."

Whatever ill tidings Kirton, a family man, might have expected, the demise of a member of his department was evidently not included. At first, he seemed puzzled; then a look of quick relief appeared on his face; and then, as the import of Trewley's words struck home, he gasped.

"Holbrook? Basil Holbrook—dead?" He fell suddenly back, clutching at the arms of his chair and breathing hard. "Holbrook—dead! Oh, no—the Squib project—and what am I to tell Mr. Woolverstone? It must be some mistake. . . ."

He closed his eyes, and exhaled in a deep, shuddering sigh. "Dead . . . But how," forcing open eyes that were dull from shock, "did it happen? And why," more passionately, "did it have to happen now, of all times? Squib—Holbrook—Mr. Woolverstone . . ."

And he shook his head in disbelief, Trewley broke in: "It seems to have been a domestic accident, as far as we know—at the moment," he added, watching the other's strained face for any reaction out of the ordinary. "We'll be making full enquiries, of course."

That ominous qualification brought a reaction which was far from ordinary. Dr. Kirton flushed scarlet, and cried:

"So you don't think it was a—an accident? And suicide—Holbrook would never—so that must mean—oh, no . . ."

He couldn't bring himself to say that last, grim word, and trailed off into a despairing groan. He slumped forward, his breath coming in jerking, agitated rasps, and his fingers groped in spasm at the empty air.

Trewley shot one horrified look at Stone, and left her to sprint to Kirton's side while he stampeded to the door, and wrenched it open.

"Miss Springs—in here, quick!"

Julia was there almost before he had finished speaking. Her startled eye fell upon the goldfish-gasping form of her boss, whose tie was being competently loosened by the quiet young woman sergeant. "His pills—let me get them!"

She darted round to the top drawer of Kirton's desk, the knob of which he had been vainly clawing as he struggled for breath. After a few seconds' frantic search, Julia snatched out a neat glass phial, unscrewed the top, and tipped two small pink tablets out on the palm of her hand.

Stone, divining her intention, held the stricken man's head and shoulders. "Steady, now," she said. "Steady. . . ."

"Dr. Kirton—Dr. Kirton, listen to me. Don't try to talk—can you manage your pills?"

"Steady," said Stone, as a low moan emerged from his throat. His lips parted. She looked at Julia. "Angina?"

"Yes—it's happened before, though never this bad. . . ." Dr. Kirton, gasping, opened his mouth. Stone held him; Julia slipped the pink tablet under his tongue. With a sigh, he closed his eyes. After an anxious few seconds, he began to relax.

"Good," said Julia. "That's right. . . . Take it easy." And, as his breathing improved and his face lost its ghastly colour, she turned angrily to Stone. "What on earth can you have said to—no, just take it easy, don't try to talk . . ."

"Is there a company doctor?" asked Stone, while Trewley hovered by the door, ready to summon more help if it seemed necessary. His sergeant didn't look too worried, though, and he generally bowed to her superior knowledge: but when Julia announced at last that she would leave Dr. Kirton in Stone's charge while she telephoned for Dr. Black, he sighed with relief.

But then his detective instincts began to stir. Was Dr. Kirton's attack—which looked, on the face of it, genuine— simply the result of shock? Or could it be that the man had a guilty conscience?

The company doctor arrived promptly, but the worst was well over by then. Kirton's breathing was more regular, his colour was almost normal, and his alarming look of pop-eyed strangulation had disappeared. Neither Julia nor Stone was panicking: the sergeant had even explained something of her personal history to the secretary, and Dr. Kirton had managed to croak the odd question as she did so.

Everyone left the office while Dr. Black carried out a brief examination of his patient, but it was not long before they were called back in again.

"He'll live to fight another day," said Dr. Black cheerfully. "Scared half to death by the local constabulary, of course, but he made his own way back from the brink—with a little help from his friends, naturally. Top marks, Sergeant—Miss Springs."

Julia smiled, and slipped from the room with a murmured promise to ring for a taxi the minute she was asked. This brought a weak protest from Dr. Kirton, and robust approval from Dr. Black.

"She's right, Geoff, you can't stay here. This is the second attack you've had within a month, remember. I don't want to see you within a mile of this place until next week at the earliest—and if it means waiting longer, then you wait. I want your own chap to give you a thorough overhaul. You're supposed to be taking things easy—no exertion, no shocks, no stress. What the devil brought all this on, for heaven's sake?"

Kirton coughed, and nodded at Trewley. "You tell him—I can't. The very thought . . ."

"Then don't you go thinking about it, sir," said Trewley at once. "Not if it's going to get you all worked up again. Dr. Black, perhaps we could step outside?"

"No!" With one word, Dr. Kirton forced himself back in command. "I'm not dead yet, for goodness' sake—and this is my department. It's my responsibility!"

Trewley looked at Dr. Black, who shrugged. "He's a tough old devil," he said. "If he insists . . ."

"I do," said Dr. Kirton. "There's no need to fuss—as I said, I'm not dead yet. Tell him, Superintendent."

"No, sir, you're not—dead, I mean," said Trewley, after a quick, silent exchange with Dr. Black. Dr. Kirton had heard the news once already: he had survived the worst: he'd be all right now. "But Dr. Holbrook is."

"Basil Holbrook?" Dr. Black showed much less surprise than had Dr. Kirton. "Dead? Well, well. Count your blessings, Geoff, because the man's in an even worse state than you are."

"Oh, how can you joke about it?" groaned his colleague. "At a time like this—the Squib project nearing completion— the police here, making enquiries . . . Surely you must see what—what it all means!"

"Of course I can." Dr. Black continued to address his friend in matter-of-fact tones. "For a straightforward accident, we wouldn't have had the privilege of a superintendent breaking the news—begging your pardon, Sergeant. So, not an accident—which leaves suicide. And I'm not," said Dr. Black, "in the least bit surprised."

Six

THEY STARED AT him. Dr. Black lost none of his certainty as he went on:

"Apart, that is, from the fact that he was a Catholic—though his faith, from what I gather, had lapsed over the past few years. But if I consider suicide purely from the medical point of view, well . . ."

Dr. Kirton seemed lost for words. Trewley said:

"What exactly do you mean, Doctor? What medical reasons could Holbrook have had to make him take his own life?"

Dr. Black shrugged. "I'll probably get my stethoscope snipped off for breaking a patient's confidence, but if the poor chap's dead, and as he had no family, I can't see that it matters, in the circumstances. Basil Holbrook, Superintendent, was a very sick man indeed. In my considered opinion, it was only a matter of time."

Kirton looked devastated. "A sick man? Suicide? But I had no idea—he never said—and Mr. Woolverstone—"

"And don't," interposed Dr. Black sternly, "let's forget that you're another sick man, Geoff—though not, fortunately, to the same degree. Provided you behave yourself, of course. But if you don't—if you can't sit listening calmly and quietly, then home you go—at once, and no messing. Understood?"

Kirton sighed, and nodded, sighing again. Dr. Black took this as a signal to continue.

"Yes, Holbrook was a very sick man. He came to see me—oh, early autumn, it must have been. Yes, some time in September, as I recall—said he had a feeling there might be something wrong—and there was. Seriously wrong. I was able to confirm that he'd need an operation, an urgent operation—any neglect could only result in . . . the inevitable. He was shocked, naturally, but said he wasn't surprised—he'd had his suspicions . . . though his symptoms," and here Dr. Black looked, for the first time, a little uneasy, "could have been masked by . . . by other considerations."

He cleared his throat with unnecessary emphasis. "Anyway, he thanked me for putting him straight, and said he'd need to think it over—about the operation, I mean."

"Would it have saved him?" asked Trewley. "Could it?"

Dr. Black pondered. "The growth was pretty deep-rooted—he'd lost his best chance by not getting medical advice—oh, a year or more back, when he should have noticed the very first symptoms . . ." He coughed again. "Ten percent at best, I'd say. If that."

"Did he know?" Trewley was starting to incline to the suicide view.

"Don't get the idea that I told him, because I didn't. Why make it worse for the poor devil? No point in saying what he ought to have done eighteen months ago! But he may well have guessed the truth—he was an intelligent man."

"He was a brilliant man," amended Dr. Kirton, in despair. "One of the most consistent achievers in the department— oh, he was touchy, moody, an individualist in so many ways—but an absolute genius when it came to metallurgy. . . ."

"And they say genius," rumbled Trewley, "is a law unto itself. I suppose, Dr. Black, it would have been a—a painful death? Doesn't the Catholic church regard suicide in those circumstances as—as not so much of a sin as, well, at other times?"

Dr. Black frowned. "I believe so, although, as I said, Holbrook hadn't been a practising Catholic for some years—not since his wife died. It would, of course— indeed, it does—require great strength of mind to wait for the climax of a singularly unpleasant illness—the pain, the suffering, the negligible hope, in this case, of recovery—not that Holbrook wasn't a man with considerable strength of mind. Cold-blooded nerve, on occasion. I can well imagine that he'd study the latest medical opinion on his condition, weigh up his chances, and opt, quite rationally, for the easy way out. In some ways, it's an understandable reaction—and particularly when you take into account that since the loss of his wife he really had little to live for . . . except his work," he added, and Dr. Kirton groaned.

"His work—it was invaluable—irreplaceable! With the Squib alloy so close to success, and now . . . Oh, dear—what am I going to tell Mr. Woolverstone?"

He was starting to breathe jerkily again. Trewley felt it would be wiser to change the subject. "How long has his wife been dead, do you know?"

Dr. Black nodded his approval of the diversionary tactic; Dr. Kirton concentrated on trying to remember.

"I forget exactly, but . . . about four years. I do know it affected him deeply. He never referred to her, or to the accident, again—not that he had been one to give much of himself away at any time, but afterwards he simply blotted out of his life everything of the remotest personal nature, and dedicated himself to his job—which was vital. Vital!" He was almost wringing his hands as he spoke. "Why did he—how could he—not tell us of this—this dreadful illness? We could have spared him some of the pressures—we could have tried to find others to work with him, share his knowledge, his theories, his methods—but he was so damnably independent, and now . . ."

"Perhaps," said Trewley, "he was overworking. Not that we're blaming you or your firm, Dr. Kirton, but if this job of his was so very . . . vital, maybe it was pressure of work—with the shock of his illness coming on top of it all—and, well, it could explain why he committed suicide. If," added the superintendent, "suicide's what it was, and not an accident." He did not list the third possibility: but it could not be far from anyone's thoughts.

Dr. Kirton was moved to protest, and his voice sounded stronger than it had done since the two detectives first entered his office. "If Basil Holbrook overworked, Superintendent, I assure you it was entirely his own choice. He was rightly proud of his importance to Allingham Alloys—he knew he was virtually irreplaceable. Not just because he had such a wide knowledge of metallurgy, but because he was so deeply committed to furthering that knowledge. If only," and he sighed, "he had not been so insistent on working at his own pace, in his own way. . . . He hardly ever made notes, you see, and the few he did make were indecipherable to anyone else. His way of—of safeguarding his secrets, or so I gathered. . . ." He forced a smile. "Though his handwriting was as bad as any I've seen on prescriptions written by a medical, rather than a metallurgical, doctor."

Dr. Black grimaced. "Getting cheeky, Geoff? You must be feeling better."

"Trying to make the best of a bad job," said Kirton. "And goodness knows how bad it's going to be, sorting out the mess—with virtually no notes, not even from his lab work, and certainly nothing in the current literature. . . . He would never publish until he could show only the final, successful results of his researches. He never wanted to give anyone the chance to spot errors or unnecessary steps that he might have made on the way—he'd done too much of that type of hatchet job on the preliminary notes of other metallurgists to wish the same thing to happen to him."

Trewley rubbed his chin. "Not one to own up to his mistakes, eh?"

"No, indeed. He would never forgive anyone who pointed out even the slightest discrepancy in his work. There is a member of our profession—I won't mention his name—who once had the temerity to say that Holbrook could have proved . . . a particular theory using a simpler, and cheaper, experiment than he in fact did. Basil Holbrook has—had—not spoken to him for the last fifteen years, Superintendent. Fifteen years! But you must understand that in metallurgical circles, his professional"—there was a slight emphasis on the adjective—"reputation was paramount. He had every reason to be proud of it, and he naturally wanted to take no risks of damaging it."

"Sounds an interesting bloke," said Trewley. "Brilliant—bad tempered—bears grudges—stubborn—conceited . . ."

"And not just conceited about his work," said Dr. Black, with a grin. "He was *not* pleased when I told him his hearing was going! He may have been a scientist, but he had no intention of believing the evidence in this particular case—though it's a far from uncommon reaction, of course."

As the three men pondered this truth, Stone, thinking aloud, said: "It's only human nature for the elderly not to want to admit their powers are fading. Perhaps, with the deafness on top of everything else, he thought suicide—"

"Have a heart, Sergeant!" For the first time, Kirton laughed. "I can't say I take too kindly to being numbered among the elderly, though I concede that to someone of your age anyone over forty must have one foot in the grave. The horrid truth is, my dear, that even if I'm not in the best of health, I could have given Holbrook five or six years."

"Good grief!" cried Trewley, as Stone blushed, and tried to frame an apology.

Dr. Black, with one quick, calculating look at Dr. Kirton, made up his mind. "An understandable error, Sergeant. Poor Holbrook was, I regret to say, subject to a condition which, in lay terms"—with a nod for Trewley, the non-medically-trained—"we might call premature ageing. Greying of the hair—some loss of hearing, sight and smell—a certain shakiness of the limbs, and—well, it can't be denied that he did look far older than he in fact was. Which, as far as I recall, was in his late forties."

"Good grief," said Trewley again. Stone looked startled. So did Dr. Kirton, though he covered it well.

"I myself am fifty-four—and hardly, Sergeant, I hope you'll agree, with even a toe, let alone a foot, in the grave?"

She smiled. "Not even the tip of a toe, sir. But—Dr. Black, surely such severely premature ageing in a man in his late forties is . . . unusual?" She glanced at Trewley; he raised no objection to her taking over the questioning. "Is there any chance that Dr. Holbrook's condition could have been the result of his illness?"

There was a long, long pause before Dr. Black replied; he seemed to be debating with himself. In the end, he favoured Dr. Kirton with an apologetic, embarrassed grimace before saying:

"No, the condition wasn't caused by his illness. In fact, I'm sorry to say—this is only an informed guess, but I'll wager a tidy sum it's correct—it was more likely that the condition would have been the cause of the illness."

"The cause?" Trewley and Stone spoke together; and Dr. Kirton, head of the Research and Development Department of Allingham Alloys, looked suddenly apprehensive.

"I have to tell you," said Dr. Black, with evident reluctance. "I know poor Holbrook was a law unto himself—I've no doubt he'd short-circuit any number of safety regulations to speed up his work . . . but it's my belief he was suffering from . . . from mercury poisoning."

Stone drew in her breath sharply; Dr. Kirton buried his face, white as paper, in his hands. "Oh, no . . ."

Trewley scowled at the others, and waited to be enlightened.

Now that he'd said it, Dr. Black was more relaxed. "To be frank, it surprises me that nobody in this department ever noticed—the loss of weight, the discolouration of the eyes, not to mention the way he was starting to slur his words as he talked." He nodded to Stone. "Of course, nobody could know whether he also suffered any of the mental side effects—the insomnia, the loss of memory, hallucinations, delusions—and it would take a medical examination to note the physiological changes—damage to liver, kidneys, heart, bowels—"

"Ugh!" Kirton shuddered, turning green; Trewley muttered something; Stone sighed. Dr. Black hurried to turn the conversation along less gruesome paths.

"As the good sergeant doubtless knows, there are many symptoms of chronic mercury poisoning—one of which, gentlemen, is progressive anaemia. And, when anaemia is allowed to progress too far . . ."

There was a thoughtful pause. Trewley was the one who eventually broke it.

"Yes, well, from what you've already said, Holbrook hadn't planned to go for treatment?"

"It would seem not. He made no mention of it to me—though you will, I imagine, be having a word with his general practitioner. I advised him to get a second opinion, of course."

Trewley grunted. "Now let me get this straight, Doctor. These—these mental side effects you mentioned. Would they have stopped him realising just how ill he was?"

"I'm sure he understood the nature of his condition—I gave you the list of possible symptoms for general information, no more. Not everyone suffering from mercury poisoning will have them all, by any means. Besides, if Holbrook had been suffering, say, from delusions, they'd be just as likely to have suggested to him that something was wrong, rather than that there was nothing the matter with him. He could . . . oh, have developed a persecution complex—heard voices, seen visions—suddenly announced himself to possess supernatural powers . . . the variations are endless. As far as I could tell, however, he was suffering from nothing of the sort."

"You said," objected the superintendent, "that he was a bright bloke. He could have hidden it from you."

"Why should he want to do that? If it were indeed the case, he would have had no reason to consult me—he could have remained in ignorance of his true condition and—and cherished, if that's the word I want, his delusions in private." Dr. Black smiled at Stone, one medical type to another, then nodded to Dr. Kirton. "I only meant, Geoff, that some of the—the more physical symptoms displayed by poor Holbrook might have caught the attention of someone in the department—but they didn't. And in any case, there was little, by this stage, that could have been done for him—which I'm reasonably certain he must have known. I repeat, he was an intelligent man."

"Brilliant," groaned Kirton, inevitably. "But—this mercury . . . Oh, dear, it was a—an essential part of his process, but—how could he have been so careless! He never dreamed it could happen to him, I suppose—the conceit of the man—the great Basil Holbrook, for whom the laws of science and nature were bound to suspend themselves!"

"And what," demanded Trewley, "about the laws of the land? Would the Health and Safety at Work Act have been . . . suspended on his behalf, as well? Just think—if the man could have proved this mercury poisoning, he might have taken Allingham Alloys right through the courts, and sued you for thousands. Millions, even!"

Stone blinked. Dr. Black stared. Dr. Kirton paled.

"Sue? But—but . . ." And he lapsed into a frantic babble of "carelessness . . . law unto himself . . . impossible to prove . . ." while Dr. Black considered this new proposal.

"It's an idea, I suppose. You could never be sure, with Holbrook. He had a—an idiosyncratic mind, to say the least of it—I imagine that's why he made such a good scientific researcher."

As a moan burst from Dr. Kirton's lips, Trewley hurried on before the departmental head could expound, yet again, on the brilliance of the dead scientist. "So a theory of suicide would be . . . pretty convenient, all things considered? You say the man had no family left. There's nobody who'd go making too much of a fuss, is there?"

"Superintendent, I—I don't know what to say."

"Oh, dear . . ."

The medical and the metallurgical doctors had spoken as one. Trewley decided to stir things up a little more.

"I reckon we'd better have a word with his solicitors about this. I'd like to know if Dr. Holbrook was planning any legal action against his employers—do you happen to know who he used?"

"I—I believe," said Dr. Kirton, in shaken accents, "his wife's affairs were handled by Gooch and Honeycombe—but you surely can't be saying—"

He was cut short. The door of his office thumped and rattled in its frame; the ceiling—the whole building—seemed to tremble; and the air was filled with the crash of breaking glass, and the shouts of startled scientists.

There had been an explosion in the Research and Development Department of Allingham Alloys.

───── Seven ─────

SIXTEEN ARMS AND legs met and tangled in the doorway of Dr. Kirton's office as everyone—including Kirton—rushed to find out what had happened. Stone, being the smallest and most nimble, broke free first; then they were all outside, gazing about them. There was nothing of interest to be seen, apart from the brown stain spreading slowly around a cup of coffee dropped near the desk—the untenanted desk—of Miss Julia Springs.

Dr. Kirton cleared his throat. "Where is everyone?" He was puzzled, but steady, and Dr. Black regarded him with a relieved expression in his eyes. Whatever further shocks were in store today, the Head of R&D was unlikely to succumb to them.

From a far corner of the enormous room, a discordant clamour of conversation rose above a cluster of excited scientists.

"Over there." Trewley stabbed a finger, and they all headed towards the hubbub. Kirton kept up well with them, though he was puffing a little as he complained:

"Explosions in R and D—whatever next! Some sort of accident, no doubt, but in all my years here—"

"Save your breath, Geoff," said Dr. Black, as the four threaded their way through the desks and work stations. "I swear I'll put you straight in a taxi and send you home at once if you don't behave yourself!"

"I have to know what's happened," insisted Dr. Kirton. "As long as I am head of this department, any—any untoward occurrence is my ultimate responsibility. . . ."

"Bob Heath's responsibility, you mean," snapped one of

the scientists, as the little party joined the chattering throng. "That fool let the picric acid solution boil dry on his hot plate—look! Glass everywhere!"

"Not to mention the noise," said someone else, rubbing his ears and wincing.

"Picric acid." Kirton nodded. "Yes, I see. . . ." As of course he did: and as the detectives did not, although Stone frowned at some faint memory. "An extremely careless and foolish thing for him to have done. Heath—where are you? And what have you to say for yourself?"

But Bob did not reply.

"Skipped off and left someone else to do the clearing up, the lazy slob," someone said.

"It could be worse," said someone else, who obviously had a Pollyanna complex. "If you think of all the foul-smelling brews he cooks up in here sometimes—and now, look—free ventilation!" He waved at the shattered windows, and some people chuckled.

Others were not so amused. "It'll let in the fog—"

"No, it won't—it's starting to clear—"

"Because it's blowing right in here with us! And if you or anyone else thinks I'm going to—"

Dr. Kirton decided it was again time for him to intervene. With a few general words, he soothed people's startled nerves; gradually, the diversion over, everyone began to wander back to their places.

"Yes," he murmured, once only he, Dr. Black, the two detectives, and Julia Springs remained to examine the scene. He probed gently among the wreckage of Bob Heath's work station. "Look—this bottle's empty. Obviously, he poured out the lot, intending to do that entire box of samples. No wonder there was such an explosion. Fortunately, however, nobody was hurt by the flying glass—fortunately for his conscience, that is." He switched off the hot plate at the wall, and frowned again at the mess.

"Pity you can't deduct the damage from his wages," said Dr. Black, thinking it was time he urged his patient back to his office. "Unless there was some . . . er, medical emergency which drove him away from the job at top speed, it looks remarkably like carelessness to me."

"So it was." Dr. Kirton frowned. "And in his continuing absence, Miss Springs, I wonder if you would mind arranging for someone to clear up as much of the broken glass as possible? And could you ring for the carpenter—boards of some sort, for the windows? And—oh, dear—really, this is a most disturbing sort of day. . . ."

Dr. Black pounced. "I warned you, Geoff! Leave everything to Miss Springs, who is more than capable of coping, and come right back to your office this minute!

"Ten minutes," he continued, once everyone was settled again in Dr. Kirton's little room. "Ten minutes, no longer—and even that's longer than I'd like, except that I know you'll worry even more if you don't know just what's what. But you've had far too many shocks today for a man in your condition—not that I think you'll drop dead, of course, but there's little sense in overdoing things. Understood?"

"If you'd rather," said Trewley, "we could always leave it for today."

But, as he'd anticipated, both men dismissed the suggestion. Dr. Kirton said he would rather have it all over and done with at once, since the police were already there; and Dr. Black, with a laugh, said that *he* would rather Dr. Kirton didn't go worrying himself all weekend about what the police would say on Monday, or whenever he next saw them. Stress, he pointed out, wouldn't help his patient's blood pressure, as Sergeant Stone would no doubt agree.

"But ten minutes," he said again, as Stone nodded, smiling, "is your lot, Geoff. I'll be having a word with your invaluable Miss Springs on my way out—you've been warned."

"Just one thing, Doctor, before you go." Trewley's request halted Dr. Black in his tracks. "Could you let me have the name of Dr. Holbrook's GP, please?"

Dr. Black grinned. "Quite right, Superintendent—check,

and check, and double-check. Trust nobody! Just like poor Holbrook," he added, and Dr. Kirton, thinking again of those indecipherable laboratory notes, sighed. "If I remember correctly, he attended the Stowe practice—and I'm pretty sure you'll find out I was right. Poor Holbrook—suicide, in many ways, was the best solution for him—though it's horribly unprofessional of me to say so. But then, I'm an atheist, myself. I've no time for a God who'll let people suffer needless torments—and I imagine many scientists, looking squarely at the plain facts of the case, would agree with me. Poor old Holbrook . . ." And he was gone.

Dr. Kirton, sighing, sat back on his chair. "Are there many more questions, Mr. Trewley? Miss Stone?"

Trewley rubbed his chin, and chuckled. "To be honest, Dr. Kirton, I reckon the first thing we'd both like to know is what caused that almighty bang just now. Picric acid, I think you said? What the devil's that? And what's it used for? None of your lot seemed the least bit bothered, once they realised what had happened."

With his mind distracted from his most pressing woes, Dr. Kirton's breathing relaxed; he even managed to appear faintly cheerful. "Now there, Mr. Trewley, is the classic example of the scientific mind in action. I congratulate you." Trewley stared. Dr. Kirton smiled. "Neither we, nor you, care for mysteries," he explained. "We both demand logical, rational explanations for everything: we need to know cause and effect. To us, the scientists, because we have additional knowledge which you do not, the potential effects of picric acid are, of course, well understood."

Dr. Kirton's own scientific mind was clearly in gear by this time. Trewley and Stone prepared to be baffled, as he prepared to elucidate.

"Let me first," he said, "explain that the crystals of picric acid, if dissolved in water or alcohol to form a solution, are very widely used in metallography for etching metal surfaces. If we wish to study the crystallographic structure of certain types of alloy, we cut a sample piece from the bar—or casting, or whatever—and then grind and polish it to a mirror finish. We then dip it in the solution. And for a number of technical reasons—with which I won't bother you," he added hastily, "we find that it's best to heat that solution before use." He had spotted the eyes of his captive audience starting to glaze over, and took pity on them.

"Yes—well! We have to heat the stuff—then we dip the sample in it, and the acid attacks the surface, destroying the mirror finish, making the crystals themselves show up more clearly. I'm sure," he said kindly, "you'll have noticed a similar phenomenon on a—a galvanised bucket, or a water tank."

They seized on these welcome examples, and agreed that they had. Dr. Kirton smiled briefly before continuing:

"Of course, our sample crystals aren't as large as that, but the effect is the same, in principle—and we use a microscope to examine them. Their size, shape and so on can tell us much of what we wish to know about the various properties of the individual alloy."

He seemed to have paused. Trewley, looking hopefully at Stone, waited a moment, then ventured:

"So you heat up this—this acid in a saucepan . . ."

"Usually a glass beaker, on a hot plate."

"You heat it up," persisted Trewley, "and you dunk your bit of shiny sample in the beaker so the acid eats away the—the bad bits . . . and leaves the bits you want?"

"Most expressively and succinctly put, Superintendent. For a layman, your grasp of the fundamentals is admirable." Kirton coughed. "Now, picric acid, as I told you, comes in crystalline form—but in that form it is most unstable. For this reason, we must keep it covered by liquid at all times. Picric acid, you know, is used in the manufacture of explosives. We always take the greatest care to prevent its drying out and reverting to crystalline form."

Trewley struggled gamely on. "And if it *does* dry out—it explodes?"

"It does, Superintendent—as you yourselves observed a short time ago. Bob Heath made the elementary mistake of allowing the solution, which he was heating in accordance with recognised practice, to dry out on the hot plate."

"So he did," said Trewley, the bulldog wrinkles of his frown giving him a most thoughtful look. "So he did. . . ."

Observing her superior off on some track in pursuit of a theory she had not yet considered, Stone said:

"*Mist. explos.*—of course! Picric acid—except that we called it trinitrophenol," she said, as astonished eyes turned towards her. "When I was a student, one of the ward sisters—a real character, one of the old-fashioned dragon sort—insisted on using a one percent solution of trinitrophenol for the treatment of burns. So that's picric acid. . . . And what," she enquired of Dr. Kirton, "can you tell us now about this—this Squid thing Dr. Holbrook was working on? You said it was important."

"Oh, dear, yes. The, ah, Squib." Dr. Kirton lost his sprightly tutorial expression, and sighed, recalling the company's unfortunate loss. "The Squib . . . and I still have to tell Mr. Woolverstone—our Managing Director. He's been most keen to follow the progress of Squib—that's to say, as far as Holbrook was prepared to tell anyone anything about it—but, in the circumstances, he followed it closely. This will be a dreadful shock to him. Perhaps I . . ."

"And Squib," said Stone quickly, "is—what, exactly?"

Dr. Kirton looked shocked. Trewley came to with a start, and remarked that he and his sergeant could be relied upon completely. Dr. Kirton sighed. He frowned. . . .

He made up his mind, and assumed an air of intense secrecy. It would not have surprised either of the detectives if he had put his finger to his lips before he spoke; he certainly glanced quickly round the room in case anyone had sneaked in, unnoticed, to eavesdrop; and he lowered his voice by several decibels, to a low murmur.

"Our new discovery, Sergeant—Superintendent. A breakthrough of literally stupendous importance! Still at the research stage, of course—but with the potential to change civilisation as we know it!"

Trewley and Stone forced themselves not to look at each other in case their expressions of disbelief betrayed them. This was science fiction—this was daydreaming! Real life, especially in Allshire, didn't happen like that.

Dr. Kirton looked unhappily at the two wooden faces in front of him. "I do rely on your keeping this confidence, Superintendent—Sergeant. A word in the wrong place could be . . ." He turned a mottled pink, and coughed.

"Not a word, sir," promised Stone. Trewley was mute. "Unless," she added, "it should turn out to be, uh, germane to our enquiries, that is."

"Oh, I hardly think it will!" Dr. Kirton's tone sounded as if he was rather hoping than thinking. "Squib, you know, is an acronym for—ahem!—Splat-Quenched Iron-Based alloy. Actually, since it's iron-based, we could have as easily called it a ferro-alloy, but"—and he permitted himself a dry chuckle—"our resident acronymist did himself an injury trying to pronounce *Sqfa*, so . . ."

He shrugged disarmingly, and his audience realised who that resident acronymist must have been.

"Squib," repeated Stone, as Trewley still said nothing. She said it thoughtfully; coaxingly.

"Ah, yes." Dr. Kirton sat up. "Doubtless you both know that an alloy is a—a combination of metals. Plumber's solder"—at Trewley's involuntary cry, Dr. Kirton blinked, but carried gamely on—"is an alloy of lead and tin, for instance. Now, alloys often have markedly different properties from those shown by their separate components: properties such as better malleability, higher tensile strength, higher resistivity . . ."

As he paused to wag a didactic finger at them, Stone—Trewley was speechless—stared up at the ceiling, musing: "Pinchbeck is a substitute for gold, isn't it? Copper and . . . copper and something?"

Kirton beamed. "Indeed yes, Sergeant! It's an alloy of

copper and zinc, and decidedly gold-like in appearance." He shot a quick look at her left hand, bare of any ornament. "Don't, I beg you, ever buy a 'gold' ring without a hallmark—you'd have a nasty disappointment were you ever to melt it down. But that's the principle behind the alloying process, you see—to obtain improved properties of, well, various sorts—or, as in the case of pinchbeck, to create an acceptable, or at least convincing, and cheaper substitute."

Stone nodded, forcing herself to sound confident. "So that's alloys explained. And the—the splat-quenching?"

"Quenching is a way of cooling a metal very rapidly. Perhaps you have watched a blacksmith quenching a horseshoe in water? Ah, it is said," and Dr. Kirton raised his eyebrows, "that the ancient swordsmiths would use—ah, human blood—for this purpose. They, ah, felt it gave the sword a keener edge, you see. In certain countries, it was the regrettable custom to keep a supply, as it were, of slaves, on standby—ahem!—so that, once the completed weapon had come from the anvil and the fire, it would . . . ah, run a few of them through. To quench the steel, you understand—that is, to harden it, in everyday terminology."

Trewley grunted. "I trust," remarked Stone, "that you use a less drastic method of quenching nowadays."

Dr. Kirton chuckled. "Indeed, yes. Water, usually—very, ah, dull by comparison. It takes twelve tons of water to make one ton of steel, you know—which, if you recall your history, was the purpose behind the Dam Busters raid of the Second World War. The intention was to deprive the German steel mills of their water supply. . . . Ahem!"

He gazed sternly at his audience. "Has that explained quenching to your satisfaction?"

Neither detective would have dared to suggest otherwise: not that Dr. Kirton would have noticed, by this time. He was growing brighter with every passing technical syllable.

"Excellent. Ah—to continue. Splat-quenching is no more than one way—an extremely fast way—of quenching. The molten metal—in our case, the iron-based alloy—is thrown upon a much colder surface, which makes it solidify quickly, which alters its basic structure—to our advantage, naturally. The cooling is so very fast that the atoms have no time to arrange themselves, as it were, into their usual crystals—they have what we call an 'amorphous' form, which accounts for some of the differences in properties between splat-quenched alloys and those made by more conventional means. . . . And there you have it."

He nodded, as if he'd come to the end of his lecture and was inviting questions from the floor.

Trewley realised that Stone wasn't going to ask. "Why splat?" he demanded, hoping he'd understand the answer. "Er . . . stands for something, by any chance?"

"Another acronym, you mean? No, Superintendent. *Splat* is merely an onomatopoeic representation of the noise made by the metal as it falls, or as in this case is thrown, upon the cold surface."

Trewley sighed, then scowled. Dr. Kirton took this to mean that his words had so far reached receptive ears. He leaned forward again, and lowered his voice still further.

"No doubt you're about to ask the point of all this. It no doubt seems, to the lay mind, fantastic—dollops of white-hot metal being splatted on cold surfaces, or immersed in water . . . but I will tell you." He was almost whispering now. "In one word: superconductivity!"

Trewley blinked. If this was the punch line, the introduction had obviously been wasted on him.

Stone, however, stirred at her colleague's side. Kirton at once directed his attention towards her. "I see you take my meaning, Sergeant. *Superconductivity:* the ultimate technological goal of the twentieth century! Once our new alloy has been perfected, it will *revolutionise*, no less, every conceivable application of electricity there could possibly be! Its generation, its transmission—industrial applications, domestic equipment, medical equipment—transport—electronics . . .

I could go on, but I won't. The list is endless. I will simply say again, any conceivable application there could ever be!"

Trewley sensed Stone's quickened interest. He rubbed his chin. His sergeant was a bright girl, though he'd never dream of telling her so: but if she thought it was worth getting worked up about, maybe there could just be something in this, after all. . . .

Dr. Kirton's face turned pink with excitement, and he forgot to keep his voice low.

"The principles of superconductivity—of the complete loss of all electrical resistance—have been known since 1911, of course." He nodded to Stone as if there could be no doubt of her, at least, sharing in this knowledge. She ventured a solemn nod in response. He smiled.

"At that time, of course—indeed, until the last few years—it was only possible to achieve superconductivity with the use of liquid helium: a method which is not only expensive, but difficult, with a required temperature very close to Absolute Zero. Minus 273.15 degrees Celsius. Ah . . . extremely cold," he translated, as Trewley still looked blank.

Stone was thoughtful. "I seem to recall something in the papers about superconductivity at temperatures a good deal warmer than Absolute Zero. . . . Using ceramics of some sort, wasn't it?"

"Exactly so, Sergeant!" Kirton seemed delighted by her feat of memory. "Muller and Bednorz—an absolutely brilliant piece of research! Justly deserving of the Nobel Prize for Physics—their discovery that, with a particular combination of certain key elements—copper, barium, oxygen and yttrium, or lanthanum—superconductivity can be achieved right up to Minus 93 Celsius. Warmer than liquid hydrogen!"

"But that's not room temperature, surely."

Once more, Kirton's voice sank to a near whisper. "You are right, Sergeant, it is not. The research continues. . . . But, while the race may still be on for a room temperature superconductor, almost all of that research is in the area of ceramics. Yet I have to tell you—and this is in the *strictest* confidence—that Holbrook's Squib—the company's new alloy—could well turn out to be the room temperature superconductor for which the whole world is searching—and it is entirely without ceramic connections!"

"Oh," said Stone, clearly impressed.

"Oh," said Trewley, trying to sound as if he knew what he was talking about. He rubbed his chin. "You mean—you mean your Squib is . . . pretty important, then?"

"Vital, Superintendent, is no exaggeration, believe me. This superconductive material—one through which electrical current could pass with no resistance, no subsequent loss of power, requiring neither power nor resistance to keep it at artificially low temperatures . . . it will be more dramatic in its effect than the transistor, in its time—than the microchip, in ours! Nothing less than the three-minute mile of the power industry! For the very first time in history, *any* electrical equipment for any application imaginable will be *totally efficient*! Absolutely no loss, no wastage, of power— cheaper to manufacture—far more compact . . . The wires carrying the current need be only a fraction of the present size! Even copper wires, efficient as they are— although silver, as a matter of interest, is even more efficient—even copper wires grow warm as electrical current passes through them—warmth which indicates so much wasted power. The thinner the wire—the cheaper, the more compact—then the more power is lost. But, with a superconductor, there is *no heat produced, and no power wasted, whatsoever*!"

"Energy conservation," said Stone, sounding gratified by the prospect.

"Among other aspects, yes. The possibilities are, literally, endless—which explains why so many people are working to achieve this end. But the ceramics on which most recent research has been concentrated use copper, which is comparatively expensive—not to mention yttrium or lantha-

num, which are extremely rare. Squib, on the other
hand . . ."

The whisper thrilled about the little room. "The Squib, you
see, is basically composed of nothing more nor less than iron
and hydrogen. Two simple, easy, cheap ingredients. . . . And
if so minor an advance as the ceramics may earn a Nobel Prize,
you can surely see that the Squib, once it has been perfected,
must astonish the world!"

And the two detectives could see that indeed it must.

— Eight —

DR. KIRTON WAS by this time thoroughly engrossed in his peroration. There had been a moment when Julia Springs opened his door and made taxi-summoning gestures, but he had waved her away as he continued to expound: it was obvious that he revelled in the secret discovery upon which Basil Holbrook had worked. Did Dr. Kirton—Holbrook's departmental head—have his own dreams of a Nobel Prize?

"So what you're saying," said Stone, "is that your Squib—your ferro-alloy—it's going to knock spots off all the new ceramics?" And both she and Trewley expected Dr. Kirton to approve this crisp summing-up of the story so far.

To their surprise, a shadow crossed his face. "There can be no doubt," he replied, "that it will do so . . . ah, eventually. But—but we have, alas, to, ah, perfect the manufacturing technique. . . ." And he sighed. Then, having made the confession, he brightened.

"It is, however, our only weak point. You see, at white heat—when certain essential structural changes occur—the metal must be protected from the open air. We, ah, blanket the metal with an atmosphere of hydrogen—some of which dissolves into the metal even as it protects it. And the rapid cooling of the molten alloy as it is splat-quenched will trap this dissolved hydrogen in the alloy. . . ."

"And that's a good thing?" prompted Stone, as he paused to savour the prospect of trapped, dissolved hydrogen.

"My dear Sergeant—it's the whole point! The hydrogen nuclei so alter the electrical properties of the alloy that it becomes superconductive!" He was on the point of beaming again, when he remembered. He sighed. "But . . . I fear that it must be through his work with hydrogen that Holbrook came in contact with . . . with the mercury. You see, if a gas can diffuse into an alloy then it can also, given time, diffuse out. And it was this diffusion rate factor which had poor Holbrook at his one disadvantage. Undoubtedly, he improved the stability of Squib, but . . . the standard test for diffusion of hydrogen out of metal is to—to immerse the sample in a mercury bath, measuring the amount of hydrogen which then bubbles out—which," he concluded sadly, "it always did. So Holbrook was always testing and retesting it. . . ." Again he sighed. "It's ironic, I suppose, that mercury, of all substances, should have been the first superconductor—though only below Minus 269 Celsius, so it can't have been of much practical use. . . ."

Trewley frowned. "Isn't there something . . . a bit safer he could have used, instead of mercury?"

"Ah, Superintendent, you have touched on a sore point." Dr. Kirton looked sorrowful. "Glycerine, it may interest you to know, is used in some countries for a similar purpose— but I fear the results it produces are less accurate than those obtained by using a mercury bath. And Holbrook is—was, I mean—almost obsessional in his demand for accuracy. The scientific mind . . ."

Stone was thinking about electricity. From her training, she remembered various items of hospital equipment; she considered their size, and the heat they generated, and she saw that the Squib would indeed astonish the world. But she also saw that there were other ways of astonishing it . . .

"Suppose," she said, "that you manage to iron out—oh, I'm sorry." She smiled. "I mean, to smooth out your, um, production problems. Suppose you make a Squib that's superconductive at room temperature. Won't it have rather . . . dramatic effects on the world demand for copper? I mean, if everything electrical, except your new alloy, needs copper in one form or another, then surely . . ."

For the first time, Dr. Kirton looked quite taken aback.

"Good gracious. I must confess the idea had never really dawned on me before—the, ah, commercial impact of Squib, that is, from the viewpoint of the copper industry, as you appear to suggest. Squib itself is so revolutionary a concept that the consequences for us—for Squib's manufacturers—would—will—be miraculous, to say the least. So far, however, we here in R and D have regarded it as more of a pure research challenge. The—the mercantile side of it we have left to others. A rather . . . naive attitude, I admit, now that you have alerted my mind to the possibility. . . ." And he pondered the possibility for a few moments.

He nodded. "You are right, Sergeant. Once our Squib is successfully marketed, I would agree there is likely to be less demand for copper than at present."

"You mean," demanded Trewley, trying to get things absolutely straight, "that nobody's going to be buying copper anymore? That sounds—"

"Oh, hardly *nobody*, Superintendent, if you will excuse me. Copper, after all, is used for many other purposes than electrical ones. Kitchen utensils, pipes and plumbing—my dear Superintendent, is something wrong?"

Stone hurried into speech to cover Trewley's involuntary groan. "From what you say, Dr. Kirton, the electrical industry wouldn't need anything like as much copper as before, would it?"

"I have to admit, Sergeant, that I imagine it would not. However . . ." Once more, the scientist sighed. "The birth, as one might say, of Squib would have been enormously exciting—we could have announced it to the world. Allingham Alloys would be famous, we could patent it worldwide . . . but now, with Holbrook's death, how much time has been lost? Oh dear—I can't think what Mr. Woolverstone will say! He's been so very insistent recently on the alloy's early success—and Holbrook, insofar as such an uncommunicative man can communicate, was almost encouraging him to think . . . To hear Holbrook talk over the past few months, you know, one could readily have believed that he was on the very point of solving the hydrogen loss problem—and then . . . "

"And then," suggested Stone, "Mr. Woolverstone could have gone public, and named his own price on the Stock Exchange. Is that it? Is that the reason your managing director's been so keen to have tangible proof of Holbrook's success with the new alloy?"

Dr. Kirton flushed. In the excitement of his narration, he had allowed his tongue to run away with him. "Oh, dear. Well—I wouldn't care to go as far as that, exactly . . ."

Trewley didn't want Kirton's death from embarrassment on his sergeant's conscience. "Well, maybe at the moment it's not that important, sir. Besides, we could always go and ask him direct, if it turned out any of this, er, stock market business had any bearing on Dr. Holbrook's death."

"You surely can't be suggesting—oh, no!"

"We're suggesting nothing, at the moment," Trewley told him, as he turned pale. The superintendent did not add that they were *thinking* a great deal: there was no need. Anyone could understand that the police must have several questions to which answers would be required. To whose benefit, for example, had the death of Basil Holbrook been? Everybody in the copper industry?

Or might Allingham Alloys have weighed a potentially damaging court case against the premature loss of their most valuable researcher now that his work, according to his own departmental head, was nearing completion? Nobody, after all, is indispensable. . . .

"So there would," mused Trewley, "be some effect, at least, on the world copper market." He set the likely legal aspect aside to be pondered at leisure. "If everyone starts using Squib, I mean. Pricey stuff, copper?"

"My dear Superintendent, it's hardly a precious metal like silver, or gold—but on the other hand a day's salary probably wouldn't fill you a bucket. Selling the scrap from our foundries would make you far richer than, say, stealing the silver from old church roofs."

Trewley looked startled. "Don't you mean lead?"

Kirton's chuckle was less hearty than earlier efforts. "Only in a manner of speaking, Superintendent. Old lead, you see, could in its time have been classed as an alloy—an alloy of lead and silver. Early extraction and refining processes were far from adequate, you see. Mind you, the silver was by way of being, ah, an impurity, rather than an element deliberately introduced—but our modern techniques manage to remove all the silver, and modern lead is hardly worth the effort of stealing. Many an old church, however, has had a new roof, as it were, for free, simply through the scrap value of the old one."

"Metallurgical research," said Trewley, stumbling just a little over the words, "sounds . . . interesting, Dr. Kirton. I expect there's a lot more you could tell us, if we only had the time—but there, we haven't. And I don't think we could justify keeping you here asking you questions out of—out of sheer curiosity. . . ."

"Ah, Superintendent, that was where Holbrook scored so very highly! He had the true research mind—alert, curious—brilliant at the inspired guess which seemed on the face of it against all logical concepts of the correct approach—but which, after careful study, would in retrospect be so blindingly obvious that you'd wonder why it had never occurred to you before. Partly, I have to say, it was because he was a very . . . close, cautious man, who would reveal not even part of his theories until he was utterly confident of success—success which he invariably achieved. And which only then would he demonstrate, step-by-step. Experiments—documentary evidence . . ."

He seemed about to lament those illegible laboratory notes again. Stone smiled. "Just like a detective story, sir. All the clues and red herrings unresolved until the final chapter!"

"Indeed, Sergeant. Poor Holbrook—he may have

been . . . temperamental, but he was a most conscientious employee. He must surely have felt confident that he was about to write the final chapter during the past couple of months, otherwise—oh, dear . . ."

"And talking of final chapters," said Trewley, "who—?"

But there came a tap on the door, which opened. Once more Julia Springs, frowning, looked into her boss's office; and this time it was clear she would not be waved away.

"You must excuse me for disturbing you—again, Dr. Kirton, but Dr. Black was really most insistent that—"

"Oh yes—yes, I know!" And the scientist began to rise from his chair, perhaps eager now to escape the attentions of the two detectives. He had told them a lot: more, probably, than they needed to know; and he felt a little uneasy. "Miss Springs," he said, "takes excellent care of me, excellent. Nobody could have been kinder when I was . . . ill on the day after the Metallurgical Society dinner. She tried to send me home in a taxi then, too, but—"

"But *this* taxi," Julia broke in, "has been waiting for over twenty minutes! If you'll only leave now, I'll do my best to keep it from Dr. Black, but you really must take proper care of yourself, or I won't be able to."

She took his pill bottle from the desk, and put it into the briefcase she had collected from beside his desk. She helped him wind his scarf about his throat, and eased him into his coat. She handed him the briefcase, and stood by the office door, looking sternly at her watch.

"We'll expect you back at work when we see you, Dr. Kirton, and not a moment before," she said. "Good-bye!"

"You know, Dr. Kirton," said Trewley, as the scientist, with a shamefaced grin, was taking his leave, "your secretary's a wonderful woman. She doesn't just take good care of you—she doesn't poke her nose in where it's not wanted, either. Believe me, there's not many women—or men, come to that," as he felt Stone flinch at his side, "who'd have two coppers come waltzing into their office, on business they'd said was to do with someone who worked there, and not have tried finding out what was going on—unless Dr. Black told you, which I doubt if he did."

"He did not."

"Then you're a woman in a million, Miss Springs."

Julia's discreet eyebrows were raised just enough to make the point. "You should not be surprised, Superintendent. Had either Dr. Black or Dr. Kirton considered it my business to know the reason for your visit, they would have informed me. Since, however, they did not, then naturally—as any secretary would—I respect their wish to keep the matter secret."

"There's no secret about it, I'm afraid," said Dr. Kirton, shaking his head. "Poor Holbrook—Basil Holbrook—is dead." He gulped. "Suicide, or accident—either way, it's a terrible tragedy for us all at Allingham Alloys."

"Suicide?" For once, Julia Springs showed some emotion. "Suicide? But—but how? I mean—how horrible! And, of course, how very sad."

Dr. Kirton turned to Trewley, who cleared his throat. "I believe you asked me the same question, sir, right at the start of our interview. Just before you were taken ill when I told you about the accident." There was a slight stress on that word. "Accident's all it seems to be, so far—yes, it could be suicide, I agree—but it has every appearance of an accident. Dr. Holbrook was . . . well, gassed. The cleaning lady found him dead in his study, with the fire not lit and the supply full on. Could be a fault in the fire, or the pipework, or the pilot light—we'll have 'em checked, of course—and that's all we know at present."

"Oh, dear." There was what sounded like genuine regret in Julia's voice. "Just think—if it hadn't been for his cold, he would have noticed when the fire went out, and then he need never have died. What a waste."

"Yes, I'd forgotten," said Kirton. "Poor Holbrook certainly had the beginnings of a cold. . . ." And he wished he could as easily forget Basil Holbrook's invariably alcoholic remedy for all ailments, serious or trivial. Then he brightened. "Yes, the cold—it may well have been an accident, despite—oh," and he turned an anxious eye upon the superintendent, "despite other considerations."

"A cold?" Trewley rubbed his chin. "Are you sure?"

Kirton and Julia both nodded. Julia said: "He was busy coughing and sneezing most of yesterday afternoon, as I'm sure Mr. Whatfield could confirm, if you asked him. Poor Dr. Holbrook—he'll have taken a couple of aspirin, I expect, and fallen asleep in front of the fire, trying to shake it off. It only goes to show that you can't be too careful—can you, Dr. Kirton?" She shook her head firmly at her hovering boss. "You still look decidedly peaky—and you're still here, instead of—"

"Yes, yes, I must be on my way. . . ."

Trewley glanced at Stone. She was not urging the scientist home: he'd risk it. "Just one moment, if you wouldn't mind, sir. I think perhaps we'd best make arrangements for locking Dr. Holbrook's desk, or his filing cabinet, or whatever he kept his papers in. Just a temporary precaution," he added, as Kirton stared at him in dismay. "To—to safeguard your Squib," he said. "As Miss Springs pointed out, you can't be too careful . . ."

"But—but Mr. Woolverstone—"

"I," Julia broke in, "will explain it all to Mr. Woolverstone. You have no need to worry about anything. It won't be for long, will it, Superintendent?"

Trewley longed to say he had no idea, but Kirton didn't look like a man who could take much more. "Well, I shouldn't think you'd be choosing anyone to carry on the good work right away—but when you get round to it," as Kirton opened his mouth, then shut it without speaking, "when you've got, er, Holbrook's successor, maybe you'd be good enough to let us know? Just for the record," he said, as Kirton opened his mouth again. "But don't you go worrying yourself about all that now."

"No," said Julia, speaking over Kirton's attempt at a protest. "The only thing you're allowed to worry about, if you insist on worrying at all, is that R and D will have to budget for some overtime cleaning this week. You should have heard the grumbling! I can only assume that close proximity to scientists must significantly broaden the vocabulary." She smiled. "Heath's office, however, looks a great deal tidier than it did before."

"Yes," said Trewley, as Kirton managed a smile for the little pleasantry. "The elusive Mr. Heath. Tell me, Miss Springs, has he showed up yet?"

"Nobody, more's the pity, has seen the wretched youth. He probably knows that there are a good many people who wish to offer him the benefit of a few well-chosen words."

Trewley rubbed his chin. "Must have been in quite a rush to have taken off like that and leave the—the acid to boil dry and explode. I suppose you've checked in the—in the obvious places, in case he was, er, taken ill?"

His delicacy was wasted on Julia. "I have already asked somebody to check in the lavatories, and Heath is in none of them. Nor is he over in the Sick Bay: I phoned some time ago to check, and I left a message for them to call me if he turned up later. They haven't."

"So," said Trewley, "no sign of him anywhere? Wonder if he's done a bunk? And why."

A flush darkened Julia's face. "I rather fear, Superintendent, that if he *is* missing, it may be my fault. You see, he was pestering me—trying to find out who you were, and what you wanted. Normally, I refuse to gossip, especially to the likes of Bob Heath, but in this instance it—it just . . . slipped out."

"That we were police?"

Julia dropped her eyes. "He'd guessed, anyway—all I did was to confirm it. Mainly so that he would go away and leave me to get on with my work—which he did, thank goodness. But—now . . ."

"Did you tell him—did he say—anything else? Do try to think, Miss Springs. This character seems to have vanished without trace. We need to know why."

Her brow puckered. "Well . . . he was very tense even before I told him you'd come about Dr. Holbrook, but afterwards . . . he was certainly startled by the news. He almost jumped in the air, and he looked rather green. And he went very quiet . . ."

"So you saying we'd come about Dr. Holbrook bothered him more than he was bothered already? Was he normally the, er, the bothered type?"

Julia's mouth twisted. "On the contrary, he took pains to cultivate a laid-back pose which was intended to impress. Whether it did or not, I can't say. It didn't impress me."

"Bothered by police presence," mused Trewley, "then more bothered by knowing we'd come about Holbrook. Then what?"

"Then he went away."

"Just went? Didn't say anything?"

"Not a word, as I recall."

"And hasn't been seen since, I'll wager." Trewley gave the hapless Kirton a modified—the man was on the sick list—bulldog glare. "Is there a security man on your gate? To stop you sneaking out with those valuable, er, bits of waste copper in your pockets. Mind asking him if he's spotted our friend Heath recently?"

"Miss Springs . . ." pleaded Kirton, looking more worried than ever. "Oh, dear . . ."

They waited while Julia spoke urgently into the telephone on Dr. Kirton's desk. She did not speak for long; she hung up, and turned to face them.

"Superintendent, you were quite right. Security say they saw Bob Heath leave the premises on his motorbike over half an hour ago. And—and they say he seemed to be in a tearing hurry, Superintendent!"

Nine

"TELL YOU ONE thing," said Trewley, as they made their way back to the waiting police car. "We may not know what's what in this case—dammit, we don't even know if it's a case at all—but we know a hell of a lot more about metallurgy than we did before." He paused. He didn't generally care to pay his sergeant compliments, in case she developed a swelled head, but there were times . . .

This was one of them. As Benson leaned over to open the door, the superintendent added hastily:

"Well, I suppose I should be thankful it was you with me, and not one of the others. I always said that fancy education of yours would come in handy, one day. To Dr. Holbrook's house, please, Benson."

"Thank you, sir." Stone was buckling herself into her seat belt. "I wouldn't want you to run away with the idea I understood any of the details, though." There was, however, no room for false modesty in police work. "The *gist* of what Dr. Kirton said was clear enough, I think. As you implied, just because I dropped out of medical school doesn't mean I don't keep up a general interest in what's going on. I try to read the science pages in the papers, for one thing, and there are one or two good programmes on television and the radio. . . . Room temperature superconductivity, if they could achieve it, really would be the breakthrough to end all electrical breakthroughs. Nobel Prizes would be just the start—but please don't ask me to explain why throwing bits of . . . of the new alloy on lumps of cold metal should stop hydrogen diffusing out of it, because I honestly couldn't."

"Splatting," said Trewley. "Blooming jargon! Omono—no, onomatopoeia—and acronyms, and Lord knows what else."

"Splat-quenched ferro-alloy," said Stone, savouring the words. "Sqfa. It's a foreign language all right, sir!"

"Umph." He could hardly argue with that. They sat in silence, pondering the mysteries of metallurgical research.

The silence was soon broken by a polite cough from the driver's seat. "Excuse me, sir, but—but would that be a—an amorphous ferro-alloy you were talking about? Bit of a coincidence, that. With me seeing something about them on Dr. Holbrook's desk, I mean."

"Is it?" Trewley sighed, and rubbed his chin. "Stands to reason a boffin'll talk boffin language like all the rest of 'em. Write it too, what's more—*and* read it. Anybody else'd take a nice hot bath to relax, but there's no telling what a scientist'll do. . . . Still, they can be funny things, coincidences. In a case like this, if that's what it is, when we're not sure what's going on and can't understand it even if anyone does try to tell us—well, it'd be daft not to take a closer look at anything out of the ordinary. Remember anything else?"

"Sorry, sir. It was all handwriting, except the title, and I know he wasn't that sort of doctor, but he might just as well have been. Really long words, I do remember that."

"Not a suicide note, then. At least, it doesn't sound like it, although . . ." Perhaps, before finally taking his life—if that's what he'd done—Holbrook had, for once, broken with his usual practice—had made some concession to the duty he owed his employers, and committed details of his invaluable research to paper. And now somebody else could carry on that research . . .

"It, er, wasn't his name on the paper, sir, from what I remember. I did check—but with all the long words, sir, and the chemical symbols, well, it didn't seem . . ."

"Needs a dictionary," said Trewley, with a resigned

chuckle, and a nod for Stone. "Here's where you earn your keep, Sergeant."

"I can only do my best, sir. But the terms we use in medicine don't seem in the least like metallurgical ones— except for being polysyllabic, of course. As I said, it's a foreign language. . . ."

Benson snorted with suppressed mirth. "Better watch out if you're going to read it, Sarge. Might choke on a diagram and do yourself an injury."

"You keep your eyes on the road, lad, and leave Sergeant Stone to take care of herself." Trewley was perhaps being a little unfair: Benson's attention had hardly wandered from the task immediately in hand. "And, talking of keeping your eyes open, we could've done just that thing for our elusive motorbike bloke, if we'd only known what he looked like." He sighed. "Pity nobody knows his number. They're all the same nowadays, inside those helmets with the visors right across their faces."

"They do," Stone reminded him, "reduce accidents, sir."

Trewley grunted. He knew very well that they did, but he was still feeling slightly guilty that the case might not be a case, after all. And at some point, he would have to justify his absence to Desk Sergeant Pleate. . . .

"Accidents," he said. "The Health and Safety at Work Act—we'd better check on that, too. We'll go and see Holbrook's solicitor—and his doctor. And we've yet to fathom why young Heath should've done a bunk at the sight of us, when so far as we know he's got no reason for wanting to leg it like that."

"As far as we know, sir," came the echo from Detective Sergeant Stone. "But—"

She was interrupted by Benson. "Heath? You mean Bob Heath, sir—we're looking for him? Why, I saw him come out of Allingham Alloys on his bike while I was waiting for you. Half an hour ago or more, I reckon it would've been."

"What?" The bloodhound growl echoed around the car. "You saw this Heath character do a bunk? On his bike? You didn't"—Trewley's voice was dangerously low—"happen to notice his number, did you?"

The tips of Benson's ears were now an unhappy pink. "Er—yes, sir. Sorry. F250 QIZ—a souped-up Cinnabar, with a stainless steel exhaust. Made a terrible racket, sir, which is why I spotted him—he was fairly motoring down the drive. Took the exit corner at such a lick I thought he'd have the rubber off his tyres."

"You didn't think to book him for speeding, of course— no, you wouldn't. Never mind. How the hell'd you work this thing?"

"Push the button to the left, sir." His two companions spoke with one voice: it was almost a reflex response. The inability of the Plainclothes Prune to work police car radio transmitters was a station byword.

"Damn! I forgot." A split second from danger, Trewley banged the handset back in place. There was an ominous, splintering sound. "Pull over, Benson—you'll have to put out the APB. And if you let on I'm in the car with you, I'll—I'll boil you in oil!"

"Like a pilchard," murmured Stone, as Benson tried to follow his instructions with a straight face and a steady voice. "Or a red herring . . .

"Which," she went on cheerfully, after the journey to Dr. Holbrook's house had eventually—that splintering sound had caused a few problems—been resumed, "I bet you Bob Heath will turn out to be in the end, sir. He's too . . . obvious."

"He's up to *something*," retorted Trewley, "even if we don't know what it is—and even if it's got nothing to do with Holbrook. Nobody with a clear conscience carries on the way he has—and, talk of carrying on, it's a fine carry-on for a nice young copper like you, Benson, knowing a rum type like him. How come? Go to school together, did you? Same darts team?"

"Er—he used to date one of my cousins, sir, ages back. Before he, er, got married."

"Had to," deduced Trewley, as Benson's ears turned pink again in the knowledge that Sergeant Stone, sitting behind him, was female. "Typical. Well, even if he didn't know enough to stay out of that kind of trouble, he's up to his eyes in another sort, if I'm not very much mistaken. . . ."

Yet trouble, for once, was not in evidence on the council estate where Bob Heath lived with his wife Tracey. Police Constable Hedges, silent and watchful, having intercepted the all-points bulletin, had taken it upon himself to go on patrol. So unobtrusive was his presence that no telephone boxes were being vandalised, no cars broken into, no graffiti sprayed on walls; but young Mrs. Heath, pregnant with her third, knew nothing and cared less for the sentinel outside.

Trewley and Stone, with Benson hovering in the background, were making their examination of the dead man's house.

"Certainly does look as if these notes of Chattisham's were pretty well the last thing he saw before he died." Trewley cast an uncomprehending eye down the handwritten sheet with its chemical symbols and neat diagrams. "Must say, I agree with Benson—it'd kill *me*, all right, having to wade through this lot. Probably only read a few words and then keeled over from shock."

Stone was subjecting the writing to closer scrutiny than that of her baffled superior. "I wonder, sir, if the Squib *is* connected somehow with this. Superconductivity, and hydrogen diffusion, and amorphous ferro-alloys together at one fell swoop—I've heard of coincidences, but this is ridiculous."

"Umph." Trewley peered over her shoulder. "Could be whatever Chattisham had to say about these alloys somehow destroyed Holbrook's fancy theory. And with him being, as Kirton kept telling us, touchy about his reputation—and a sick man, off balance to begin with . . . well, then he goes broody, realises all his work's been a waste of time, and it just tips the balance in favour of killing himself. . . ."

"Once this lot's been, um, translated, sir," said Stone, "we could know, one way or another."

He rubbed his chin, and scowled at the neat, bewildering scrawl on Basil Holbrook's blotter. "I don't know—there's something, somewhere, that isn't right—though I haven't the foggiest notion what, or why, or how. Benson, you were here first. Can't you think of anything at all . . . off?"

Benson scratched his head, then shook it. "Sorry, sir. Nothing, except what I told you before. Everything was all locked up when the milkman broke in—er, I thought it'd be best to say nothing about that, sir, not unless this turns out to be a case. I mean, he might just've been in time to save the poor bloke's life. . . ."

"You're learning, lad. Poor bloke, indeed." Trewley chuckled, remembering the various names an embattled young Benson had previously called Basil Holbrook during that tipsy genius's campaign of letters to superior officers, the threats of approaching the chief constable. "So, the milkman picked the lock—but apart from that, the house was secure?"

"He and Mrs. Mint both said it was, sir."

Trewley rubbed his chin. "This cleaning lady—you've got her address, of course. Bright little body, is she? The sort to spot anything a bit different? Does she know if it was his usual way of going on at night, to lock himself into his study?"

"Well, sir, she wasn't surprised that he did, though I'm not sure she *knew* he did. She kept on about how careful he was with his scientific papers, and worried they might be disturbed—but *she* was more worried, sir, about how she'd most likely lose out on her money for this week. I told her she'd best talk to his solicitors about it. . . ."

His ears were turning pink once more. He coughed. "She . . . well, I dunno if you'd exactly call her bright, sir, not exams and things—though she's sharp enough. Something in the air, maybe. She says Holbrook made his own computer and telly and video, all from bits and pieces sort of lying around the house. Doesn't seem to have realised he could've bought ready-to-assemble kits for half of it— except he'd have had to buy 'em, of course, and she said he didn't like parting with his money. He might have been exploiting her over the years, you know, sort of looking down on her and not bothering to treat her right because . . ." He blushed again as he remembered his moment of embarrassment. "The poor old biddy can't read or write, sir, and . . ."

"Umph. There's quite a few like her, of course, missed out somewhere along the line. A hiccup in the system just at the wrong time—illness, interrupted schooling—that sort of thing. If a real need arises later, they generally learn easily enough, because it's not that they're thick, they've just been unlucky. If anything, they're brighter than most, because they can sometimes go on for years coping without anyone finding out. Not very nice if Holbrook took advantage—though we've only her word for it, of course. But I don't doubt she'll be sharp. People whose minds aren't cluttered up with letters and long words and numbers and diagrams can often see a damn sight more clearly than the educated types."

Stone knew he wasn't getting at her: he was stating no more than a fact. The cleaning lady's memory could well—if this case proved to be as complex as she was starting to believe it might—be invaluably clear and uncluttered. . . .

Benson said, "Well, sir, between the three of us—her and me and the milkman—we couldn't spot one thing different from what an accident, or a suicide, would be like—and surely you can't think it was murder?"

Trewley hesitated. "I can," he said at last, "but I'm not sure if I do. It's early days yet—but something's not right, I'll swear, only I just don't know what. Appearances can be deceptive—looks like an accident, could be suicide—but

I've got the strangest feeling we were *meant* to be deceived. . . ."

"Talking of deception, sir," said Stone, as he stared in perplexity about the silent study, "haven't you—we—been skiving off long enough now? When we don't even know for sure it's a case. Sergeant Pleate—"

"Sergeant Pleate be—be bothered, Sergeant Stone. If you're trying to get rid of me, you'll have to try harder than that." He chuckled. "You're not happy about this, any more than I am, are you? Want to hog all the fun for yourself? You're not superintendent yet, you know."

"No, sir." Stone suppressed a smile. Her tone gave no indication of exactly what she was denying.

Trewley sighed. "You're right, though, we ought to get back to the station . . . to pick up our car," he added, as her smile broke through, "and to let Benson go back on patrol. But, just to keep you happy, I'll check out properly this time—before we go to Holbrook's solicitor. And then his doctor, I think. Between the pair of them they might have a clue to what's going on . . .

"If anything is," he added, and rubbed his chin again.

The offices of Gooch and Honeycombe, Solicitors, were all that legal chambers should be: oak-panelled, deed-boxed to the ceiling, and dust-powdered by history in so artistic a manner that it could only have been deliberate policy on the part of Mr. Garland, the senior partner. And Mr. Garland, too, was perfect for the part: a musty, shrivelled, bespectacled little man with a stoop, and a dry cough, and the habit of rubbing his hands together.

"But I must advise you, Superintendent, that I am not your man," he said cheerfully. "Dr. Holbrook's affairs were handled by Mr. Kirkwood—who is, alas, indisposed at this particular moment. And I fear it will be some considerable time before he is able to return to work."

"Nothing too serious, I hope, sir."

The senior partner responded to the courtesy with a

mischievous smile. "He has concussion, Superintendent, and a cracked skull." He rubbed his hands, clearly delighted by the effect of his words. "He is in Allingham General, feeling very sorry for himself—though there is, fortunately, no doubt whatever that he will survive. He is young, and fit—which is, I dare say, just as well, in the circumstances."

"Circumstances?" Trewley's mind leaped to conclusions. "You mean the man was attacked?" Lead pipe, brick, sandbag, spanner . . . or was it just too much of a coincidence?

"A deed-box fell on his head." There was a malicious, self-satisfied gleam in Mr. Garland's eye as it twinkled towards a distant part of the room. "The one at the very top of the pile—over there. Fearnehough and Jones." He sighed. "A most valuable, well-documented portfolio—and, as a result, very heavy. Very."

"Umph." Trewley scowled at the innocent white letters. "As you say, sir, right at the top. A long way to fall."

Mr. Garland nodded. "Particularly so when there is somebody underneath. Most distressing . . . but it was, I assure you, an accident, a most regrettable accident. Naturally, our insurance will compensate Mr. Kirkwood for any little inconvenience he may undergo. We are, of course, thoroughly covered against any risk of such an occurrence." Mr. Garland smiled, and once more rubbed his hands.

"Funnily enough, sir, it was about, er, industrial injuries that we wanted to talk to your partner. About the Health and Safety at Work Act, I mean. Perhaps we could have a few words with you instead?"

"I doubt it, Superintendent." Mr. Garland sounded almost pleased at his inability to fill the shoes of Mr. Kirkwood. "The duties of the partnership have always been most clearly defined. Most. Wills, inheritance, and trusts on my part: and the more, ah, urgent and distasteful requirements of the law—drunken driving, the conveyancing of houses, that sort of thing . . ." Airily, Mr. Garland dismissed the notion that any client of Gooch and Honeycombe might indulge in murder, robbery, rape, treason, or piracy.

"And of course," he continued, "any *business* matters. Contracts, mergers and so on . . . all these were the province of Mr. Kirkwood. Health and safety would have been his pigeon, Superintendent. Naturally, I have *read* the Act, in what one might term a general sense—but for a truly informed opinion"—was that a gleam in his eye?—"I regret that I must refer you elsewhere. Unless, of course, you wish to wait for the return of Mr. Kirkwood."

"You mean you never discuss your cases?" It was an appalling thought. How long could the superintendent survive without a faithful sidekick to use as a sounding board?

Mr. Garland regarded him with a reproachful eye. "Client confidentiality, Superintendent, is both *ex*pected and, let me assure you, *re*spected. Abstract theorising over some abstruse and interesting point of law may be one thing, but idle chitchat and gossip are quite another. Quite. I have every confidence in Mr. Kirkwood's ability to function without my perpetual, ah, supervision—and I devoutly trust that he has the same faith in me."

"Oh." Trewley rubbed his chin. "Then you can't help me at all?"

"It is always," allowed Mr. Garland, with evident reluctance, "possible." He sighed. "I suppose." He brightened. "But I must emphasise that anything I may say can by no means be taken as an informed opinion."

Trewley was a little nettled. "I can't believe it's all that difficult, sir. What I want to know is, do you know, or can you find out, whether the late Dr. Holbrook was about to undertake any legal action against his employers because of injuries—or rather damage to his health—sustained at work?"

"Aha!" Mr. Garland rubbed gleeful hands. "No, Superintendent."

"No you don't know, or no you can't find out for me?"

Mr. Garland smiled an evil smile. "Let that be a lesson, Superintendent. Never pose an ambiguous question to a lawyer—why, it positively begs for confusion!" Then he saw the bulldog's jowls begin to quiver, and made haste to relent. "What I meant," he temporised, "was that I did not know—though I have little doubt," he added, "that you will be pleased to learn that I could, if I so wished, find out for you. But first," as a query trembled the bloodhound dewlaps, "I must ask a question of you, Superintendent. Ha!" That rubbing was going to drive Trewley mad before long. "Ha—one question only! Is this important?"

Trewley tried not to grind his teeth. "Could be, sir. It's early days yet. But if you'd be kind enough to check Mr. Kirkwood's files, or whatever you have to do . . ."

"I could always," began Mr. Garland, "enquire as to your search warrant—but I won't." The bulldog's eyes had a decidedly red glow in them now. "I have, ah, faith enough in the probity of our police force to suppose that your reasons for asking the question must be pertinent. . . . If you will be so good as to wait?"

Since Trewley could hardly insist on following the solicitor into the far office—and indeed had no wish to do so—it was easy for him to be so good. He spent the expectant minutes moaning quietly to Stone that he'd heard about Garland, and never met the man before, and didn't much care how long it was before he met him again. Stone ventured to remark that Mr. Garland must be considered a great loss to certain classes of Allshire society. It was a pity (from the point of view of the local crooks, she meant, not that of the police who wanted to convict them) that Mr. Garland so plainly considered criminal work beneath him. The man would be (she felt) invaluable in decimating—at least—the number of successful prosecutions in local courts. It was a fortunate circumstance that he preferred leaving that side of the practice to his partner: she refused to credit that one small firm should produce two attorneys of so devious a nature, and trusted that she and her colleagues could rest easy in their beds . . .

The voice of Mr. Garland broke in upon Trewley's groan. "Now I may answer your query, Superintendent. Was the late Basil Holbrook contemplating suing Allingham Alloys over a breach of the Health and Safety at Work Act? As far as Mr. Kirkwood's notes and client files have been able to inform me . . . he was not."

Ten

"NOT?" TREWLEY COULDN'T keep the disappointment out of his voice. "Not even a—a casual enquiry?"

Mr. Garland looked horrified. Behind his spectacles, his eyes glinted. "Nobody, Superintendent, should *ever* make a casual enquiry of a solicitor! Of what use to anyone can be knowledge thus obtained, beyond the fleeting satisfaction of idle curiosity? A waste of time for all concerned! And Dr. Holbrook was a most efficient, methodical man—most. One might, indeed, almost say ruthlessly so. Any queries he may have had on such a subject would have been posed, let me assure you, with the intention—the fullest intention—of proceeding."

"Umph." Trewley frowned. "I see."

"That will be all, will it, Superintendent?"

He was not going to let himself be dismissed so quickly. "Not just yet, if you don't mind. Another thing I'd like to know—Dr. Holbrook's next of kin. We understand that he had no immediate family, but—"

"He had none at all, Superintendent."

"None at all?" Trewley stared. "Nobody? But everyone has some relations."

"An orphan does not," countered Mr. Garland at once.

"Ah. An orphan." That would explain the cold-blooded character of the man, of course. "Brought up in an institution or something, was he?"

"He was not, Superintendent." Mr. Garland didn't exactly smirk, but his aura of smugness seemed almost to fill the little room. "I merely," said Mr. Garland happily, "cite the orphan as one example of a person with no relatives—a

state in which you evidently found it difficult to believe.
You yourself, and your sergeant, are no doubt blessed with
large and flourishing families, all living. Dr. Holbrook, on
the other hand, was already predeceased by his nearest and,
ah, presumably dearest.

"If," he went on quickly, before Trewley could open his
mouth, "you were to ask the source of my information, I
must protest my inability to quote you chapter and verse—
but, since his entire Estate, according to his Will, is
bequeathed to charity, it is a not unreasonable assumption.
It is no more than prudence—it is the standing policy of
Gooch and Honeycombe—to induce our clients to leave a
token sum to anyone with the slightest possible claim to a
share of their estate, so that future claims to overthrow what
might be seen as unfair disposal of moneys would be
difficult to pursue through the courts."

"Oh." Another motive apparently down the drain—
unless . . . "Could you tell us which charity, Mr. Garland?"

"Ah. Which charity." For the first time, the solicitor
appeared discomfited. "Perhaps a—a slight slackness of
definition? It would probably be more accurate to say that
this bequest is for the foundation of a charitable trust, a
scholarship to read Metallurgy at his old university—
Grantaford," he added, before Trewley could ask. "The, ah,
Basil Holbrook Bursary, to be precise."

"Yes, of course." Trewley saw the chance for revenge.
"Solicitors should always be, er, accurate and . . . precise,
shouldn't they?"

Which sudden turning of the constabulary worm so
surprised Mr. Garland that he never even thought to
comment on the tautology until after Trewley and Stone had
left.

They were buckling themselves into their seat belts when
the car radio, popping, emitted a peculiar whistle.

Trewley looked at Stone. "After all that," he growled,

jerking his head in the direction of the Gooch and Honeycombe premises, "I'm not up to it, girl. You carry on."

Grinning, she leaned across, and seized the handset. It
would, she knew, be more than her job was worth to ask
Trewley to push the switch. . . .

"Preliminary report on the Holbrook postmortem," came
the disapproving tones of the misanthropic Voice in Allingham Police Station's radio control room—even more misanthropic and disapproving than usual, Stone noted with
interest. Whatever was in that report must be dynamite. . . .

"*How much?*" she cried. The crackling airwaves repeated
the figure. An unspoken temperance lecture throbbed in the
ears of the Voice's startled audience.

"Good God," said Trewley at last. The Voice emitted a
shocked tut-tut of condemnation for the blasphemy. "Why,
the bloke was as drunk as a lord—no wonder he never
noticed when the fire went out!"

There came the sound of a pointedly cleared throat.
"Plus," said the Voice, "considerable quantities of aspirin in
the blood." And there came a very audible click.

"Oh, dear." Stone tried not to giggle as she replaced the
handset. "Somebody's feelings are hurt, sir."

"Never anything else."

She shook her head. "I think you've pushed your luck a
little too far this time. What's the betting somebody's
trotting down the corridor right now, ever so casually
mentioning to Sergeant Pleate on the way past that you're
out with me instead of—"

"Oh, God!" She was right, of course. Trewley squared his
shoulders. He scowled. He gave a sudden snort, and
chuckled. "My life won't be worth living once I'm back at
the station—so let's get it over with, girl. And don't forget
to put in for a spot of promotion, then I won't have been
sacrificed in vain."

"You don't want to go to the doctor's first, sir?"

"I want to think things over quietly," he said, as she
started the car. "Accident looks a sight more likely, now.

Everyone said he was hatching a cold, didn't they? Dosed himself up and just—just drifted away. Any fool knows you can't mix alcohol with drugs like that. The man was asking for trouble. . . ."

"He certainly got it." Stone frowned. "He was a scientist, though—I really would have expected him to know the risks. Of course, there might have been some idiosyncrasy—an allergy, whatever—to give him a quicker response than usual in his feverish state, make the aspirin knock him out faster and deeper than he intended. The postmortem should pick up any histamine traces, any mast cells and so on—but it'll take time."

"Umph. End result's the same, isn't it? Allergy or gas or booze, or all three—Holbrook's dead."

"Yes, sir." There was a pause. "And the other business too, sir—what Dr. Black told us, about the mercury, and the rest. We'll have that confirmed later, as well. . . ."

"Still dead," grumbled Trewley, though his mind was on other matters. He rubbed his chin. "The world's lost a remarkable man, Sergeant. You saw the empty whisky bottle by his desk, didn't you? And the medical evidence shows he must've downed the lot within an hour or so of his death—yet that didn't stop him having a go at reading that Chattisham stuff about your precious ferro-alloys. If that's not remarkable, I don't know what is."

"The likely state of his liver, sir," she returned. "Or so I should imagine. If he regularly drank as much as that— which we know, of course, that he did . . . Poor Benson."

"He was a menace on the roads, too," mused Trewley. "In a car or on a bike . . . vindictive, with it. Things could've been awkward for the lad if we hadn't known what Holbrook could be like—but there, we did. You know, it beats me. The bloke spent most of his time, the last few years, in a permanent fog of booze—yet Allingham Alloys say he was a—an irreplaceable genius! Like I said, a remarkable man. . . ."

• • •

Having sneaked into the station through the back door, they sat in Trewley's office, theorising over cups of canteen tea. Out of consideration for her superior, whose wife and three daughters had ordered him on another diet, Stone nobly refrained from opening the packet of chocolate digestives she had brought in only that morning: but it was hard, with the last wisps of fog still swirling outside. She reminded herself that suffering was supposed to be good for the soul, and waited for Trewley to pronounce.

"There's too much, and too little, about this case, both at the same time," he grumbled. "If it *is* a case, I mean. And where the hell do we start sorting it all out?"

"I'm as baffled as you are, sir—but," said Stone, who thought he needed cheering up, "things could be a great deal worse. Isn't it much better to be baffled in private, here, just the two of us, rather than in an open plan office with everyone staring at us, wondering why we haven't come up with the answers right away?"

Trewley sighed, and agreed that the very thought of Desk Sergeant Pleate and the Voice watching and waiting for him to pull a rabbit from the hat was more than enough to chill the blood—which was cold enough already. He sipped his sugarless tea, and shuddered.

"It's hardly your fault, sir, if there's a frost in November." Stone thought again of her chocolate biscuits, and sighed. "But it's a pity there was, because if there hadn't been, Holbrook might not have died."

"He wouldn't have had the fire on, if it'd been warmer," Trewley agreed. "He'd've wanted to save the money. So even if he had dosed himself up with aspirin and booze, he wouldn't have been gassed when it went out. . . ."

"Er—suffocated, sir," said Stone. "If you'll excuse me. Suffocated, not gassed, strictly speaking. This isn't the coal gas you remember, sir, the sort that poisoned you in the good old-fashioned way with carbon monoxide. Heads in ovens, that sort of thing. This is different. It just, um, displaces all the air, and leaves you breathing in . . . well, gas. Mostly methane, I think it is. It's the same mechanism as putting a plastic bag over your face. Once you've run out of air to breathe . . . you stop breathing."

Trewley shrugged. "Suffocated, gassed—he's dead, and I don't like it. It's too . . . tidy. No signs of forced entry, no violence, no clues worth speaking of . . ."

"Could be the perfect crime," Stone said gravely. Trewley shuddered again.

Stone made up her mind, and opened the drawer of her desk. "Sir, would you like—?"

She broke off, as there came a tap on the door, and the superintendent growled for the tapper to come in. PC Benson put his head inside the office, and ventured a grin.

"Wasn't sure if you were back, sir," he said. "Sergeant Pleate said he hadn't seen you, when I—sorry, sir."

Trewley swallowed his second oath, and snarled at the young man to come right in and shut the door. Did he want to let the whole damned station know what was going on?

"Sorry, sir." Benson smothered a grin as, behind Trewley's back, Stone winked at him. In he duly marched, his cap under his arm, his buttons bright. Before Trewley's desk, he stood to attention, his spine ramrod stiff.

"Er—report on Heath, sir. Robert." He paused.

"You've found him?" Trewley brightened. "Where is he? Have you got him outside?"

PC Benson flushed. "Er—he's . . . er, in hospital, sir. Allingham General—in Casualty."

"What?" exploded Trewley.

"What for?" enquired Stone, more practical.

A grateful Benson turned towards the former medical student. "For observation, Sarge. He's got concussion, and shock, and a broken leg. And, er, he's unconscious, too."

"I'm not surprised," murmured Stone, though Benson could not catch her words above Trewley's irate bellow.

"Good God, lad, you were told to bring him in, not batter him to a pulp! You weren't even meant to arrest him, just let us question him. He can't have been resisting—so what the hell happened?"

What had happened was that Bob Heath, after his speeding panic flight into the countryside, had realised that it was no use disappearing in so ill-prepared a fashion. He'd had time to think things over—his story ought to stand up now—but he would not, could not return to work just yet: he would go home.

He went home. And there, outside his house, he saw a waiting police car—waiting, he knew, for him. He lost his nerve completely, slammed on his brakes, skidded, and made a desperate turn. PC Hedges, inevitably, spotted him. There was a chase. Bob had a considerable start. PC Hedges radioed ahead for help . . .

And around the next corner, just as PC Benson appeared, there also appeared a patch of black ice.

Bob got halfway across the patch, but no farther. Somehow, he and his bike engaged in a somersaulting competition. Unfortunately, the bike proved the more agile, and ended up on top. . . .

PC Hedges, being nearer, had administered first aid; PC Benson, horrified, called on his radio for an ambulance. The two police officers accompanied the ambulance to the hospital, and eventually elicited details of the victim's condition from Casualty Sister. These—the two friends having tossed a coin—it was now PC Benson's duty to impart to an incredulous Superintendent Trewley.

"A broken leg, sir, and two fractured ribs. A badly cut arm—he was lucky there, it could've been an artery. The fastening on his helmet was faulty, or his head might've stood a better chance—as it is, sir, it's a wonder he's not dead, so they told us."

Trewley glowered. "He'll live, I hope?"

"Oh—yes, sir, only they can't say when he'll recover consciousness. And—well, they don't know how much he'll remember of what happened before the accident, either."

"Very convenient," snarled Trewley. "For him."

"What I don't understand," Stone hurriedly interposed, "is why he bolted in the first place. Did Hedges say something rude to him? I find that hard to credit." PC Hedges was notoriously the least talkative officer on the force. "Did he shake his fist with intent to threaten—or make funny faces—or even flash his headlights?"

Trewley rolled his eyes, but Benson ventured to respond with a grin. "Heath probably didn't want to have to face his wife, Sarge. She's—well, she's a real horror, if you ask me."

Stone raised his eyebrows. "You dare to disparage one of my gender? Watch your step, Constable, or I'll have the sex discrimination people after you."

Benson grinned again. "A real horror," he reiterated firmly. "When I went to let her know about the accident—we thought she was bound to find out, being local, you know the way folk talk on that estate—well, as soon as she came to the door you could see what sort she was."

"And what sort," enquired Stone sweetly, "was that?"

Trewley grunted. "No welcome on the mat, I gather."

"No, sir—and not because of the uniform, either. For a start, the front garden was a mess, and the door could do with a lick of paint—but she was grubby too, and the kiddies. Slippers all down at the heels, fag in the corner of her mouth, didn't look as if she'd brushed her hair for a week—and she was absolutely enormous with another kid on the way, and the one she'd got with her not more than a few months, and the other only just toddling, sir."

"She was doubtless too wearied by the demands of domesticity to bother overmuch with the niceties of life," Stone said, trying hard to sound reproachful.

"So what," demanded Trewley, "did she say when you came banging at the door to tell her her old man was in the hospital and lucky to be alive?"

PC Benson shook his head in disbelief. "I had to shout,

sir, with the radio on full blast and her not bothering to turn it down, but . . . when she understood what I was trying to tell her, she gave me a right ear-bashing. Only it wasn't the way you'd expect—I mean, she didn't act shocked or upset or anything. Once she knew he wasn't going to kick the bucket, she never spared a minute to ask, like, when she could go to see him. All she seemed to be bothered about was whether there'd be any sick pay from work, and how long he was likely to be off, and whether they'd have to pay for the bike or if the insurance would cover it—and moaning because they'd probably lose the No Claims Bonus, sir. You can understand she'd be a bit worried about money, with the kiddies and everything, but . . ."

"Charming," said Trewley. Stone, still making up her mind how to respond, thought it safer to keep quiet. "And I suppose she tried to hint the accident was all our fault, and she'll be writing to the chief constable or one of the other high-ups to complain and ask for her money back?"

Benson blinked. "How—how did you know, sir? That's almost exactly what happened!"

"Human nature, lad. Some folk'll do anything for money, and some'll do anything just to make life awkward for other folk, if they think there's the slightest chance they can get away with it."

"Let's hope," said Stone, "that she doesn't go pestering her husband about all this. Whether he's concussed or convalescent, it won't do him any good at all to have to think about writing letters, or balancing the household budget."

Benson gave a snort of disgust. "He won't be pestered until next week at the earliest, Sarge. Tuesday, she said. Honest!" as Stone stared.

"Tuesday?" Trewley barked. "Good God, it's only Friday! Is he that bad?"

"Oh, it's nothing to do with that, sir. It's just Tuesday's her Antenatal Clinic at the hospital, and there isn't anyone she wants to look after the kiddies till then—she's got a sitter arranged for Tuesday, you see, and she says she can't pay her for extra."

"Money again." Trewley rubbed his chin. "We'd better organise a policewoman, if there really isn't anyone she can ask, though I'd have thought on that estate they'd all be willing to muck in together. But—"

"Er—beg pardon, sir," Benson broke in, "but I did take the liberty of suggesting something like that." He blushed from the tips of his ears to the lobes. "But—well, when I did, she . . ."

Trewley sighed. "All right, lad, we can guess what she said. You needn't repeat it—but good thinking, anyway."

"I must say," he remarked, once Benson had departed, "if it won't offend your sensibilities, she sounds a thoroughly unpleasant piece. If your young What's-his-name had ended up in hospital out cold, I hope you'd have the decency to raid the piggy bank for the bus fare if there was no other way of getting to see him. . . ."

Stone had to smile at his reference to the officer from Traffic with whom she shared her life. For some reason best known to himself, the superintendent always professed to be ignorant of the young man's name. . . . And he was right in his assumption. If raiding the piggy bank was what it would, in certain circumstances, take, then raided—without question—that piggy bank would be.

She shut her mind to the awful possibilities that would render such a course of action essential. "Surely, sir, it can't just have been the—the sheer ghastliness of what he was going to find at home that made our friend Heath go off like a rocket when he spotted Hedges on guard. I'll accept that he might have lost his nerve, but it must be more than that—it must be!"

"A guilty conscience, that's what it was," said Trewley. "He didn't want to talk to the police—I told you there was something wrong, only I didn't know what . . ."

"With Benson and Hedges keeping a bedside watch," said Stone, her eyes sparkling, "we'll know the very minute he says anything about what on earth's been going on. Or we'll know soon," she amended; but Trewley did not appear to be listening. He was brooding.

"We know what's been going on, girl," he said at last. "Didn't I say it all along? Something not right—something that didn't fit . . .

"Murder," he said, and rubbed his chin in thought.

Eleven

FRIDAY NIGHT BROUGHT its usual quota of Allingham drunk-
ards, popped into the cells to sober slowly for Saturday
morning in an atmosphere of plumbers' solder and hasty
ventilation. Saturday and Sunday were quite as cold as
Friday, though without the fog. Smoke from Guy Fawkes
bonfires hung heavy in the air, which was chilly and dank.
Not until Monday, when a grey quilting of cloud blocked
out the sun, was the earth, paradoxically, made warmer.

On Tuesday—another mild morning—with her head
down, watchful for potholes, her hat pinned earnestly to the
back of her head, Mrs. Mint once again rode her bicycle
towards Dr. Holbrook's turning. And, once again, she was
spotted by the milkman in the near distance. He wondered
fleetingly what she could be doing there, since it was not
one of her three customary days, but his thoughts soon
turned to the ravishing redhead further along the road, and
he forgot Mrs. Mint altogether.

Mrs. Mint swerved across to the right, and this time
reached the gateway of the Holbrook residence without
incident. Once there, she paused to look about her in a
furtive manner before lifting the latch with great care. The
gate creaked accusingly as she pushed her bicycle on to
now-forbidden territory, and the caution with which she
shut it behind her would have told anyone watching that her
conscience was far from clear.

At the porch, she fumbled hopefully beneath the flowerpot, but found, as she'd feared, nothing. She tried the front
door, with equal lack of success; scuttled round to the back;
and returned, downcast, a few minutes later.

With a gleam in her eye, she looked swiftly all around; then raised her hands to her head, and withdrew from her cherry-bobbing hat a long, forceful hat pin . . . and bent to the old-fashioned lock of Dr. Holbrook's front door.

With memories of the milkman's earlier triumph to inspire her, she pushed the pin, she twisted it, she poked and twisted and pushed again. Something inside the lock clicked, then lifted. The door swung slowly open . . . and into Dr. Holbrook's house tiptoed Mrs. Mint.

She soon tiptoed out again, proudly carrying her pink bag of cleaning impedimenta, dropped and abandoned in all the excitement of Friday's discovery. Not for Mrs. Mint, with her mistrust of Authority, the official request to Them—the police permit to retrieve her own property—the long delays for triplicate forms and red-tape demands. "Nosey-parkering, that's all it is," said Mrs. Mint.

"What's that, Missus?"

The sudden male voice from just outside the porch made her screech with fright, and she dropped the bag again. The postman stared at her, holding out an elastic-banded bundle of letters, grinning.

"Spot of extra overtime, eh?"

He was doing no more than pass the time of day, but Mrs. Mint's heart thumped. "Here y'are, then. Dunno who's to bother with this lot, after Friday, poor old basket—but they're for this address, so that makes it legal. Besides, it ain't my problem, is it?"

As the postman stumped, cheerfully humming, back down the path, Mrs. Mint moaned softly. Letters! All delivered to the front door—and she'd accepted them! Trembling, she forced herself to sort through the bundle. Her heart sank. She could recognise unimportant coupons and circulars, but some of these looked official indeed—typed addresses and machine franking—and one, she felt sure as she studied its brown envelope, was a bill. And she'd taken it herself from the postman's hands! At that moment, the words *To Account Rendered* seemed the most terrible she had ever heard. . . .

A wiser woman, less panic-stricken, would have locked up the house at once and left the letters on the mat, just as they might have fallen in the normal way; would have trusted to some authorised person to discover and deal with them in due course. But Mrs. Mint, conscious of her illicit entrance as she hadn't been before, couldn't bring herself to do it. The postman had *seen* her with the bills in her hand—they were now her responsibility—she was already out-of-pocket with being owed the money for last week, and here she was being plunged even deeper into debt. . . .

"Cheer up, Ma." The milkman leered at her from over the fence. "Never say die!"

She muttered something noncommittal, and turned back into the house, the post still clutched in her hand. What should she—what could she—do? Who would advise her?

She peered out of the window, waiting for the milkman to go on his way. She must see nobody else, so that nobody else might see her with those ominous letters and bills. If only she could read them, she would know better just how serious the matter was likely to be. . . .

Then her guardian angel winged his way past, and relief flooded into her heart. PC Benson, to whose smile and kindly presence she had warmed—Benson, who knew of her handicap and wouldn't ask awkward questions—was out on patrol. And she felt sure she could tell him all about it—that he would understand, and help her. . . .

And so, wearing an aspect of virtuous calm beneath her cherry-bobbing hat, her hat pin well concealed, Mrs. Mint, her pink bag hanging from her handlebars, cycled slowly back the way she'd come, and carried on until she reached Allingham police station.

Now that the plumbers had been, Desk Sergeant Pleate was as willing as Mrs. Mint to face the world calmly. Observing the newcomer, he mentally docketed her as Lost Property, and was minded to deal with her himself: there was always the chance she could be his secret weapon in the war he perpetually waged with Superintendent Trewley . . . and never mind that Trewley had spent the entire weekend grumbling about the place with Sergeant Stone, muttering of murder and insisting that there had to be proof somewhere. The man must stop messing about with theories, argued Desk Sergeant Pleate: he should face up to his responsibilities.

But, once the cleaning lady had fully explained her insistence on speaking with PC Benson by giving the address where she'd been working—together with a satisfactory gloss for her purpose in being on the premises in the first place—Pleate had realised the possible importance of what she had to tell. For once, his superior might be right. . . .

"Gave her a receipt for the lot," said Trewley, brandishing the bundle of envelopes, "and sent her away happy. We'll be passing everything on to the solicitors before long, of course—but with Kirkwood off sick, and Garland not that interested . . ."

"It wouldn't do us any harm to take a look, would it?" supplied Stone at once. "And it's so nice to know you and Sergeant Pleate are on speaking terms again, sir." There had been more than calendar reasons for the chilliness of the station atmosphere during the past few days.

"Umph." Trewley glanced sideways at his smiling subordinate. "Yes, well . . ." He opened his desk, and took a wooden ruler from the top drawer. Paper knives, he would say from time to time, made him nervous.

He slit the first envelope, and pulled out a magazine. "*Which*—yes, from what everyone said he'd be interested in getting value for money, though I'd've thought he'd do better looking at the library copy for free . . . *New Scientist*—the man was a boffin, of course . . . *Materials World*—technical stuff. Tax-deductible, probably."

"Cynic," said Stone, leafing through *New Scientist* as she spoke. "You're right, though, sir, it probably is. Perhaps we ought to read it before we hand it to Gooch and Honeycombe—we might learn something."

"About your pet alloys?" Trewley chuckled as he passed *Materials World* across the desk. "Help yourself, if you can bear the jargon. . . . I know what *this* is, all right." He scowled at a garish yellow envelope slashed with red lettering. "We had one this morning—some offer for all-singing, all-dancing double glazing. Kid you they'll do a special offer to install it in your home if you answer within so many days, but they don't let on until the small print you've got to let them use your house afterwards for demonstration purposes. Don't you and young What's-his-name fall for it, girl, whatever you do."

"No fear of that, sir." Stone had abandoned *New Scientist* in favour of *Materials World*, and was contemplating the index with some interest. "It always pays to read the small print. . . ."

"Coupons for kitchen stuff—soap powder, bleach, one of those concentrated washing-up liquids—and a money-off form. Pity he missed out on that. *Buy your film from us and have it developed free!* Sounds right up his street."

Stone emerged from *Materials World* to shake her head. "The small print, sir," she said gently. "They don't say anything about having it *printed* free—just developed. Besides, if Holbrook was half the boffin they say he was, I bet he could have developed his own films with no bother at all."

"Just another catch," he growled. "Typical. . . . A couple of bills. These'd best go straight to Gooch and Honeycombe, I think. We don't want a petition for bankruptcy served on a dead man, or the bailiffs sent in, all on account of police negligence."

"Goodness, no. How urgent are they, sir?"

"One's the Water Board, and the other's a general handyman's account for—hey!"

"Sir?"

"Listen, Stone. This bill—not the Water Board, but the one from the odd-job man. It's for fixing a gas fire!"

There was a long, pregnant pause. Stone abandoned *Materials World* completely, and scanned the sheet of headed paper her colleague now held out to her. She frowned, and read it again.

"Of course, sir—there's more than one gas fire in the house. It could be one of the others . . ."

"Rubbish! It's a coincidence, dammit, and you know what I think about coincidence. I don't like it, but if it's there, then it means something. I told you I had a feeling about this case. That it *was* a case, I mean. . . . Let's have another look, please. 'To fitting of new valve to gas fire supply pipe, £37.48 plus VAT at 17½ percent, settlement at your earliest convenience' blah, blah, blah." Trewley waved the paper under his sergeant's startled nose. "I've got to say this, Stone—I told you so!"

"So you did, sir. Um—what put you on to it, exactly?"

He chuckled. "Wait till you've been a householder for a few years more, my girl. Then you'll know what's wrong with this bill—because right now you don't, do you?"

"He charged too much?"

"No, no. You've got an honest mind, that's your trouble—try thinking like a villain, for once. What's wrong with this bill is that it *is* a bill! On paper!"

"Well, sir, they generally are. I wouldn't expect the average Allingham odd-job man to start sending out invoices by electronic mail—I mean, I can't see he'd ever justify the cost of the equipment, for one thing."

"You mean?" Trewley chuckled. "Mean—that's the word all right! Everyone's gone on and on about how close Holbrook was with his money—and it's the way of the world for your average odd-job type to say, 'If you give me cash on the spot and I don't give you a receipt, it'll work out cheaper for both of us'—because he doesn't have to charge you the Value Added Tax and spend hours afterwards doing the paperwork!"

"Oh," said Stone. "Yes, of course . . ."

"Of course," echoed Trewley, losing some of his cheerful mood as he pondered the deeper implications of this discovery. "It's just another blasted fiddle—the Black Economy, dammit. The sort of offer that's always being made—and accepted by a sight too many people, if you ask me. But a bloke like Holbrook, mean as they come—he'd never have missed the chance to save himself a few quid by paying cash on the nail, instead of settling a properly sent in account like this one."

Stone frowned. "I can see that, sir, and I agree, but—perhaps he didn't have enough cash in the house at the time. Or maybe he wasn't even around to have the man make him the offer in the first place. If he was half as secretive and paranoid as people say he was, would he have trusted Mrs. Mint to pay it for him?"

"Umph." Trewley didn't like to have his theories overturned, even though he generally relied on Stone to play Devil's Advocate when he was in full flow. "Yes, but he trusted the woman with the run of his house—all except his precious study, anyhow, but he trusted her. . . . So, if *he* obviously wasn't around when this valve was being installed—and *she* presumably wasn't . . ."

Stone nodded. "Then maybe, sir—just maybe—somebody else was."

"Somebody," concluded Trewley, "who'd got no business being there. . . ."

"You said all along you thought something wasn't quite right, sir." Stone was studying the odd-job man's bill for the second time. "And now you come to point it out, I can see . . . Holbrook was a pretty fair handyman himself, by all accounts. So, even if he didn't exactly build things from scratch, he must have known his way around a tool kit. Anything to save money . . . and surely someone like him could have at least *fitted* the valve for himself? Listen, sir. 'To fitting of new valve'—not a word about *supplying* the thing as well, sir. And you know what builders and garages and so on are like. 'To supplying, fitting and adapting one silver-plated widget, three hundred pounds' . . . And wasn't I only saying just now you had to check the small print?"

Trewley rubbed his chin, thinking of the odd-job man's account, and the shaky truce with Desk Sergeant Pleate. "Well, Sergeant, if you're coming round to the idea there's something suspicious in all this . . . I reckon the sooner we go and investigate, the better!"

"Hexperimental, he said it was, Mr. Trewley." Mrs. Bert Gadgett spoke wearily: she wasn't sure she liked the idea of a police investigation into her husband's handiwork. "Some new design what they wanted to try out in a—in a proper house, like, instead of up at the factory."

"Mentioned Allingham Alloys by name, did he?"

She seemed startled at his eagerness. "Course he did! They'd made but this one small batch, see, and given him one to write a report, or summat, only with him not being too sure how to fit it, he said he wanted my Bert to do it for him—so that's what he did. And nothing more."

Her Bert—a quaint little button-eyed, silent body, nodded confirmation of her words. Trewley and Stone surveyed the pair with satisfaction: trustworthy, trusting, and not too bright, Mr. and Mrs. Gadgett were a criminal's ideal choice.

If, indeed, a crime had been committed. But, as the conversation advanced, it had become increasingly likely. . . .

"So what did this man look like—the one who asked you to fit the valve at Dr. Holbrook's house?" enquired Trewley. Stone had her notebook and pencil ready.

Mrs. Gadgett's mouth dropped open. She stared.

Stone smiled. "We don't need a detailed description," she reassured the odd-job man's wife. "But if you can give us just the general idea . . ."

Mrs. Gadgett blinked. She glanced at her husband. Bert

shook his head, and said nothing. Mrs. Bert made up her mind.

"Dunno as I can, Miss, because I'm not much of a one for describing folk, not unless they're stood in front of me. 'Sides, I don't understand why you're asking. You know as well as I do what he looked like. Surely I told you before it was Dr. Holbrook himself?"

Twelve

"HOLBROOK?" ROARED TREWLEY.

"Are you sure?" cried Stone.

Mrs. Gadgett regarded the two detectives with some scorn. "Everyone knows the old gentleman, wobbling about the town on that bike of his and terrifying folks in his car—him and his white hair, and poking his head down to peer at you with being so tall, and his squeaky voice—only this time, o' course, it was all muffled up with a scarf—"

"A scarf!" Trewley's triumphant eyes met those of Stone. *Disguise* . . .

"Starting a cold, he was." Mrs. Gadgett ignored the interruption. "And no wonder, being November—that bad night still to come, mark you, but there was change already in the air. Enough to make anyone ill, if they're inclined. Take my lumbago, now—started playing me up summat cruel, it did, and that was well before." She massaged the small of her back, and prepared to enlarge on her sufferings. "Two days before, easy, and—"

"Yes, of course." Neither Trewley nor Stone required details of her lumbago: there were more urgent matters to consider. "So," said the superintendent, "you saw—er, Dr. Holbrook when he brought in the valve, did you, Mrs. Gadgett? And how about your husband?" He turned to Bert. "Did you see him at the house when you went to fit the valve in the gas fire pipe?"

Bert shook his head, and obviously thought this answer enough. His wife interpreted for him.

"Told us how he'd be out to work that day, and nobody at the house to let my Bert in, so he'd leave the key under a flowerpot in the porch, and please to put it back when he'd finished."

"That bloody flowerpot," groaned Trewley. "I might have known!"

"The whole town seems to have known about it," agreed Stone. The Gagdetts simply stood and stared.

Trewley sighed. He thought of something. He turned to Bert. "Look here, Mr. Gadgett. What day of the week was it when you fitted this valve for Dr. Holbrook?"

"He asked particular for the Tuesday," said Bert's wife, as her husband looked towards her for guidance. "Special job, he said it was. Said it was usually a quiet day at work, so he might be able to get time off to come and see for himself how it was done—but he never. Did he, Bert?"

Once more, Bert shook his head. Trewley asked:

"Are you sure he said Tuesday?"

Mrs. Gadgett gave him a long, slow stare, then reached under the counter and withdrew a black-bound daybook. "One week ago last Saturday, it was when he came in," she muttered, turning back the pages one by one. "Saturday . . . look! So what does that say, if it don't chime exactly with everything we've told you?"

Trewley studied the daybook. It had not been written in copperplate, or script, or italic. Medical people were used to illegible scrawls . . .

He nodded to Stone, who moved forward to follow Mrs. Gadgett's pointing finger. *"Fit valve on downstairs pipe in study,"* she read, in a voice she tried to keep steady. *"Afternoons preferred, Tuesday next if possible."*

"And was it?" barked Trewley.

Mrs. Gadgett drew herself up to her full height. "Tuesday he said, special, and Tuesday he got," she insisted. "Very particular about it, he was." And, at her side, Bert nodded again.

Trewley looked at Stone, who looked back at him. Tuesday: Mrs. Mint's day off. An empty, unguarded house—and, underneath that infamous flowerpot, the only door key Basil Holbrook possessed, his parsimony preventing his acquiring a spare, his caution keeping it where it could always be found . . . whether by him, or by anyone else . . .

Trewley was rubbing his chin. He coughed. "I think," he said, "we'd like to take a look at this—special valve, Mr. Gadgett. If we ran you back to the house, d'you reckon you could take it out for us?"

For the first time, considerably startled, Bert spoke. "If you're implying, Mr. Trewley, as there was anything amiss with my work, then I take leave to tell you you're mistook. That there valve was fitting as safe and careful as any could wish—just like Dr. Holbrook said he wanted!" And at his side his wife stood, and nodded.

She nodded again, scowling, when Stone, with a hurried apology, ran back from the police car into which she and Trewley had managed to coax her indignant spouse, and asked if she could take down full details from the relevant page of the daybook.

"It might," she explained, "be evidence, you see. . . ."

But Mrs. Gadgett said nothing. She and Bert appeared to live their lives in a perfect loquacious equilibrium. Once her husband entered the conversation, she evidently thought it unnecessary for her to utter another word: and now Stone found it difficult to reassure her, as she must, that no blame—come what may—could attach itself to Bert Gadgett, Odd-Job Man. . . .

Back at the Holbrook house, Bert set to work, with Trewley and Stone eagerly watching his every move. The gas had been turned off at the main; it wasn't too difficult for him to undo what he'd done just a few days before. He dragged the heavy bookcase away from the wall, and turned his attention to the gas pipe running along the skirting board. It was only a matter of minutes before he produced, to everyone's satisfaction, the mysterious valve he had fitted on that particular and special afternoon.

"But I ask you," said Bert, displaying the object on a

grubby palm, "what's so special about that? Looks just like an ordinary valve to me—dunno why he made such a fuss about it. No, nor why you should, neither."

"Maybe it's made from some special metal," said Trewley. "A new alloy, or something."

Bert weighed it thoughtfully in his hand. "Might be a bit heavier nor some, perhaps—but I'd not swear to it," he added quickly. "Being as it was experimental from Allingham Alloys, like Dr. Holbrook said, it wouldn't surprise me. But if you really want to know, why not ask them?"

Why not, indeed? It was now beyond all reasonable doubt that Basil Holbrook's death had occurred as a result of suffocation by gas: the autopsy results had confirmed this, as they had also confirmed Dr. Black's diagnosis of the state of Holbrook's health. Was it likely that this valve could have contained a nerve gas, or an untraceable poison unknown to medical science? Trewley had to admit that it was not. In fact, since he'd received the full postmortem report, it had been only his niggling sense of something not right that had made him refuse to consider the case closed. Stone, for one, had been slowly coming round to accepting the original theory of suicide or accident . . .

Until the bombshell of the odd-job man's bill.

"I'm surprised," said Trewley, "he didn't ask you for a cash discount. The old VAT dodge, I mean." And he forced a chuckle, to which Bert responded with a wink.

"You'd've thought he might—I've had 'em say it for a hundred quid or more, not to mention a tiddly sum like this. Only with him not being in the house, see, there wasn't nobody to say nothing to, was there? So I sent in my regular bill, or rather the wife did, same as always when she makes up the books at the end of the week."

Trewley looked at Stone; Stone looked at Trewley. She could almost read the superintendent's mind. *Every criminal makes one mistake.* . . .

"Then I think, Mr. Gadgett, we'll drop you off on our

way," said Trewley aloud. "Thanks for your help. We'll do what you suggest. We'll ask Allingham Alloys about it."

Bert shrugged. "S'all right—though I still can't see what the bother's about, meself. Just an ordinary valve, if you ask me, and I'll say the same to anyone. Nothing odd about it at all."

"Oh, yes." Dr. Kirton poked at the valve with a pencil before handing it back. "It is, as you supposed, one of Allingham Alloys' Memory Metal valves. There's nothing at all remarkable about it, as far as I can see."

Trewley's bulldog wrinkles writhed in disappointment. "So it's not made from this, er, Squib of yours, then?"

Dr. Kirton had seemed a little peaky, despite his weekend's rest, as his two visitors arrived. He now smiled, and at once looked far brighter. "Dear me, no—most definitely not. Squib, I must remind you, is hardly past the experimental stage, while the principles of Memory Metal have been well-known in metallurgical circles for forty years or more. Much longer than the time for which it has been commercially viable, as it is now—it was quite a party piece for us as students, almost a joke. And Squib, I assure you, is far from a joking matter."

Trewley turned the valve with its copper-coloured spring over and over in his hands. "So there's nothing special you can tell us about this particular valve?"

"I'm sorry, Superintendent. I don't think so."

Trewley sighed. Stone said:

"You called it Memory Metal, Dr. Kirton. I haven't heard of that before. Could you tell us how it works, please?"

The scientist smiled again. "With pleasure, Sergeant. The principles, as I've already said, are easy to grasp—indeed, I believe I may best illustrate them by an example which should have considerable appeal to the detective instincts of yourself and your colleague. Let us suppose, Sergeant Stone, that you wish to become a superintendent. Your path to promotion is blocked by Mr. Trewley here. You resolve to ease that path by disposing of him—but you know, none better, the risk of discovery. Let us therefore suppose that you resolve to commit the perfect crime. . . ."

Trewley's bloodhound face looked decidedly unhappy at this resolution, but Stone smothered a giggle as she nodded to Dr. Kirton to continue.

He was delighted to do so. "Shape Memory Effect Metal, to give it its full name, is a metal—an alloy—which is so structured, crystallographically, that it can be programmed, as it were, to respond to the stimulus of temperature variation by, ah, changing shape. And its built-in memory means that, once the temperature returns to normal—why, so does the shape.

"For example, we have supposed on your part, Sergeant, a homicidal inclination towards the good superintendent. You design a dagger—a dagger of most unusual type, unique and easy to identify. Curved at an odd angle, perhaps, or with a shape in cross section like no other. But"—and Kirton tapped an emphatic forefinger on his desk—"when you *make* this dagger, you fashion it—to the outward eye—in the, ah, conventional form. A simple, ordinary dagger—except for the fact that you have programmed the metal to react to a temperature of, let us say, forty degrees Centigrade. And when the weapon is immersed in water of this critical temperature, it will alter its shape from the conventional to the unconventional one . . . and then, my dear Sergeant, you stab Mr. Trewley to the heart!"

Trewley stifled a groan. Stone coughed. Dr. Kirton hid a smile, and hurried on:

"Leaving, as you of course appreciate, a sickle-shaped, or an oddly angled, wound. A unique mark from the weapon for which your colleagues will hunt high and low—in vain. For you will have hidden its secret by cooling it down again—dropping it in the domestic freezer, perhaps, for speed, whereupon it reverts to its former simple shape. You may hang it upon the wall for decoration—use it as a paper knife—flaunt it under the very noses of your friends, if you wish. You may do so in perfect safety. To all intents and purposes, the mysterious murder weapon has disappeared forever!"

Trewley shuddered at the thought. Stone shook her head, and sighed. Dr. Kirton chuckled.

"The perfect crime, with the untraceable weapon! Or . . . is it? Take care, Sergeant Stone, that by some mischance the dagger does not fall into water of the critical forty degree temperature. Should it do so, I fear that it would revert, only too readily, to its original murderous form to bear witness against you."

There was a stunned silence.

Stone cleared her throat. "I'm not sure . . . Dr. Kirton, have I understood this correctly? This—this memory lasts forever? The metal can go on changing shape, backwards and forwards, entirely according to the temperature? Forever?"

"Broadly speaking, Sergeant, yes. It will, as it were, remember the other shape—both shapes. Which is why it is known as Memory Metal. Ah . . . like the elephant, you know, it never forgets."

"Memory Metal," repeated Stone.

"Memory Murder," growled Trewley.

As Dr. Kirton blinked, wondering if he'd heard correctly, Stone hurried to enquire:

"Apart from, um, the manufacture of untraceable weapons, Dr. Kirton, what can this metal do that's not a party piece? You said earlier that its commercial applications have been realised only quite recently. If firms such as yours . . ."

Dr. Kirton beamed at this enthusiasm. "There are many areas where Memory Metal can be used, Sergeant, particularly in these days of energy conservation. Take temperature regulation, for instance. Large greenhouses have a great number of vents it would be most time-consuming, and uneconomic, to open and close by hand. Memory Metal can close these vents automatically if a sudden frost should occur, even in summer—and they can, conversely, be opened wider, if it becomes too hot inside. Or take the humble domestic kettle, which switches itself off when the water boils—the metal here is programmed to the temperature of steam, you see.

"In the area of health and safety at work," he went on, "there are numerous types of cutout valve in industrial fluid transport systems—and, again in domestic use, there is the basic thermostat which you have here . . . And," he added, with a smile, "I believe that an enterprising manufacturer of, ah, ladies' foundation garments has utilised the Memory Metal principle in the, ah, support structures of . . . of certain garments which are frequently washed at higher temperatures than the normal body's thirty-seven point five degrees Celsius. No matter how the, ah, brassiere may be tumbled about in the machine, as soon as the lady in question puts it on it will, ah, mould itself to her individual requirements, which it remembers. Memory Metal . . ."

Both detectives sat and stared with increased respect at the object on Dr. Kirton's desk. Trewley prodded it with a thoughtful finger.

"Goes on changing shape forever," he mused. "Amazing."

"Amazing indeed, Superintendent. But, in the old adage, truth can indeed be stranger than fiction."

"So let me get this straight, Dr. Kirton." Trewley prodded the valve again. "If a room got hot—and then got cold again—and if this thing had the right sort of memory . . . I can't help thinking it's a pretty lethal sort of gadget to set near a gas fire."

Kirton tut-tutted. "I do beg your pardon, Superintendent. I fear my explanation has misled you. Radiators, not gas fires. The valve is controlled by the temperature of the room, and in its turn controls the flow of water through the central heating pipe—it's a common enough fitting on modern radiators to regulate the flow rate, and consequently the heat, in the system at any given point. Energy conservation, as I remarked earlier. But I assure you that one would never fit a valve like this to a gas fire."

"You wouldn't?"

"Are you sure?"

Trewley and Stone spoke as one. Dr. Kirton stared.

"Of course not. Why, if the temperature of the air in the room reached a critical stage, the valve would shut off the gas supply—the fire would go out—and, when the air cooled down and the gas came on again . . ."

His voice tailed away. He gulped, and turned faintly green. "Superintendent—Sergeant—don't say . . . You can't be trying to tell me . . ." He took a deep breath. "This—this Memory Metal valve . . . you didn't find it . . ."

Trewley didn't care to see the man suffer any longer than necessary. "Dr. Kirton, I'm afraid we did. This valve was fitted, at the time of his death, to the gas supply pipe of the fire—not the radiator—in Dr. Holbrook's study." He glanced at Stone, whose eyes were wide. He couldn't keep the note of triumph out of his voice.

"It's an old-fashioned fire, without a pilot light, without any of the safety devices you'd expect nowadays. It's so old-fashioned I doubt if you could have them fitted, even if you wanted.

"But this valve was fitted, all right. Caused to be fitted," he said, in the traditional words, "by person, or persons, unknown. . . ."

It was murder, after all.

──────── Thirteen ────────

Tracey Heath, bulging and blowsy, trudged along the hospital corridors following sign upon sign for the Antenatal Clinic. She carried a string bag stuffed with magazines and sandwiches; a discreet specimen bottle rattled against a flask of coffee. Never mind that her appointment wasn't for an hour or more: she'd managed to get shot of the kids for the whole morning, and meant to enjoy every minute of peace and quiet. Feet up, slumped in a chair, her much-thumbed love stories at her side, she would indulge herself to the best of her ability in her one chance for an uninter-rupted, undemanding, un-child-filled rest.

It barely crossed what passed for her mind to enquire after her husband. She had telephoned last night, to learn that his condition was unchanged: *still unconscious, but no cause for alarm.* Casualty Sister had sounded disapproving down the wire, but that didn't bother Tracey, enveloped with imminent motherhood and basic human selfishness. . . .

"You're an early bird this morning, Mrs. Heath!" A voice accosted her brightly from the rear as she passed pair after pair of rubbery swing doors, plastic peepholes through which the curious might inspect the arcane world of the sick and convalescent. "You've come to see your husband, of course," the voice went on. "Well, dear, you were in such a hurry, you've walked right past him! He's in a side room off this ward—head injury, you see, he has to be kept quiet. I've just this minute been having a little chat with Sister about you both."

Cursing inwardly, Tracey turned to confront the beaming countenance of her gynaecologist, a good-hearted individual whose imagination could never conceive that a wife might not wish to visit her invalid spouse. Circumstances beyond the poor girl's control might have prevented her coming before, but here she was at last—and so keen to see him, she'd overshot her target.

"In here, you poor dear." The gynaecologist beckoned and smiled. "There's a policeman with him, you know, still waiting for details of that dreadful accident, but nobody's going to mind if you sit with him for a while. Only you mustn't go upsetting yourself, remember—it's bad for you, and for the baby."

Having thus unwittingly provided Tracey with an escape route, the gynaecologist ushered her into Bob's room. Poor child—so near her time, and so distressed—as anybody was bound to be, seeing their husband lying so still and white in bed, with tubes and instruments all round him.

And with a bright-buttoned bobby at his side. . . .

"Sister says," mumbled Tracey, "he'll be okay as soon as he's come round. A matter of time, she said, and I didn't ought to worry over him, being as he's in the best place to get better and they know what they're doing. Which so they should," she added, aggrieved. "I mean—it's their job, innit? 'Sides, the insurance is going to pay for the bike, so it don't much matter he's not earning for a bit, with the Social Security and all. We can manage—and he don't cost nothing for feeding, neither, when he's like this. . . ."

Even as she uttered this feeble apologia, she moved in slow motion towards the motionless bed on which Bob lay, his breathing so shallow it was almost imperceptible. Monitored and trussed about with octopus arms of tubing and wire, he was a frightening enough sight without the huge white bandage wrapped about his head.

Yet Tracey wasn't frightened. She'd seen it all before, on the telly, hundreds of times, the same old thing: why should she worry? She was getting her money, and Bob would get better, that Sister'd said so. What was she doing, wasting her time with him this way?

"Might as well be going," she muttered, having refused the offer of PC Hedges to take his bedside seat. She began backing towards the door. "Stuffy in here, innit? I can't breathe proper . . . the baby . . ."

"Your husband," explained her medical escort, "is still in a state of shock. We really can't risk opening a window—the chill, you see. Perhaps, if you feel unwell, you'd be better off coming back a little later."

PC Hedges, who sympathised a little with Tracey's feigned distress, nodded at her encouragingly, and mimed a frantic loosening of his tie. She did not smile.

She did not smile: she grinned, wolfishly, and retreated a few more thankful steps. She reached for the doorknob behind her—too quickly, carelessly. Somehow, she missed her footing, stumbled, and nearly fell. Her heavy bag, swinging, banged against the door.

Tracey cursed. The gynaecologist gasped.

"Mrs. Heath! Are you all right?"

"Yeah," said Tracey. "Fine. Don't worry."

She had forgotten to keep her voice low. There was a sudden, convulsive jerk from the bed. Bob twitched again, and moaned.

Strange voices . . . chatter and bustle . . . he was in his open plan office at Allingham Alloys, and someone was asking if he was all right. How was he supposed to answer, when he was flat on his back—and in the dark, too?

Bob Heath opened his eyes, and stared ahead of him. He blinked, and groaned. Gradually, his sight focussed.

"Oh," he mumbled. "Hello, Trace."

"Hello yourself." Her hand was still on the doorknob; her voice was still far from tender. "All right, are you?"

"Dunno." He tried to lift his head, and failed. "Where am I? What's happened?"

The gynaecologist hurried over to give the traditional reply, adding that Bob had only had a very slight accident, and would soon be fine again, and wasn't, on any account, to worry.

This platitude brought Bob's eyes swivelling weakly from the distance of his wife to the bedside presence which had addressed him. With another groan, he turned his head. The uniformed watcher on the chair came into view.

"Oh, blimey," moaned Bob Heath. "Bloody copper . . ."

"Whatcher done to him?" demanded Tracey, shrill and angry. "He's out cold again!"

And the gynaecologist, after checking his responses, had to agree that he was.

"Dr. Kirton," said Trewley, after Stone's nod had reassured him that the scientist wasn't about to succumb to another attack. "This Memory Metal. Anyone employed here would know how it worked, would they?"

The wretched head of R&D swallowed twice. "Oh dear, yes—but"—as he saw a gleam of hope—"so would many, many others in metallurgical circles, as I told you before. This effect has been known since the early fifties, remember. I should hate to think that anyone at Allingham Alloys was . . . was suspected of . . ."

He choked, and fell silent. Trewley regarded him with some sympathy.

"We understand, sir—but think about it from our point of view. You're a scientist. Look at the facts. This is the sort of valve you say is a standard radiator fitting, but we found it in the supply pipe of the gas fire in Dr. Holbrook's study. What's more, the odd-job man who fitted it is prepared to swear that he had special instructions to fit it there, and not in the radiator pipe—in fact, there aren't any radiators in Dr. Holbrook's house."

"He could be mistaken," said Kirton. "Or he could be lying, for some reason. To—to think, to say that anyone could even have dreamed of such a thing . . ."

"And according to you, sir, almost anyone could have dreamed it, couldn't they? Any metallurgist, I mean. If these valves are standard fittings, it could have been anyone in your department—in your company—anyone from outside it, come to that. Though I'd better remind you, sir," as the scientist began to look slightly less distraught, "that this person, whoever it was, must have been at least acquainted with Dr. Holbrook to want to kill him." Dr. Kirton winced. Trewley went on:

"I'm not going to insult your intelligence by suggesting it was some random homicidal maniac. There's a connection between whoever had this valve fitted, and the death of Dr. Holbrook—and what we have to do is find that connection. And prove it," he added, rubbing his chin. "Well, it's our job, of course. Just give us time."

"This odd-job man," began Kirton, hopefully; then he paused. "I, er, take it there can be no question . . ."

"Shouldn't think so," said Trewley. "Not the type at all, I'd've said. Which is why we've got to start looking for more personal motives—or professional. Tell us about Dr. Holbrook, please. What was he really like? And don't," as Dr. Kirton looked unhappy, "let's have any of the speak-no-ill-of-the-dead nonsense, which won't get us anywhere. If you're a scientist, you've got to be honest. Right?"

Dumbly, unhappily, the departmental head nodded. Stone had already slipped her notebook and pencil from her pocket. Kirton gazed vaguely in her direction, and sighed.

"Basil Holbrook . . . was not a popular man, Superintendent. He was far from easy to work with. I have already told you of his high self-esteem, his jealousy for his professional reputation—his vanity, if you will. . . . And I said it was more than justified by his undoubted brilliance in his field, a brilliance which was widely acknowledged—and which served, indeed, in many ways to . . . not to excuse, but at least to explain, his sometimes . . . odd behaviour. His moodiness—his irritability—his disregard for the opinions of other people . . ."

Dr. Kirton drifted to an embarrassed halt. Stone, who over the weekend had found her old textbooks and researched the symptoms of chronic mercury poisoning, gave him an encouraging nod. Trewley said nothing. He left medical matters to the experts, and Stone knew much more than he could ever understand. She'd given him the condensed version, though; and with what Dr. Black had told them the previous Friday when he'd learned of Basil Holbrook's death . . .

"He seemed," said Kirton at last, "to have grown more— more eccentric, of recent years. Obsessional." He sighed again. "Withdrawn—almost reclusive. Antisocial, some might have called him—definitely tetchy, on occasion— jumpy, imagining insults where none had been intended . . ."

Trewley thought of Dr. Black's remarks, and Stone's confirmation, on the topic of delusions and hallucinations. He nodded, but said nothing. Dr. Kirton looked even more unhappy than before.

Then he brightened. "He had, of course, always been . . . vindictive, never able to forgive or forget. Fifteen years' refusal even to mention the name of—of our metallurgical colleague, the one who challenged his method of experimentation . . . But it had come to manifest itself in such—such petty ways, if one can use so demeaning a term about so great a brain . . . and I have to admit that there was, sometimes, provocation, one might say."

Trewley's eyebrows twitched, and he rumbled a question. Dr. Kirton, only too eager to enlarge on an argument which might be seen as proof, from the mercury poisoning point of view, that Allingham Alloys need not be as much to blame as he had at first feared, spoke with fluency and excitement on the subjects of Dr. Fishwick's coat, and Mr. Tilbury's sink.

". . . favourite cloakroom peg . . . Fishwick new to this department . . . Holbrook late one rainy day . . . coat thrown from peg to floor without explanation . . . Fishwick arrived an hour early next day to stake claim . . . forced to provide individual coat stands for offices . . . civil war only prevented by move to open plan . . ."

It had been a similar saga with Oscar Tilbury. Dr.

Holbrook had decided—for reasons which he thought good but which, as in the case of Dr. Fishwick's raincoat, he had failed to explain in sufficient detail to the other person most directly concerned—to reserve a particular sink for the preparation and disposal of etching reagents which he used in his metallography. Mr. Tilbury had set up his reflux condenser with its water flowing to waste in the identical sink—arguing (with some justification) that since it was right next door to the place where he worked, he had a certain claim for preferential use.

Dr. Kirton, smiling ruefully, shook his head for the folly of his fellow metallurgists. "Holbrook and Tilbury are barely—oh, dear, of course I mean *were*—on speaking terms, though it must be ten years ago by now. They almost came to blows about it, I'm told. Standing face-to-face and shaking each other by the lapels—very childish, I fear. Fishwick, I suppose, could have been excused—just—on the grounds of ignorance—but not in Basil Holbrook's opinion. He refused to contribute to Fishwick's wedding present when we had a whip-round four or five years back. . . ."

He looked hopefully at the two detectives, who had been listening with close attention and growing disbelief to his catalogue of scientific squabbling. Police officers though they were, accustomed to human nature in all its weaker moments, they yet found it hard to credit that educated adults, dedicated not to self-indulgent hysteria, but to logic and dispassionate judgement, could really behave in so small-minded a manner.

"I assure you that they did." Kirton sighed. "Without any encouragement from me, let me add! But what use was it for me to try to reason with them? Holbrook is—was—too valuable a man to lose, and he was perfectly capable of resigning if he felt he'd been slighted . . . and I would never have dreamed of suggesting that the others resigned, or even of insisting that they should apologise, when there were undoubtedly faults on both sides. These matters generally blow over, with time—at least to the extent of developing some sort of working relationship. . . . Generally," he added, with yet another sigh. "In this instance, I fear, they merely avoided one another—and that was that. And it was all a long time ago," he concluded, firmly. Was this firmness some subconscious attempt to lessen the arguments in favour of recent mercury poisoning as having an effect on the erratic behaviour of Basil Holbrook, genius?

"I know there's never a good reason for murder," Trewley said. "And I know we've seen enough crazy reasons in our time—but surely none of your lot would bump off a bloke for a daft thing like a sink, or a coatrack? And if he was always picking quarrels—all right," as Dr. Kirton protested feebly at the brutality of the phrase, "if he was a touchy sort of bloke all round, there must be dozens of folks who weren't exactly in sympathy with him. And I just don't see . . . No, we're going to need something a bit more definite than that, for murder." He rubbed his chin, and the bloodhound jowls quivered in thought.

"Dr. Kirton," he said at last, "I meant to ask you the other day, only I didn't. Who's been chosen—who did you have in mind, at any rate—to continue Holbrook's work on the Squib project?" Maybe, if the personal motive didn't so far seem much of a starter, there'd be something more helpful on the professional side.

The head of R&D looked uneasy. When, as requested by Trewley on that grim Friday morning, he had duly telephoned on Monday for police permission to unlock Holbrook's files to his successor, no thought of sinister possibilities had even entered his mind—particularly so since Trewley, who'd had time during the weekend to think things over, had unhesitatingly given his consent.

"But just let us know, would you, if the papers have been tampered with? Bits missing, alterations, that sort of thing . . ." And Trewley had added to Stone that it didn't seem worth sending anyone along to keep an eye on things, as there was nobody on the strength with even half a qualification in metallurgy, and nobody they sent would understand anything of what was going on. Far better to let things take their natural course, he'd reasoned . . . to the relief, at the time, of Dr. Kirton.

But now—when he hadn't before appeared to be bothered about it—the superintendent seemed to be suggesting that there might, after all, be some doubt about Squib. . . .

Dr. Kirton coughed, and spoke with evident reluctance. "I've asked Mr. Whatfield to take over, for the time being. He's one of our newer men, only been with us since September—he's barely found his feet within R and D, and isn't too deeply involved with anything else. A nervy chap—excitable—but, in his own way, nearly as brilliant as poor Holbrook. He came from Grantaford with excellent references—quite overshadowed his, ah, unprepossessing interview. . . . Grantaford has one of the finest metallurgy departments in the country, so it would hardly be in their interests to, ah, mislead us about a candidate's worth. The professional reputation again, you see. We've had a number of our best researchers from among the Grantaford graduates."

"Including you, Dr. Kirton?" enquired Trewley, as the scientist paused. A smile, proud but shy, crossed Dr. Kirton's face.

"Ah . . . I worked my way up through the ranks, as it were, Superintendent—started as a lab assistant, and took my qualifications on an external basis—though with the full knowledge and support of the company, of course."

Trewley was intrigued. "Easy, is that? Sort of thing someone like young Heath could do?" And then, having accidentally raised the topic of the absconding—and now unconscious—laboratory assistant, he added:

"By the way, d'you know if Bob Heath had any particular reason to bear a grudge against Dr. Holbrook?"

———— Fourteen ————

KIRTON STARED, THEN forced a smile. "None that I know of, apart from the fact that Holbrook refused to contribute to the young man's wedding collection on, ah, grounds of immorality. It was, ah, a shotgun affair, the lad had only just come to us from school—and Holbrook was, or at least had been, a Catholic, you see." He added, "Though I have to ask myself how much of his, ah, protestations served to conceal his undoubted parsimony. . . ."

Trewley and Stone did not return the wavering smile. It was hard to treat lightly that characteristic of the dead scientist which seemed to have brought to police notice the strange manner of his passing.

Trewley pondered. "We've still got to find out why he took off like that when he knew we were here—but we don't stand much chance of knowing until he comes round again. So let's try another tack. Professional rivalry, Dr. Kirton—in a general sense, I mean. Is there another firm you know of that might be about ready to launch their own Squib type of alloy? Those ceramics people you mentioned, for example. Would it be worth their while trying to slow up your lot's work to stake their own claim first? Is it even likely anyone from outside would have known how close Holbrook was to getting this superconductor of yours ready to roll?"

"Room temperature superconductor," he was gently reminded. "For that is the important thing, Superintendent—the ability to do entirely without liquefied gases to achieve the desired result! However"—as Trewley stifled a groan at the idea of further lengthy explanation—"that is hardly germane, I would have thought, to your question. The ceramics researchers have really been most generous in sharing their findings with interested parties—most. But their work is of such a kind that it will be ten, fifteen years before it could be commercially applied—and, what is more, though they are certainly working towards the same end—superconductivity at room temperature—the medium used is very different from ours. Squib, remember, is a metallic, not a ceramic, conductor.

"As for your second query . . ." He coughed, and wriggled on his chair. "Well . . . sooner or later, of course, word of a scientific breakthrough, no matter how closely guarded, gets around, even when the researcher is as secretive as Holbrook had increasingly become. But he had developed the idea of Squib, you know, from previous work he himself had published in one of our metallurgical journals—he saw further possibilities for a different application of the basic principle. . . . With hindsight, of course, we could say he might have done better not to publish, but the development came later . . . and then, of course, from time to time we have visitors. Someone might well have noticed the new equipment, or overheard something—competent specialists are capable of putting two and two together in the scientific world just as easily as in, ah, real life . . .

"And then . . ." He sighed, and lowered his gaze. "This, I fear, reflects rather badly on me. I do hope it won't be necessary to allow this to go any further, but . . . quite recently, I was asked to confirm the rumour that Allingham Alloys—that Holbrook in particular—might be working on a room temperature superconductor. . . ."

"And you said he was?" Trewley ignored the scientist's flush. "Who asked you?"

Dr. Kirton turned from red to purple. "Mr. Trewley, I—I very much regret that I . . . don't remember. I, ah, attended the annual dinner of the Metallurgical Society last

month. My doctor had warned me not to, ah, indulge too
deeply—but with meeting so many old friends . . ."

Trewley nodded: he could sympathise. There had been
one or two festive gatherings with long-lost colleagues he
certainly wouldn't care to quote chapter and verse for.

"I can imagine the rest," he said, as Dr. Kirton gulped,
and looked wretched. "You needn't go into the gory details.
I imagine you had a pretty good time—and were, well,
maybe tempted to boast a bit, under the influence?"

Kirton's face writhed with embarrassment. "I'm—rather
afraid I may have done. If only"—embarrassment turned to
anguish—"I didn't now have the dreadful feeling it might
have been through my careless talk poor Holbrook was
brought to his death. . . ."

The scientist's eyes were narrowed, his voice faltering,
his expression strained. His breath came in uneven bursts.
Stone, at Trewley's side, gave her superior a worried look.
He said at once:

"Well, it's only one theory, Dr. Kirton, and I wouldn't say
it had any more going for it than the personal motive, as
things are. Don't forget, you were asked to *confirm* the
rumour, so it must've been already known. If it wasn't you,
believe me, if these folk'd wanted confirmation, they'd have
found out some other way.

"Mind you," he added, rubbing his chin, "it'll be interesting if it was only after that dinner your managing
director—Woolverstone?—began chasing you and Dr.
Holbrook to get a bit more, er, definite about Squib. Is it?"

Dismayed realisation dawned on Dr. Kirton's face.
"This . . . is terrible, Superintendent. Oh dear—your
guess is absolutely correct. Mr. Woolverstone began pressing us both for a preliminary patent application, or at least
a written paper—publishing would stake our claim, you
see; indeed, he was pressing for anything we could use in
public—two or three weeks ago. Until then, he'd seemed
happy enough to allow Holbrook to work, as he always did,
at his own pace, and in his own way."

"Umph." Trewley glowered at the toes of his shoes, in search of inspiration. "Perhaps we'd better have a talk with Mr. Woolverstone—and with Mr. Whatfield." At Dr. Kirton's shocked gasp, he looked up. "Only because he's the one you've picked to replace Dr. Holbrook, nothing sinister. Just routine enquiries. We've got to start somewhere."

Kirton looked anxious. "If you must, then of course you must—but I should prefer, if you don't mind, to . . . have a word with Mr. Whatfield before you interview him. He is a—a temperamental man, as I said earlier, and I wouldn't want him . . . upset just as he comes to start work on the project. I wouldn't want him to think . . ."

Trewley nodded: what difference would it make? Whatfield either had his story ready—if he needed one at all—or he hadn't. The mind of a man who could plot a crime like this one probably wasn't going to be caught napping by the first bout of police questions. But once they'd dug about a bit, they'd have a better idea where they were going. It would be the second, maybe even the third, time of asking that got results. . . .

On the other hand, they might not need to go that far. If Whatfield was a nervy man—and guilty—then having advance warning the police were about to grill him could be a big help—to them. Could be he'd get so flustered to realise his plans had been discovered that he'd give himself away. It wouldn't do any harm at all to let him pickle. . . .

So Kirton spoke to Julia, and Julia spoke to Mr. Woolverstone's secretary. And, before long, Trewley and Stone were in the office of the managing director of Allingham Alloys.

Richard Woolverstone had deep blue eyes, dark blond hair, and an internal dynamo which drove him at hyperspeeds guaranteed to cause ulcers in everyone who tried to keep up with him. Under his guiding hand, Allingham Alloys had grown and flourished; but it was still only a second-class power as yet, and (he explained to his visitors) he wanted it to be Number indisputable One.

"This would have been our takeoff," he said. "We were about to float Allingham Alloys as a public company! It was all set to go, barring the final stages—rumours spread in confidence, potential major shareholders approached, patent experts ready with a Notary Public to register the world's first ambient-temperature superconductor—with Squib as a sweetener, they would have been clamouring for a piece of the action! Our shares would have soared—enormous capital input—new plant, new research staff, the chance to expand into a world leader . . .

"And now everything's been set back. And for how long? Until Philip Whatfield finishes what Basil Holbrook began—whenever that will be. Months—years, maybe—wasted!"

"Let's hope not, sir." Trewley didn't want another depressed scientist on his hands. "Dr. Kirton seems to think pretty highly of Mr. Whatfield's abilities. Perhaps Squib will be ready sooner than you think."

Woolverstone shrugged. "We must wait and see, Mr. Trewley. Let's hope you're right—the potential applications for room temperature superconductivity are endless! But, you know, it was the name of Basil Holbrook that would have held so much of the attraction. Who's heard of Philip Whatfield, apart from the universities? Industrial research is quite another animal from the academic, believe me. Here, one must be prepared to work under pressure, to meet deadlines. Is anyone going to wait for the unknown Whatfield? I'm afraid they may not."

"Umph. If you're as worried as all that about losing him . . . Might it have been in a business rival's interests to stop Holbrook completing his research?"

Woolverstone stared for a moment, then chuckled. "Maybe a slight touch of melodrama there, Mr. Trewley. As far as I know, nobody else was ever seriously studying Atoms—sorry, that's our jargon—Ambient Temperature, Only Metal, Superconductors." Another of Dr. Kirton's little efforts, deduced Trewley and Stone. "Atoms were Holbrook's original concern, in a far wider field. He only stumbled on the Squib idea by chance. Most other recent research into superconductivity has been with ceramics. In fact, for a long time we found it hard to concede that he could make anything of his earlier Atoms work when, as far as we knew, what he'd already published in the literature was his final word.

"Except, of course, that in the scientific world it is hard to have the final word on anything." Mr. Woolverstone smiled. "After one or two papers had appeared, and before he shut off communications, as it were—even to me—he provoked a very lively correspondence, though only from one or two groups rather smaller than we are. Companies who haven't the capability to carry out the intense research required. It needs a genius of inspired guesses—as poor Holbrook was—and they come rather thin on the ground, I'm told. He was, in a subject full of specialists, a superspecialist, if you understand me."

Stone could tell that her superior was becoming baffled by the technical nature of the conversation. She said:

"What did he specialise in—before Squib, and Atoms?"

Richard Woolverstone's blue eyes expressed no surprise at a question from the female half of the detective team. "Dr. Kirton, Sergeant, could tell you better than I could. You may have gathered that I rely very heavily on his judgement—in scientific matters, at least. As far as I recall, however, Holbrook's lab reports used to mention something called . . . Direct Reduction and Powder Composites— whatever they might be." He chuckled. "All I know is that we were forever authorising the purchase of hydrogen in those huge red cylinders that are so awkward to store properly."

"Hydrogen." Stone nodded. "He worked with mercury as well, didn't he?"

Trewley suddenly saw what his subordinate had been driving at. He waited eagerly for Mr. Woolverstone's reply.

"Mercury? Yes, I believe so." Either the possibility of a

prosecution for mercury poisoning hadn't occurred to the managing director of Allingham Alloys, or the man was a good actor. "Still, I'm no expert, as I said. Have a word with Kirton, if you want the details. I do know he used to mess about with vacuums and glass burettes and magnets and so on, but I really couldn't say exactly what he was doing, most of the time. Nor, of course, did I care, provided that he came up with the results."

Stone subsided, and allowed Trewley to put his next question. "He'd almost done that, with Squib, hadn't he? Come up with results, I mean? He was trying to make an alloy that was an improvement on copper, wasn't he?"

"He'd been trying for years," agreed Woolverstone. "On and off, that is. That's how the Atoms acronym came about: it was an extra layer of secrecy, because he had a great dislike of risking anyone catching him out halfway through a project. But once he got as far as endowing the results of his research with the Squib name . . ."

"You thought," supplied Trewley, "that he'd pretty well sorted the problems out, didn't you? You and Dr. Kirton— Holbrook wouldn't have let on until he was sure, a bloke of his sort—he was happy for the pair of you to know a bit more about what he'd been doing, over the years. But then how many other people knew he'd come up with something that could knock the bottom right out of the copper market? I should think there have been a few worried suppliers around the place recently. . . ."

Woolverstone, that astute man of business, chuckled. "So your theory, Superintendent, is that Squib's imminent launch might be a motive for disposing of poor Holbrook? Your reason for wanting to see me? No, no. This sort of thing happens all the time, I assure you—but nobody ever needs to murder anyone. There are far easier ways!"

Trewley's stare was sceptical, in the extreme. Richard Woolverstone smiled. "Suppose that somebody invents a genuinely reusable match—or an everlasting light bulb— or," with a smile for Stone, "tights or stockings which neither ladder, nor hole. The invention is leaked, once it's been patented, to the firms most likely to be commercially hurt by it—who almost always adapt the circumstance to their advantage. Either they buy out the rights of the invention, and freeze the patent so that nobody else can exploit it—or, as will be—would have been—most probable in the case of Squib, there's a topflight takeover bid for the whole firm. A partnership, perhaps—but *we* get the money, *they* maintain their monopoly. They can either market the invention there and then, or they hold off for a while. If the inventor's upset by the suppression of his brainchild, he's told it would be uneconomical to carry it out on a commercial scale, or that the firm will eventually exploit it themselves, when the time is right.

"Which," he explained, as Trewley gave him a disapproving look, "is once they've exhausted the possibilities of the original thing the new invention supersedes. Or, of course, when they believe they'll make even more money by using the new thing, even if it means closing down their old business. It's very simple, I assure you. Common business practice, nothing more."

Trewley was thankful his business was good, old-fashioned crime. Big business was another sort altogether. Open plan offices, double-dealing and dishonesty under fancy names, rigging the market . . . give him catching crooks for a job, even if the money wasn't as good.

"Common practice it may be," he said aloud. "But from what you say, there must be some companies who're going to show a definite interest in Squib, whether it worries them or not." He wasn't convinced by Woolverstone's protestations that all would be sweetness and light among the traders in copper, or the manufacturers of electrical goods. "Have you had any hints of a takeover bid? Any approaches—maybe through a third party?"

"A couple of nibbles, yes." Mr. Woolverstone gestured smugly. "You have to realise, however, that neither party would wish to show its hand until that patent had been properly filed. For a proper bargaining point, you see. It is a matter of confidence, you understand—but," as he caught the full force of Trewley's glare, "I think it would not be . . . unethical to say that Chattisham Copper were the first to put out the old feeler. Then there was—"

"Chattisham Copper?" cried Trewley and Stone together. Richard Woolverstone jumped.

"Why, yes. Only to be expected, of course—they're one of the three largest users of copper in the country, and Edward Chattisham has a doctorate in metallurgy. He'd be one of the first to appreciate the potential of Squib—far more quickly than any of his rivals, I'm sure. His company—he's a true rags-to-riches type—is still run by people who know just what they manufacture and sell—unlike Allingham Alloys, as you may have guessed." The blue eyes twinkled; the firm mouth curved in a wry grin. "I may be a good businessman—indeed, without any false modesty, I am—but my metallurgical knowledge is . . . haphazard, to say the least. You see, I, er, came here from domestic plumbing. . . ."

And Mr. Woolverstone was considerably startled when the superintendent's reaction to this little pleasantry was a smothered, hollow groan.

Philip Whatfield was waiting for them when they returned from their talk with the Managing Director. He hovered in the area of the main entrance to R&D, his hands in his pockets, his shoulders stooped, his feet fidgeting against the rough pile of the heavy-duty carpet. Trewley was quick to apologise for having inadvertently delayed him.

"We didn't expect you to come to us, Mr. Whatfield—and we certainly never meant to take you away from your work like this. Didn't Dr. Kirton explain we'd be along to your office as soon as we'd finished talking to Mr. Woolverstone?"

"Oh . . . I didn't mind waiting." The scientist straightened, trying to meet the detective's shrewd brown gaze. He almost succeeded. "You, uh, wouldn't really have wanted to talk to me . . . in my office, would you? People . . . might have heard," he added, in a pleading tone. Trewley sighed, but then remembered Kirton's warning that Whatfield was yet another temperamental man.

"I won't suggest that you see him here," the head of R&D had said, indicating his own discreet office. "Even though it might seem, to you, the most suitable place for such an interview. . . . He's . . . an odd sort of chap. He'll probably be more than happy to let you sit right down at his desk and grill him on the spot—and I'm sure his neighbours will be tactful enough to leave the immediate area. . . ."

But this suggestion had not appealed to Trewley. At the time, he'd wondered about it; and now he regarded Mr. Whatfield with a curiosity he tried to keep hidden.

"It's not so private here, come to that," he pointed out. The main doorway of any busy department is bound to be full of eavesdroppers en route. "People can hear just as well as they could in your office, I'd've thought."

Behind his tinted spectacles, Mr. Whatfield's eyes were anxious. "It . . . it isn't such a bad morning, Mr. Trewley—Sergeant. We could go for a walk around the block," he offered, so hopefully that the detectives knew this was what he'd wanted all along. As he caught the way their quick glances met and passed a silent message, he flushed, and ran a jerky hand about the open collar of his shirt, and started to babble confused excuses for this preference for alfresco privacy. Trewley held up a restraining hand as he tied himself into verbal knots.

"Don't worry, Mr. Whatfield, a breath of fresh air won't do us any harm, so long as we don't stand still." He tried to set the man more at his ease. "Bracing. And, who knows, it might just ginger up a few ideas for perfecting Squib, as well. It can't be easy for anyone, having to carry on the work of a genius like Dr. Holbrook, and—"

"Genius!" In his emotion, the scientist spluttered the

word, and his feet tripped. "A conceited know-all—self-centered—spiteful! Genius, indeed!"

"That's a bit hard on a man you've only known for—how long? A couple of months?" returned Trewley, wondering if this vehemence was a murderer's double bluff.

Philip tripped over his feet again, but managed to meet the superintendent's inquiring gaze almost calmly.

"A couple of months, Mr. Trewley? Good heavens, I've known Basil Holbrook far longer than that. Twenty years, it must be—if not more."

Stone simply gasped. Trewley barked. "Twenty years?" The clicking of handcuffs was almost audible.

"Why . . . yes." Mr. Whatfield gulped. He seemed to retreat into his ill-fitting clothes at the urgency of the response. "I thought . . . I mean . . . that was why you wanted to talk to me first, wasn't it? Because I . . . . I know more about Basil Holbrook than anybody else here?"

Fifteen

TREWLEY AND STONE stared at him. He gulped again, forcing himself to speak. "We were . . . at Grantaford together. He was older than me, of course, but we—we crossed by two or three years. . . . He was doing his PhD at the same time as I was an undergraduate." He shrugged. "So, being both in the same department of the university . . ."

"Metallurgy," said Trewley, setting the record straight. Mr. Whatfield nodded.

"He was . . . always on hand in the labs, either working for his thesis or assisting with student practicals. . . . And then . . ." He coughed, and stared down at his feet as they trudged along. "We were both members of GADS—that's the Grantaford Amateur Dramatic Society. . . . My cousin Sylvia was a member, too." He hunched his shoulders defiantly, took a deep breath, and announced:

"She married Holbrook—or, rather, he married her, I should say. It was to . . . to fix his interest with her that he joined GADS in the first place. He was never really keen on acting, the way she and I had always been, from children. . . . And then, poor girl, he married her—and gave her a dreadful time, I know he did." He stopped, and turned to face Trewley with something like desperation in his eyes. "We . . . disliked each other, you might as well know now. If I'd remembered he worked here when I applied for the job, I would have thought twice about accepting it, even allowing for . . . Well, I'm not sure I would have wanted to come here. And he . . . I suspect that if he'd had any idea I was applying for the post, he would have done his best to dissuade Allingham Alloys from employing me. . . ."

"No love lost between you." Trewley rubbed his chin.

"You're very . . . frank about all this, Mr. Whatfield." Too frank? Could he be hiding something stronger than dislike, behind all this uneasy chatter about the past?

Philip spoke now in a tone of bleak resignation. "Basil Holbrook was a Roman Catholic, Superintendent, and Sylvia was a staunch convert to the faith. She and I . . . none of our family wished us to marry, you see. Cousins . . ." He kicked moodily at a pebble, and missed. "Our mothers were sisters, identical twins—everyone said it was better . . . And Holbrook gradually came to recognise that Sylvia—had married on the rebound, I suppose you'd have to call it, if anything so terrible can be summed up in such a . . . an ugly phrase. Of course, she put a brave face on it—she tried to make the marriage work—but he took it out on her, poor girl, and never forgave her for . . . for taking him as second best." The scientist's drooping spine straightened, and he held his head high, in a brief moment of pride that in this, at least, the renowned Basil Holbrook had not been the preferred choice.

Trewley rumbled softly, encouragingly: "I expect you'll be pretty glad of this chance to complete the Squib project, then. The chance to improve on what Holbrook began—to experiment with your own theories and maybe find out they're better than his. It'll make your name, I imagine, if that's what happens!"

For once, Philip's tone was sharp. "Too much importance is attached to the—the value of a reputation, Superintendent, whether commercial or academic. Holbrook was . . . was excessively conscious of his own worth. He . . . he despised me, for example—dismissed me as an untrained mind—when he was fully prepared to give my brother-in-law's ideas every consideration simply because he was a PhD. Never mind if a man has practical experience, or specialist knowledge—it was always paper qualifications which made an impression on that—that conceited snob!"

"But surely . . ." The superintendent was puzzled. "From the way Dr. Kirton talked, I thought—I thought you had a degree, Mr. Whatfield?"

The scientist hesitated. "No. No, I haven't. . . . Not exactly. Things . . . can happen, you understand . . ."

"But Dr. Kirton still feels you're the right man to carry on Holbrook's research," Trewley said, before Mr. Whatfield's embarrassed silence could become acute. "The electrical industry will never be the same again, he told us, once the Squib has been perfected!"

"If," came the flat correction. "The most recent work with ceramics has really set me thinking . . . Holbrook could well have become so fixed in his ideas that he refused even to consider the results from America and Japan—and China, of course—but he was like that. Blinkered, single-minded—stubborn. The undue emphasis on the hydrogen content—maybe a completely metallic alloy isn't the answer, after all . . . a possible combination of the two methods . . ."

Trewley and Stone barely understood one word in three of this scientific rambling, but didn't dare stop him, now that he was at last speaking freely. He might just let slip something which could have a bearing on the case as they'd so far managed to make sense of it. . . .

Philip seemed suddenly to recall their presence, and came to with a gulp. "Oh—I'm so sorry. . . . Thinking aloud—concentrating ideas—technical interest only—intending to develop from Holbrook's work . . ." He brightened. "And if we can only show that the great Basil Holbrook might, just once, have been working in the wrong direction, it will be a—a splendid chance to relax the—the stranglehold a few of your *names*, Mr. Trewley, have on the whole field of metallurgy!"

"We?" Trewley echoed, picking up the clue and wondering if it had been deliberate. "Well, I must say, Mr.

Whatfield, you're a quick worker, if you only took over the project on Monday."

The scientist achieved a shaky grin. "It's been a—an open secret in the trade for a while now. Things soon get round, even garbled versions, when there's any secrecy or mystery—and Holbrook was always paranoid about secrecy, though I've heard he was far worse in the past few years."

Stone nodded silently at Trewley's side. Her weekend reading had been most informative on the likely mental, as well as physical, results of prolonged exposure to mercury.

"He had disappeared from view ever since . . . Sylvia, . . . died," continued Philip, with a sigh. "There were rumours, of course, that he must be busy with something . . . special, and I felt sure they were justified. I knew it couldn't be a . . . an excess of grief that made him hibernate—not when he'd hounded my poor cousin into her grave the way he did, I know he did!" His voice rose, and shook. Trewley and Stone eyed him with interest, and looked at each other, but said nothing. After taking a few deep breaths, Mr. Whatfield continued in a calmer tone.

"My brother-in-law's by way of being a metallurgist as well. Once he'd heard I'd come to work here, knowing that Holbrook was up to something, naturally he was interested to learn what was going on. He—he's been staying with me for a few days—last week, it was—and of course we've had a few general talks—but nothing detailed, I can assure you," he added urgently. "For one thing, how could I know what Holbrook was doing, when he barely spoke to me until the other day? So our talk—Ted's and mine—was always on a theoretical level only—although, between us, we managed to rough out notes on various ferro-alloys, and I let Holbrook look at them—it might have given him new ideas, saved time by suggesting shortcuts, pointing out errors— though he hardly cared to listen at first, of course." Mr. Whatfield was bitter now. "No doubt he regarded any suggestions *I* might make as—as professionally insulting . . .

but once he realised that it wasn't plain Philip Whatfield who'd written the notes, but *Doctor* Edward Chattisham, he seemed all at once to—"

"Chattisham!"

At the startled cries of the two detectives, Mr. Whatfield's narrative, which had slowly settled into something approaching normal conversation, became once more confused. "Ch-chattisham? Why—why, yes. He's a PhD—I told you. That is . . ."

"A metallurgist, you said," Trewley retorted. "Copper, by any chance?" But he had already guessed the reply.

"Yes, he's Chattisham Copper—which was another reason for not talking about Squib in any detail, you see—professional discretion—loyalty to my employer—but it did no harm just to talk," pleaded Chattisham's brother-in-law. "And even Holbrook saw no harm in it—why, the afternoon of the day he died, he actually came along to my desk to talk to me without prompting—admitted there might just be something in what I'd been trying to tell him before, that he'd thought things over and might have been hasty in dismissing my ideas out of hand . . . but I know," he concluded, in bleak tones, "that it was only because of Ted's professional qualifications he was prepared to read the notes. If Holbrook *had* been in any way . . . mistaken with his research, he could never have put up with the idea of owing it to *me* that he discovered his mistakes and had the chance to put them right. He—he would have hated it."

For two very good reasons, thought Trewley. A man as conceited as Holbrook seemed to have been would never rush to admit he was wrong about anything; and there was the ghost of Cousin Sylvia to reckon with, as well. Holbrook hadn't much cared—according to Whatfield—for being her second choice; had borne a grudge, most likely. In fact, if Holbrook had murdered Whatfield, it would have been a good deal less surprising than any idea that Whatfield—from what they'd found out so far of his character—should even think of murdering Holbrook. . . .

He pulled his wandering wits together. "You said your brother-in-law's been staying with you, sir. Maybe you'd care to give us a few more details of his visit?"

The question seemed to puzzle the scientist. He blinked, and frowned, tugging at the collar of his shirt as he pondered. "He came down . . . last Thursday or Friday week, I think it was—today's Tuesday, isn't it? About ten days ago, then. I know he left me Friday morning, because I stayed to see him on the right road for London, and when I found afterwards I had a puncture I could have done with his help—I'm not very practical, you see, unlike Ted—but he'd left early, because of having to allow for the fog. But"—and he looked all at once alarmed—"I'm sure he'll be able to give me an alibi for Thursday night, you know. I'm sure he will."

"So you think you need an alibi for Thursday night, do you, Mr. Whatfield? Any particular reason?"

Mr. Whatfield ran a hand around his collar again, and licked lips which had suddenly gone dry. "Well—surely—everyone in the company must know by now that Holbrook's death was—was unexpected, and I've told you enough about our relationship for you to . . . But, believe me, nobody who knows me could ever seriously suppose that I, of all people, could—could lock a man into a room . . . could shut him in, and turn on a gas tap!" A violent shudder shook his loose-limbed form, and again his footsteps stuttered as he walked. "To do such a thing . . . impossible! Holbrook and I loathed each other, but—never, in this world!"

Yet, despite these earnest protestations, Trewley and Stone made the same mental note: *check up on Whatfield and Holbrook at Grantaford.*

They decided to break off their questioning of Philip Whatfield . . . "For the moment, sir, thank you," as Trewley put it. The scientist had told them much, and set them thinking; but at an emotional cost to himself. He looked worn and grey, uneasy with more than the customary nervousness of the interviewee. Neither of the detectives cared for cruelty. Stone had no real need to catch her superior's eye: in silence, they came to the mutual decision to return indoors; and, as they readdressed their steps, the topic of conversation was changed to that Squib research which Mr. Whatfield was to undertake. Knowing his sergeant to be much better at this sort of talk than himself, Trewley left the honours to Stone, who soon set Philip once more at his ease. His replies, at first tentative, became slowly more abstruse and confident. By the time the three had returned to R&D, he was in full theorising flow; he nodded a courteous, but abstract, farewell, and shambled off to his desk with the light of inspiration gleaming through the thick-lensed tinted glass of his spectacles.

"We'll just pop back to Dr. Kirton," said Trewley, "and then—yes, Miss Springs. Anything wrong?"

"There was a message from the hospital—one of your constables rang in. . . ." She took a neatly written sheet of paper from beneath her pencil-holder, and handed it to the superintendent.

"Oh," was all he said for now, as he read the report of PC Hedges on the strange effect his presence appeared to have had on the semiconscious Bob Heath. "Here, Sergeant."

Stone took the note, read it in turn, and murmured, "A guilty conscience, sir? Wish we knew why, if it is."

Julia discreetly ignored the speculation. "I'm glad," she said, "to learn that Heath has come out of his concussion. After all, I feel a little to blame for his accident—not a lot, but a little. And I certainly don't want Dr. Kirton worried about anything more at present. *He* has a conscience, if Heath has not. He takes his responsibilities here very seriously. He's a kindly, hardworking man—too hardworking, in fact. His state of health leaves a lot to be desired." She smiled suddenly. "I've appointed myself a censor, you know, until things settle down again—but even the most devoted secretary couldn't keep her boss from finding out about a second death in the department!"

Trewley nodded. "Glad to see he's not the only one to take their responsibilities seriously, Miss Springs—and if that's a hint to leave the man in peace for a bit, well, I'm not slow to take a hint. If you wouldn't mind passing on our, er, thanks to Dr. Kirton—I'm sure you can word it so he won't get in a state. . . ." An idea flashed into his mind. "Have you been with him long, Miss Springs? You and he seem to make a pretty good team."

"Only since I've been at Allingham Alloys—since the middle of September." She appeared gratified at one professional's recognising the professionalism of another. "But we hit it off together almost immediately."

"I'm sure you did." The superintendent nodded, then turned to Stone. "By the way, Sergeant, can you remind me of that query we had about the key to Dr. Holbrook's house having been lost at work?"

She duly riffled through her notebook, managing to hide her surprise. How had Julia Springs just added herself to the superintendent's list of suspects?

"Benson said something," prompted Trewley, as his servant seemed doubtful about where precisely she should look. He gazed at Julia in an apparently absentminded way as he continued to jog Stone's memory. "The cleaning lady told him—Holbrook lost his spare key, or wouldn't have one made, or something . . ."

Just as he'd hoped, the efficient Miss Springs couldn't resist supplying him with the answer. "Oh, yes, of course—people used to make jokes about how he kept it hidden under some ridiculous flowerpot in the garden! I would have expected a scientist to have more sense, but . . ."

"So would we," murmured Stone, who had just found the right place in her notes. She couldn't hide a smile as she remembered how talk of the flowerpot had distressed her superior. "Yes, that's what she said—only the one key, because he'd lost the other at work."

"Wonder how long ago that was?" Trewley's calm tones

could not deceive his colleague; but Julia did not know him as well as Stone.

"From the way everyone joked about it, some years ago, I imagine." It was a casual response to a casual question. "Certainly it was general knowledge around here—he was lucky not to have been burgled, I'm sure."

Stone felt confident that this remark would meet with her chief's approval, and was puzzled by his evident disappointment as he said: "Do you think Dr. Kirton could confirm it for us? Or, if you think he ought not to be disturbed, could somebody else?"

Julia's eyes gleamed at the suspicion he didn't trouble to keep out of his voice. "Feel free to ask anyone you wish, Superintendent. I can promise you that Dr. Holbrook's front door key was lost a considerable time before I came to work at Allingham Alloys—just ask anybody you like!"

Sixteen

"AND," LAMENTED TREWLEY, as they finally drove away, "she was telling the truth." He scowled. "I suppose people do . . . sometimes—but . . ."

"But it's a pity." Stone smiled in sympathy. "Another fine theory gone west, sir . . . or maybe it hasn't, after all. Maybe everyone we asked was . . . was lying about the key. It's a conspiracy, sir!"

"Conspiracy be damned." The rebuke was automatic, and she didn't take offence at his tone. "You seriously expect me to believe in a murderer who plans his crime three years in advance? This is real life, Sergeant. I don't. Especially," he added, in tones of utter despair, "when the bloke could've had a spare key cut for himself any Tuesday or Thursday during the day. Any time he wanted!"

"Flowerpots," murmured Stone, just loud enough for her chief to overhear.

"Don't push your luck, girl—oh, what's the use?"

"Cheer up, sir. I don't know what was behind that business with Julia Springs, but surely we can regard the key—in a way—as a clue? For one thing," she said, above his groan, "doesn't it confirm the mean streak in Holbrook's nature? Always saving money where he could—which ties in beautifully with the bill from Bert Gadgett . . ."

"So it does." For a moment, he sounded almost cheerful. "And then, I suppose, if we think about it . . . for three years or more, that blasted key's been under that perishing flowerpot outside Holbrook's damned front door, with the whole of Allingham knowing about it—except us, of course." His face registered acute mental suffering. "So think about this, Stone. What made someone suddenly take notice of that key—and use it? And arrange Dr. Holbrook's death in such a—a damned devious way that, if we hadn't spotted the business about the bill, it could have passed for an accident?"

"Or suicide," she reminded him. "Except, of course, that nobody seems to have found a note."

"And suicides usually leave a message of some sort." Trewley was becoming animated. "Well, for the sake of it let's argue that he *did* leave a note. Would it make sense for Mrs. Mint—or that milkman, picking locks left, right and centre—or even young Benson—to destroy it? Like hell it would! It'd be plain daft, with us knowing who was first on the scene—we'd be even quicker to suspect something fishy than we'd normally be, having our noses rubbed in it that way. Daft, like I said. And whoever our murderer is, he's *not* daft, hatching a crazy scheme like this one that almost had us fooled. . . . So, let's rule out suicide for a bit. . . ."

"Let's," said Stone. He barely heard her.

"But Holbrook was noted for never putting anything on paper if he could avoid it. Could be he even felt the same way about suicide notes. . . . And, given the poor bloke's recent state of health, we still might just have accepted suicide—or even accident—if it wasn't for that valve. Which was deliberately fitted in the wrong place . . .

"So Holbrook was deliberately killed—right?"

"Sounds logical, sir."

"Umph." He sighed. "Logic's all very well, but I prefer facts. I like things set out fair and square, and what I want to know is—why *now*? What's happened, what changes have there been in Holbrook's life, or his work, or . . . or any other circumstances, during, say, the last six months? I told you, I'm not going to believe, unless I've got to, in someone planning a murder much earlier than that."

"Whatfield," supplied Stone, after only a brief pause. "They'd known each other before, and they couldn't stand the sight of each other. Whatfield suddenly turned up . . ."

"And so," cried Trewley, having waited to see if Stone would enlarge on the Whatfield angle, "did Julia Springs! A right classy piece of goods, if you'll allow me to say so, Sergeant. Sleek—a looker—and efficient with it. September, she said she joined the company. . . . I'd dearly love to know where she came from."

"I agree, sir, she's very attractive." Stone was sufficiently liberated to raise no objection when a member of the opposite sex made a purely factual comment about a member of her own. "But what would be even more interesting, if you ask me, is what happened to the previous girl. The vacancy seems to have occurred at a jolly useful time for someone or other—if what you're saying's anywhere near true, sir."

"Useful for someone, yes." He rubbed his chin, frowning with unseeing eyes at the road ahead. "But which particular someone? What's the most likely place for Miss Springs to have . . . connections going back to before she joined Allingham Alloys?"

It took Stone five seconds to find the answer. "Chattisham Cooper, sir. Right?"

"Right." He chuckled. "I could see you wondering why I suddenly went for her back there at the factory. Mind, it's only a theory, but—"

"But anything's possible! She could easily have been Chattisham's secretary, sir—or his mistress—even his daughter, or a niece, or something. We've already had a couple of coincidences. Why not one more?" Her eyes were bright as she entered into the spirit of the superintendent's guess. "Whoever she is, somehow or other Chattisham's heard about the Squib, and—oh. How did he hear?"

Trewley's time was four seconds. "He was the one Kirton babbled to at that dinner when he got tight."

"Brilliant, sir—I mean, no," she amended. "Remember, Dr. Kirton told us how Miss Springs helped him during his angina attack the morning after? She was already working at Allingham Alloys by then.''

"So she was. Damn." The bulldog bore no grudge that she'd shot down part of his theory: it was, after all, her job to act as a sounding board. "So Chattisham couldn't have planted her as a spy—yes he could, though. Rumours had been flying about, hadn't they? Even while the thing was going under its earlier crazy name . . ."

"Atoms," she reminded him. "Double-code-named for added secrecy—all part of Holbrook's paranoia, sir, consistent with the suspected mercury poisoning."

"Yes. Right." He didn't want her enlarging again on the wide variety of symptoms Basil Holbrook could have displayed: they'd had one run-through already, and once had been enough. "So Chattisham sets up Springs to find out for sure—you're right, we'll check what happened to the other girl—and Springs reports back that Holbrook's doing some important work, only she's not qualified to understand just how important it might be. Chattisham pumps Kirton at the dinner, learns it's really as big as all the rumours had been hinting—and brother-in-law Whatfield already works for the firm. Now, did he go there of his own free will . . . or was he pushed? Chattisham could be any kind of devious blighter. If he's responsible for Holbrook's death, then he's as devious as hell. A bloke like that'd think nothing of—of infiltrating the opposition. . . ."

"Yes, sir, but if he, um, infiltrated Whatfield into Allingham Alloys, he wouldn't have needed Springs as well, would he? If you want a really useful spy, surely you find the best person first time around? You've—we've—deduced that she's unlikely to understand the details of Squib, which would be what Chattisham wanted. And probably all she could do would be pick up the odd idea. She seemed pretty bright, but not that sort of bright. Unless . . ."

"Unless," rumbled Trewley, "she's somebody else with a metallurgy degree! We're going to find out all we can about

Miss Julia Springs . . . if that's her real name, for a start. It might not be easy . . . But, talking of finding things out, that's what Chattisham's done, I'll wager. Found out from brother-in-law Whatfield, who's so muddleheaded he won't even have known he was being pumped, for all his fine talk about—about company loyalty, and professional discretion."

"Brilliant, sir." And this time, Stone did not amend her words. "So your theory is that, having confirmed just how valuable Holbrook's research was, Chattisham's tried a—a desperate piece of sabotage—and killed the poor man? Leaving Whatfield, the newcomer, as the logical person to take over. And I agree, sir, he isn't exactly the suspicious type—I bet Chattisham could run rings round him." She sighed. "You know, sir, we've got a tremendous amount of checking up to do, on all sorts of people and every kind of information . . .

"And I know jolly well," she added softly, as the car slowed for the turn into the police station, "who'll end up doing most of it. . . ."

They crept—Stone suggested *sneak* as a fair description of their progress, but Trewley ignored her—in through the back door, avoiding Sergeant Pleate on the front desk. The superintendent then dropped tea-drinking hints, and spoke wistfully of chocolate digestives. Stone bargained for a fairer distribution of the imminent information-checking, and gave permission for him to rootle through her desk while she made her way to the canteen.

Once cosily settled, they further discussed the theory.

"Industrial espionage," said Trewley, thoughtfully waving a biscuit in the air. Stone grinned at his heroism in not immediately eating it. "Chattisham," the superintendent enlarged, "wants to discover the exact lay of the land before putting in his takeover bid . . ."

"So he decides sabotage wouldn't be a bad idea, because—oh, because it's too expensive for him to buy them out the way Mr. Woolverstone suggested, sir, or even to try poaching Holbrook from the firm. Is that it?"

The superintendent, the happy taste of chocolate on his lips, nodded. "Instead of, er, buying the goose that lays the copper eggs—or, er, even poaching the things. . . ." He paused for her to appreciate his little joke. "Yes. Well, he can't, because he's short of cash, for some reason. That's another matter we'll have to look into. He removes Holbrook from the scene, leaves brother-in-law to carry on and find out exactly what's what with this wonder alloy . . . But he'll have slowed things up enough for . . . for whatever he needed to slow 'em for. Time to set up a—a consortium of shareholders . . ."

"Conspiracy, just as we said, sir."

"As *you* said, you mean." He chuckled, and helped himself to another of her biscuits. "Well, why not? They're supposed to teach 'em to use their brains at university, aren't they? Takes brains to organise a conspiracy. . . ."

"I wonder where Chattisham did his PhD?" Stone frowned. "There must be a reference list of metallurgists somewhere, the way there is for doctors . . . but I'm afraid, sir, that if it turns out that he was at Grantaford, too, we'll have to conclude he's not our guilty party."

"Good grief, girl. Why not?"

"Coincidence is one thing, sir, but this would be ridiculous. Melodramatic in the extreme . . . oh!"

"Oh? Oh, what?"

She hesitated. He glared. She said slowly: "Well, sir, melodrama . . . Whatfield was in the Grantaford Amateur Dramatic Society, wasn't he? Along with Holbrook and dear Cousin Sylvia. And Holbrook . . . everyone knew him, didn't they? He had some very—very identifiable mannerisms—easily mimicked. And that man who called on the Gadgetts with the valve . . ."

"Umph." Trewley regarded her with some interest. "Have to be tall, for a start."

"Whatfield *is* tall—taller than you, sir, if only he took the trouble to stand up straight. Like Holbrook—I mean tall, and droopy—and, well, there you are. Two tall men— squeaky voice, muffling scarf—easy, sir!"

The superintendent nodded. "The almost perfect crime." He grinned. "As good as a book. . . . A tall man, now. Wouldn't be young What's-his-name, by any chance?"

"No, sir, it wouldn't." She eyed him sternly. "But it could have been anybody who felt like putting on a bushy white wig and wrapping a scarf round his face—Whatfield knew Holbrook had been hatching a cold, didn't he? The perfect excuse for staying muffled up! He rode a bike—imitated that stooping walk—"

"Ride bikes a lot at Grantaford, don't they? One of the features of the place—students, and so on."

Stone's student days had been spent far from Grantaford, but everyone knew the picturesque ways of the old university town. "Yes, sir. And he—whoever he was—took care to go in on a Saturday, when it was likely the Gadgetts would be busiest—and less likely to spot if there was anything odd about him." She was warming to her theory. "And, if our suspect is in full-time professional employment, then Saturday would be his only chance—unless he wanted to risk finding them shut on his lunch break, or arriving late at work and drawing attention to himself."

"Chattisham stayed with Whatfield for several days, so Whatfield said. He could have gone to the shop anytime during the week, if he'd wanted."

She had to think about this one. "Yes, sir, but they're not an especially busy firm, are they? Nor overbright— probably why he chose them in the first place. A weekday might have been too quiet. They'd have had time to pay too much attention to him."

He rubbed his chin. "So doesn't that argue for local, not outside, knowledge? And when you take that perishing flowerpot into account—sitting on his front door key like a chicken on a blasted egg . . . *and* he knew which days the cleaning woman didn't go to Holbrook's house!"

She listened as he continued to enlarge on her theory. "Whatfield more likely than Chattisham, I reckon. Now I've thought it over, girl, I rather like your conspiracy idea. Maybe the new boy at Allingham Alloys stands to get a hefty rake-off from brother-in-law once the dust has settled."

"There's always the money motive," she said, thinking of her mortgage. "They say everyone has their price, sir. Didn't you think Whatfield kept on a little too much about how he only discussed Squib on a purely theoretical basis with Chattisham?"

"Could be. He was an odd sort, and no mistake, but—we need to know more. Get the computers buzzing, or whatever it is the damned things do. Too many loose ends, all leading nowhere. No real line to follow. Now, if—"

"Ouch! Sorry, sir—pun. *Reel* line—fishing—red herrings . . . sorry, sir. I was only trying to look a bit more on the bright side, but—inexcusable, I know."

"Yes. We've got more important things to think about— like checking up on Julia Springs, and Chattisham, and the, er, Grantaford connection."

He looked slightly embarrassed as he spoke the final phrase, but she didn't smile at his inadvertent composition of a likely thriller title. She said:

"Oh, dear, I've just remembered something else, sir. More's the pity."

"That sounds bad." He absently helped himself to the last biscuit to build up his strength against whatever fell blow his subordinate was about to deliver.

"Confusing, sir, to say the least. Whoever impersonated Holbrook had to be a tall man—right?"

"Right."

"Our friend in hospital, sir, the one with the guilty conscience—the one who goggled at us so hard in Allingham Alloys and bolted when he saw Hedges outside his house . . . he was rather on the tall side, too, wouldn't you say?"

"Oh," said Trewley, scowling. "Blast! Yes, I would!"

A trip to Town was indicated. London was an hour and a half from Allingham by InterCity train with, in theory, time for a detour via Grantaford on the return journey. Trewley and Stone had put their various enquiries to the computer: past experience had shown them it was seldom in a hurry to reveal what it knew: they were not prepared to sit around and wait.

Moreover, Sergeant Pleate was on the warpath.

"A laboratory specimen," groaned Trewley, flinging himself into a corner seat while Stone, their tickets clutched in her hand, dropped beside him, breathing hard, and worried for her companion's blood pressure. They'd made the train by the skin of their teeth, with the desk sergeant's accusations still ringing in their ears. . . .

"A dog," he went on, his eyes wild. "A barrister's outfit, wig and all—a motorcycle—a kitchen sink, for the dear Lord's sake—a pair of stuffed gerbils—a stag's head, fully mounted . . ."

He was unable to continue. Stone, sighing, obliged. "A windsurfer's board, a glass eye, three sets of false teeth, and a wooden leg, sir. Not to mention numerous umbrellas, books, pairs of spectacles, gloves—singly or in pairs—and overcoats . . ."

"I wish," rumbled Trewley, "he'd never found that back number of *The Daily Telegraph*. Just because folk leave that sort of rubbish on London trains doesn't mean they're going to do it in Allingham. They've got more brains, in our part of the world."

"Sergeant Pleate certainly has." She stifled a giggle. "Pretty bright of him to use that list as a Lost Property argument, you have to admit."

He groaned again. "Over my dead body! He can argue

till he's blue in the face—that cupboard he's got's quite big enough for one month, and there's no need for three. No need at all."

"No, sir." Her eyes surveyed the compartment, empty of any other passengers—and, at a first glance, of lost property. "Should I just check, before we get too comfortable?"

"Never mind gerbils and stags' heads and barristers' wigs. We've got better things to look out for. Miss Julia Springs, for one—we want to find out all we can about that young woman. We'll pop along to Somerset House, or whatever they call the place now, while we're in Town, and take a look at the registers, if that's what you do. There'll be someone to tell us, I dare say. Not so much the births and deaths, but the marriages—and the divorces."

"We could always try her Personnel records at—oh, no, I suppose"—she corrected herself in mid-suggestion—"if she's come as a spy, she'll have concocted some cover story, won't she?"

"Somerset House," said Trewley. "After we've seen Chattisham, that is—though now I'm not so sure it was a good idea, ringing ahead to make an appointment. He could have skipped the country . . . or else he'll have worked out some blasted clever-dick alibi with Whatfield, and we won't be able to touch either of the blighters."

"Yes. . . . Alibi, sir. In a way, perhaps that's a point in Whatfield's favour. That he should think we wanted an alibi for Thursday night—because that trap with the valve was set up days before. All the murderer had to do was wait for the first cold night. . . ."

And Trewley shuddered at the memory of that cold night, and cursed her for reminding him, yet again, of the station plumbing, and of Desk Sergeant Pleate.

Seventeen

THE SECRETARY, A motherly tweeded dumpling, wore half-moon spectacles in gold frames. She welcomed the detectives with a smile. "Mr. Chattisham's expecting you," she told them, and promised to intercept all calls, messages and visitors until their business with her boss was complete.

"You've got a very efficient secretary, sir," said Trewley. "Very helpful, too. Has she been with you long?"

Edward Chattisham—a plump, blond teddy bear of a man with a genial ginger beard—beamed at his two visitors in delight. "Oh, she's absolutely my right hand. I couldn't run this place without her. She started as my clerk-typist when I first set up on my own, more than fifteen years ago. What she doesn't know about Chattisham Copper simply isn't worth knowing, I assure you!"

"Let's hope none of your competitors tries to steal her, then." Trewley settled back in his chair as if he'd made a casual observation, but he remained quietly watchful.

The ginger beard seemed to pale at the thought. "What! Daisy Locket let herself be bought? Impossible! The most loyal and trustworthy of my employees . . . she'd no more contemplate such an idea than I would! Utterly honest and reliable—she's worth her weight in gold!"

"Shouldn't you say *copper*?" enquired the superintendent, with an attempt at a twinkle. "Being in your line of business, I mean—isn't copper quite a valuable commodity?"

The Chairman of Chattisham Copper smiled. "Oh, yes, I like that—worth her weight in copper, indeed!" He chuckled, then sobered. "However, I'm sure you haven't come all this way to talk to me about my secretary, have you?"

"I said on the phone it was to do with the late Basil Holbrook," Trewley reminded him.

Chattisham nodded. "My brother-in-law told me of his sudden death—a great loss to the profession—why, he was nothing less than a genius! A research worker of the very highest quality. . . ." He favoured his two visitors with a shrewd look. "Allingham Alloys are very fortunate to have a researcher of Philip's calibre on hand to carry on where Holbrook, ah, left off."

"You think Mr. Whatfield's fully capable of continuing Dr. Holbrook's . . . work, then?"

Chattisham smiled. "Such discretion does you credit, Mr. Trewley. Shall I say it for you? The ferro-alloy which is intended to be a room temperature superconductor—yes, I know about that. I've been hearing rumours—everyone has—for the last few years, and, naturally, when Philip landed the job there, I asked him if he could tell me anything to confirm that Allingham were indeed on the verge of a breakthrough. Poor Philip! Even from the way he went quiet on me and refused to give any details, I knew Holbrook must have cracked it—my brother-in-law, you see, has absolutely no gift for dissimulation! His sister—my wife—is just the same. If I don't know what my birthday present is, and where it's hidden, as soon as I walk in through the door, I take it as a sign I'm sickening for something."

"Odd," said Trewley, "when you were all in the Grantaford Amateur Dramatic Society together. I'd've thought . . ."

Chattisham seemed genuinely flummoxed. "Grantaford? Oh, yes—I believe Philip indulged himself a little in Amateur Dramatics while he was up, though I think there was a lady in the case to account for the aberration—I can't imagine he was any use except as someone behind the scenes. He's certainly never shown any thespian tendencies since then, that I know of! But I'm not one of the lucky Grantaford graduates—I went to one of Bernard Shaw's nonconformist holes down in Wales for my first degree, and took my PhD as an external student while I was working in industry. My interest at that time, you see, was in precipitation hardening—it seemed sensible to work on a larger, more commercial scale."

"Precipitation hardening—ah!" And Trewley shook a sorrowful head. "Too technical for the likes of me."

Stone hurried to speak before Chattisham could begin yet another complicated scientific translation. "Excuse me for asking, sir—but why do you call yourself Mister Chattisham? If you're a PhD, you're entitled to call yourself Doctor, aren't you? Like Kirton and Holbrook?"

Chattisham grinned, and winked. "Business tactics, pure and simple, Sergeant Stone! I was never all that keen on research for its own sake—unlike the two you mentioned, who show little sense of, ah, commercial necessity. My interest was more on the money-making side, but, with a handle to my name, business people tended to dismiss me as a head-in-the-clouds academic with no chance of serious consideration for promotion. So I decided to drop it, for most purposes. Sometimes, you know, it can pay to be able to pull the wool over someone's eyes . . ."

"Ah, now I understand!" He chuckled again as she looked startled. "Those notes on the diffusion rates of hydrogen in ferro-alloys. Philip let Holbrook have them to study, and they were still with his body when it was discovered. . . . Believe me—word soon gets round!"

"Seems it does," agreed Trewley. Stone was inaudible.

"Well, I'm sure you've heard more than enough about the special alloy Holbrook was hoping to perfect—Atomic, or some such name. Naturally, you can see it would be in my best business interests to slow him down for a while. I wanted to put in a bid for Allingham Alloys—I wanted Chattisham Copper to have full control when the thing was finally launched—but, even though I'd heard all the ru-

mours, I only made certain of my facts a few weeks
ago—and it takes time to raise that sort of capital for such
a takeover. I hoped to buy a little time by introducing just a
few doubts in Holbrook's mind—get him to start checking
a few basic concepts, go back over his research—and then,
when I was ready, well . . ."

Trewley, brooding on business ethics, nodded slowly.
"Well, indeed. But I don't understand how—if Mr. Whatfield's as loyal and discreet as you suggest—you managed
to make certain of your facts. How you managed to confirm
that Dr. Holbrook had indeed discovered this—this wonder
alloy."

Chattisham winked again. "About three weeks ago, Mr.
Trewley, the Metallurgical Society held its annual dinner."

Light dawned. "*You* were the one who pumped Dr.
Kirton!" Trewley clapped himself on the forehead. "Of
course. . . ."

Chattisham was amused. "Yes, of course I pumped
him—wouldn't anyone? Not that he needed much encouragement to brag. We all admit Holbrook's value, but
Kirton's opinion was always exaggerated, I felt. Philip
Whatfield, in his own way, is as good a metallurgist as the
late doctor—I'm glad for his sake that he has the chance to
prove himself at last, after all his . . . bad luck. . . . But,
to be fair to myself and to Geoff Kirton, he didn't really tell
me much more than what I already knew, or had managed
to gather from the grapevine. He was, ah, more than three
sheets to the wind when we talked together, but he was the
soul of discretion, considering. Dick Woolverstone would
have been proud of him . . . and certainly *he* doesn't
blame poor Kirton for that little slip of the tongue."

"And how you can be so sure of that, sir?"

Edward Chattisham regarded the superintendent with a
pitying smile. "Because I had a go at pumping him, too, Mr.
Trewley. Why else do you suppose I should spend so much
of my valuable time in a place like Allingham? No
disrespect to your home town, but . . . I was a spy on

enemy territory, you see. I let Allingham Alloys know I
might just be in the running for a healthy offer, for a
majority shareholding—though Philip, of course, hasn't the
least idea. He still believes I came down for a breath of
country air!" And Mr. Chattisham of London laughed
heartily.

Woolverstone had certainly kept very quiet about this,
thought Trewley. Hardly surprising, under the circumstances, but annoying for police investigating the murder of
one of the man's own employees. "Did Mr. Woolverstone
give serious consideration to your talk of a possible takeover?"

"He played it very close to his chest, Mr. Trewley—just
as I would have done in his place! You need a poker face
and nerves of steel to succeed in business—and we're two
of a kind, Dick Woolverstone and I. But, for what it might
be worth—I'd say he ended up with the impression it could
be in the copper industry's interests to form a consortium to
buy the rights to Holbrook's patent—and that Woolverstone, ah, wouldn't be forgotten when the board came to be
set up. I know that the sales and marketing side of business
is what's always appealed to him, rather than the pure
development aspect."

It takes one astute businessman to recognise another,
Stone told herself. But, if Holbrook and his Squib research
were so essential to Woolverstone's advancement, is it likely
that the risk of prosecution for mercury poisoning would
outweigh the personal factor? If Whatfield really is capable
of carrying on where Holbrook left off . . .

She exchanged a quick glance with Trewley, who nodded
his permission for her to put another question. "This
takeover must be pretty important to you, by all accounts,
Mr. Chattisham. How exactly would the marketing of this
new alloy—once it was launched—affect the price of
copper?"

The tycoon replied without much hesitation. "Roughly
half the copper used in this country is bought by the wire

and cable—the electronics and electrical—industries, Sergeant Stone. So I think you'll agree that a fifty percent cut in our sales would be quite a bargaining point to boost Allingham Alloys' value—as Dick Woolverstone knows!"

"He'll hold out for a good price, then," said Trewley. Mr. Chattisham nodded.

"Naturally. I can't say I blame him. This stuff will have as great an impact on modern technology as the invention of the transistor in 1948, if not more. Mind you, we could still end up in a race with the ceramics people—but that won't do either side any harm. A bit of healthy competition can only encourage sales, once we get the whole thing moving. Once we've bought out Allingham Alloys, that is."

"And the time," Trewley said, "wasn't right—or you wouldn't have tried to delay the completion of Holbrook's work by . . . concocting those notes of yours."

"I can't say I care for your choice of words, Superintendent." Chattisham chuckled, to show he'd taken no real offence. "*Concocting* sounds as if I'd just fudged something together and didn't really know what I was talking about. My brother-in-law may not have a doctorate in metallurgy, but don't forget that I most definitely have!"

Trewley thought about returning his smile, then didn't. "You stayed with Mr. Whatfield because you needed a base for your, er, forays into the Allingham Alloys territory. How long were you there?"

"Ah, yes. May I repeat, Superintendent, that I'm no fresh-air fiend—a week in your no doubt charming county town would have been far too much for me all at once, even if I could have spared the time from my own concerns here in London. I asked Philip if I might stay for about a week—a tactful evasion, I thought—and first went down on Thursday evening of the week before poor Holbrook died. That gave me a couple of days to make my—preliminary sortie, shall I call it?—and then I came back to Town—"

"When was that exactly, sir?"

"Saturday afternoon—my wedding anniversary. We went out to dinner with friends—and I hope you won't be making too many enquiries about the length of time it took me to drive from Allingham! I don't mind being a suspect in a murder case, but it would be embarrassing to have my licence endorsed."

"I don't believe the word was mentioned, sir," remarked Trewley at once. "Murder, I mean."

"Maybe not by you, but Philip was on the phone to me in one of his frantic states the very minute the rumours reached him yesterday. He wanted me to acknowledge the fact we'd spent Thursday of last week—the, ah, relevant week—together at his house—which we had, of course, though poor Phil was in such a state he would have asked me, I suppose, to alibi him even if it wasn't true. Which it is," he said, in tones of utter conviction. Or so, the two detectives thought, he hoped. . . .

"I had, as you'll gather, returned to Allingham," he continued, "on the Wednesday night, and left for Town on Friday morning—so we were certainly together on the vital Thursday night when Holbrook . . . met his end."

"You could be in it together," Trewley said, with one quick look at Stone. "Conspiracy, now—that'd be it."

Chattisham shrugged. "What possible motive would I have for wanting Holbrook dead? From the business point of view, it's absurd—and I hope you aren't suggesting that it could have been for the sake of giving Philip the chance to take over the research! Yes, I know about that, too—he rang me again, most excited, poor chap. He—he's a nervous type, brilliant but unstable—though the firm could have done a lot worse than give it to him."

"Perhaps," suggested Trewley, "you could have guessed it would be your brother-in-law who'd be asked to take over the work. He hasn't been with them long, and Dr. Kirton told us that in a couple of months a new man wouldn't have become too busy with anything else. Mr. Whatfield was bound to be the obvious choice—as you must have known, Mr. Chattisham. Known and—maybe—relied on it?"

A burst of laughter filled the room as Chattisham dismissed any notion that he might have rid the world of Basil Holbrook to give Philip Whatfield his big break. "Apart from anything else, Mr. Trewley, my wife is only his half sister—the link isn't particularly close. I told you, he's a man of . . . unusual temperament. Erratic. Likeable enough, for all that, if you can overcome his shyness—but hardly a reliable tool for the ruthless schemer you postulate! I do see your point, though. . . ." With a scientist's approval of the detective's interpretation of the facts. "How lucky, then, for Philip and myself that we *can* vouch for each other's movements on Thursday night—and no wonder he's been ringing me in such a tizzy every five minutes! I thought at first he was simply being his usual paranoid self—but I think I'm going to advise him, after you've gone, to get in touch with a solicitor."

"You don't seem too bothered on your own account, sir."

"Why should I, Superintendent? I didn't kill Basil Holbrook—and life's too short, and my time too valuable, for me to start worrying about what may never happen!"

"A cool customer, sir," observed Stone, as with Trewley she made her way down Kingsway, towards Aldwych and the Central Register of Births, Marriages, and Deaths, now to be found in St. Catherine's rather than in Somerset House.

"Almost as bad," growled the superintendent, "as that blasted Garland, for playing tricks. Frank as you please one minute, doubling back on his tracks the next—I wonder if he *did* plot with Whatfield to make that elaborate alibi, or not—rushing backwards and forwards between Allingham and London the whole damned week. . . ."

"He was still with Whatfield on Saturday, remember, sir. He didn't leave until the afternoon. It could have been Chattisham who called into that handyman's shop with the valve—"

"Wrong shape, Detective Sergeant Stone." He only ever addressed her by her full title when he knew he'd scored a point. "And that's just the first thing!"

"What? Oh, of course." She grinned. "Silly of me, sir—and the beard, too. I should have realised. On the other hand . . ." Her tone was dreamy as she gazed into space. "I once read a detective story where someone shaved off his beard to commit a crime, so that everyone would think, um, what you've just thought, and then he turned up again wearing a false one, and all his friends said it couldn't possibly have been him—"

"Amateur dramatics!" interjected Trewley, before he saw the gleam in his sergeant's eye. "Oh, yes, very clever, my girl. Chattisham's only about five foot nine, of course."

They stopped at the swing doors, and Stone ventured to look her superior up and down. "At a guess, sir, he weighs . . . rather more than you do, too. And Holbrook was a tall, thin man . . ."

"You're getting as bad as my wife, Sergeant. Can't a bloke ever have a minute's peace from nagging women?" There were times when Mrs. Trewley put her spouse on a rigid diet; he had seldom been known to enjoy the experience. He pushed her sharply between the shoulder blades, rather harder than necessary. "Ladies first!"

She was still grinning as Trewley showed his official card to a peak-capped personage of imposing appearance. This helpful individual listened without interruption to the problem as posed by the superintendent, then said kindly:

"I can't leave this desk, see—security. Though why anyone'd want to nick a load of old registers of names and dates beats me. They're only bits of paper, after all, and they've been copied on microfilm, in any case. There's no secrets to be kept hidden around here, I tell you straight. Hoy, Alf! Alf!"

Another uniformed personage emerged from some hidden cubbyhole. "That's me," he said calmly.

"Here's the Law after you for them seven wives you got

abroad in the Navy, see, and wanting to check up in our records for 'em. Lend a hand, will you?"

Alf ignored the slander, and cheerfully beckoned to the two police officers. He led the way past stacks of leather-bound volumes of great weight and width, with handles in the centre of their well-worn spines. Cramped between each pair of stacks was a long, sturdy, double-sided, sloping worktable: about which clustered a studious, muttering crowd of genealogists, with sheaves of notes in their busy hands, and open registers before them.

"They want to find out who their grandfathers was," said Alf, with a jerk of his head. "Me, I reckon it's best to live and die in ignorance. Never know what you might find out! Seen 'em in tears I have, more than once. . . ."

"Good grief," was the only remark vouchsafed by the superintendent, restraining his curiosity with an effort. "Well, there's a fair bit we want to find out, about one particular person—and we don't know where to begin. We rely on you to, er, help us with our enquiries. . . ."

He'd guessed from the way Alf first greeted them that here was a colleague after his own heart. He hadn't been wrong. Once the problem was explained, Alf threw himself with enthusiasm into the task of learning all there was to learn about the birth and marital status of Julia Springs. It was a hot, dusty process, involving much manoeuvring of the enormous registers from shelf to table and back for another volume when the first proved useless.

"We start at 1837," Alf said, "but your party'll be a sight later than that, I reckon. How old is she?"

Trewley had three daughters. "Thirtyish—maybe twenty-eight." And Stone did not correct him.

"Then we start here," said Alf. "And we look her up in every book—knowing her surname, see, it'll be easy. It's all here, filed by quarters of every year. You can cross-check as well if you want, not to mention microfilm, if you need it. . . ."

He was delighted to display his expertise. Deftly, he

hunted through quarter after quarter, removing and replacing the great volumes with a back-bending, arm-swinging motion that spoke years of practice. Stone found herself rubbing her back in sympathy, but Alf seemed to enjoy himself without reservation. It was not long before he found the record of Julia's birth, thirty years before.

"And her mother's maiden name was Hemley—see?" Alf pointed to the line with a grubby finger. Trewley looked with a regretful eye at Stone.

"Not Chattisham. Pity. Oh, well—let's see if she's ever been married to him, shall we?"

"Can't nobody get married till they're sixteen," said Alf, as he led the way to the Marriages section. "So we'll have to start there, and work forward. . . ."

It took time; it grew hotter, and Trewley found it hard to believe Alf when he informed him that they certainly did have air-conditioning. He loosened his tie, and unbuttoned the collar of his shirt. He caught Stone giving him an anxious look.

A woman fainted just behind them; somebody scooped her out of the way, and nimbly took her place at the crowded table.

"Sir," said Stone, "I'd better—"

"Got it!" cried Alf in triumph. "Springs, Julia Clare—here you are! She got married all right . . ."

Stone abandoned any thought of offering first aid as two attendants appeared from nowhere, and helped the fallen woman to her feet.

"Married," agreed Trewley, peering over Alf's shoulder at the open page. "Using her maiden name now, though." Was this because she was a spy? Or . . .

"Divorced," suggested Stone, squeezing in beside him. "Or separated. Perhaps she wanted to, um, cancel out her past mistakes. It's understandable enough, sir."

"Sometimes, Sergeant, your touching faith in human nature makes me despair." He turned to Alf. "Why ever she changed herself back, how can we find out the name of the bloke she married?"

"Why, there he is, right under your nose. Third column— and no need to bother cross-checking, if it's just the surname you want. . . ."

"Oh," said Trewley and Stone together.

Julia Springs had been married to a gentleman who bore the name of Shufflebottom.

"I take it all back, Sergeant Stone," said Detective Superintendent Trewley, with a chuckle. "I couldn't agree with you more. I understand perfectly well why the woman got divorced!"

─────────── Eighteen ───────────

THE METALLURGY AND Materials Science Department of Grantaford University was set in splendour on the top two floors of an eight-storey block dedicated, in futuristic lettering, to the Faculty of Applied Science, and housing also the Civil, Mechanical and Electrical engineering departments. It was a flat-topped, large-windowed, air-conditioned building designed, from the solar panels on its roof to the automatic doors in its entrance lobby, to shelter the keenest, richest young brains of their generation—a building whose sole purpose was to further, and to bear witness to, the white heat of the technological revolution.

Both lifts had *Out of Order* signs on them.

This was not a good start. Stone tried to look on the bright side. "They're not very big," she remarked as she allowed her appraising eye to pass from the lift to her superior, and back again. "It, um, might have been a tight squeeze, sir. . . ."

Neither detective was pleased to learn that Professor Vulcan's office was on the top floor of the eight.

"It would be," grunted Trewley, as they began the climb.

"We could do with the exercise," Stone comforted him; but this was before they had crossed the boundary of the Civil Engineers, two floors up. After that, she saved her breath for climbing, and silently marvelled at the scampering boffins who passed them, book-laden and cheerful, without visible effort in either direction.

Fortunately for constabulary dignity, Vulcan proved to be a pedagogue intent on fitting a quart of instruction into the pint pot of a lecture hour. Everyone else in the building might be ready to go home; but this one room, against the outer wall of which the two detectives leaned to recuperate, echoed and re-echoed still with the incomprehensible and flowing polysyllabic utterances of Applied Scientific tuition.

Floor-scraped chairs and eager feet at last announced the end of the lecture. The lately liberated crowd came pouring out in a talkative stream, suggesting to the keenly listening Trewley and Stone that, shaky though he might be on matters of punctuality, Professor Vulcan had a fine mind, and could speak accurately, with a good marshalling of the facts under review.

"Let's hope he's as sound on the events of twenty years ago," muttered Trewley, as they entered the lecture hall. "What we want's the truth, the whole truth, and nothing but!"

"Hear, hear," murmured Stone by his side; and, at their regulation tread, Vulcan looked up.

Drugs was his first, inevitable, thought; followed by *Rag Week Excesses*; and then—horror—*Double Yellow Lines*. But he faced up squarely to the impending doom, greeting the pair with a courteous smile.

"Good afternoon. How can I help you?"

"Good afternoon, sir. We're police officers . . ." The professor's heart sank as Trewley made the introductions; as he made the explanation, it bounded with relief.

"Basil Holbrook's death? You surprise me—but, yes, of course I remember him. A great loss to metallurgy."

Did nobody mourn the loss of Holbrook, the man? Professor Vulcan's visitors thought it a sad reflection on the late doctor's character that everyone spoke of him only in scientific and professional terms. Had he, in the end, been nothing more than a warped, brilliant brain?

"Some personal details?" Vulcan looked puzzled. "Well, I can tell you what he was like as a student, but . . . as for the present, a man may change, in twenty years! And I don't understand"—he shot a questioning look at the two detectives, his expression shrewd—"why you should have come all this way to ask me . . ."

"There's been talk of suicide," Trewley said, with perfect truth. "But he didn't leave a note—and we wanted to find out what made the man tick. We don't like mysteries any more than you scientists do, Professor. And Dr. Holbrook doesn't seem to have had any close friends in Allingham we could approach."

Vulcan nodded: the admission did not seem to surprise him. He sighed. "Of course, yes . . . so you have to come back twenty years or more to discover why such a man as Holbrook would want to kill himself. He wasn't an easy person to understand, I know—and I probably knew him as well as anyone, in those days. I was his supervisor. . . .

"Even here, he found it hard to make close friends—he was too good, too soon; and took himself too seriously, or so it seemed to me. He had an excellent brain, clear-cut, logical—he came here with a First Class degree of the very highest quality, and was expected to do brilliant research—we were pleased to have him apply to Grantaford, if the truth be told. He interviewed extremely well—courteous, intelligent, confident in his own abilities but not cocky—he was good at athletics, too, a Blue from his original university. Just the right build for running, hurdles, all the activities I believe go under the collective title of Track and Field events."

It was hard to recognise, from Vulcan's description, the Basil Holbrook who had lately graced the streets of Allingham white-haired and unsteady, gangling and absent-minded. If his past had indeed been so splendid, no wonder he'd taken the easy way out, rather than be reminded of his lost glories . . . of the cruel contrast of passing time.

Professor Vulcan must have sensed the incredulity of his audience, for he smiled a rather dry smile. "This picture does not remind you of the man you knew? Well, I'm hardly surprised. As I said, people *may* change—but I don't think Holbrook did. It's my belief that, while he was with us, he was simply playing a part—putting on an act of superficial popularity. Call it glamour, if you will—which he had, I will not deny . . . but somehow, once I came to know him, I always doubted his sincerity. I felt that he was pretending—that his brain had exactly calculated what his behaviour should be for maximum benefit, but that beneath it all there was . . . no real heart. Others, perhaps, suspected it too, when they came to know him as well as ever he would let them. But he was a cautious man—tried not to let people get too close, to run the risk they might find him out—you could call him cold-blooded, even ruthless, in that way—a great scientist, but a less than great human being."

He shook his head for the human failings of Holbrook the scientist. Trewley stared at him, fascinated. He'd wanted someone who wasn't a speak-no-ill-of-the-dead sort—well, he'd certainly found one. . . .

"Of course," continued the professor, "as a scientist he was one of the very best. He had an almost photographic memory, which helped—though it hindered, too, on the human side. He could never forget a slight, an insult, even where none might have been intended. And he had, as well, a grudging, jealous, vindictive streak which I always felt would have grown more intense with age, as his reputation and personal dignity increased in the way we all believed was inevitable. And, since you say he had no friends in Allingham, I suppose that our apprehensions were founded on more than instinct—or that the instincts of those who came to mistrust him were justified—if 'mistrust' is quite the word I want."

Trewley made noncommittal noises, encouraging him to continue. Vulcan was now well into his narrative stride; and his eyes looked back twenty years into the past with a hint of regret for the lost splendours of the dead man.

"A difficult man to like, Superintendent—but, as I said, he did his best to keep you at a distance, so that mostly what people could see to admire were the outer things—the sports, the academic results, the great brain, the abilities. He was a worker even when he didn't need to be, with a mind of his calibre—but he was a Roman Catholic, with the dedicated intensity of purpose which sometimes accompanies religious strength . . . and yet, even there, I wondered . . . a hint of some spiritual bleakness somewhere, of something lacking—making parade of his beliefs because inside himself, he had doubts . . ."

"We've been told he lost his faith in recent years," said Trewley. "Or at least that he'd, er, lapsed."

Professor Vulcan nodded. "Again, that's no surprise. The ultra-scientific mind, you see, always demands proof—which, of course, religious faith, by definition, cannot provide. And if anybody had a scientific mind—Holbrook was the one!"

"But," said Trewley, "we heard he was a member of your Dramatic Society. I grant you the sports, but—an actor? Isn't that a bit . . . a bit frivolous, for the cold-blooded type Holbrook seems to have been?"

Vulcan smiled. "Ah yes, but after Sylvia Bannister appeared on the scene even Basil Holbrook unbent a little. It was all part of his plan, you see; that single-minded nature of his which always made him take everything so seriously. She was a lovely young creature—black hair, wonderful grey eyes with a depth of expression in them few could equal. A born actress, in a—an honest way, unlike Holbrook. Who acted a part, to my mind, during his whole time with us. . . .

"Yes, she was a lovely girl, and could have gone far if she'd gone on the stage professionally, I suppose, except for a—a certain weakness, mental instability—no, let's call it a lack of balance. . . . Academically, she was sound enough—but something in her family background, perhaps . . . there were certainly indications—"

He broke off, frowned, and shook his head. "But you don't want to hear all this, I'm sure. It's the character of Basil Holbrook which is your main concern."

"But he did marry Miss Bannister," said Trewley. "And anything could be of help, in a case like this."

Vulcan sighed. "No doubt you know your own job best." He stared into the past for a moment, and sighed again. "Yes . . . Sylvia Bannister. They were introduced by their parish priest, I believe. She was a convert to the faith. Perhaps she was searching for the . . . the stability she felt she lacked, I couldn't say for sure; and converts to a faith are always the most punctilious in observance, aren't they? She was impressed—dazzled—by Basil Holbrook . . .

"He was doing his PhD when they met, and had the reputation of a coming man. He was a good-looking young fellow in those days, too. Tall, black hair, classic features—they made a handsome couple, he and Sylvia. And he was older by several years than her other swains, more polished in manner—he may have been as smitten as anyone, but he had obvious advantages over the rest—as well as being more inclined to make the definite decision that she was the sort of wife who would be suitable for whatever place in society he hoped in the end to fill: Sir Basil Holbrook, chairman of the railways, or Lord Holbrook of British Steel, perhaps. He had a high opinion of himself and his abilities, and certainly no false modesty!"

"Seems he never developed any, either." Trewley's tone was bleak as he recalled what he'd heard from Kirton and Black about the incredible vanity of the dead man.

Vulcan smiled. "I fear you will come to regard me as a gramophone record, Superintendent, but—yet again, I have to say I am not surprised. I said that people *can* change as they grow older, but in my experience they merely consolidate those characteristics which they displayed when young—and frequently," he added in a wry tone, "intensify them." Trewley and Stone had the distinct feeling that it wasn't only Holbrook to whom the profession referred; he clearly knew not a few persons who displayed this tendency—probably colleagues. And they wondered what sort of man Vulcan had been in his youth. . . .

"Yes, indeed, Basil Holbrook had good reason to anticipate a glorious future—and there, well, you asked me why he might have committed suicide. With all his high hopes having come to nothing . . ."

"Why was that, do you reckon?" enquired Trewley. "If he was so good at hiding what he was really like as you seem to think he was. . . ."

The professor shrugged. "Who can say? Perhaps he grew tired of forever acting a part, and let his true self show through. He was certainly always impatient with fools, with people less able than himself—and if that sort of reaction is too obvious, why, naturally it's resented. Perhaps, once he was married, he found he no longer felt able to keep up the pretence . . . I honestly don't know. Suffice it to say that, after the wedding—a glamorous, expensive affair, for her family was, you may know, definitely not on the, ah, breadline—"

He gazed at his visitors, who failed to respond to whatever small joke he'd evidently just made. He continued with barely a pause. "Yes, after the wedding he carried on working for his doctorate, insisting that his wife should complete her own studies without planning to take them any further." Stone shifted irritably on her chair, but she said nothing. Trewley glared sideways at her. Vulcan appeared not to notice.

"The new Mrs. Holbrook was to be a—an asset, but no more than that. She must offer him no competition, even though their fields of interest differed widely. And she was, at first, so . . . besotted—dependent . . . that she made no complaint, that I know of, about his attitude—though she may well have come to begrudge her loss in later years." Stone bit her tongue. Trewley grunted. Vulcan said:

"As to that, of course, I couldn't say for certain. It was, however, without doubt one of many reasons her cousin Philip Whatfield, whom you have met, found for disliking Basil Holbrook, to say the least."

"It was Mr. Whatfield who told you about Dr. Holbrook,

was it?" Trewley deduced. The professor had expressed some surprise at police interest in Holbrook's death, but had said nothing about being surprised by news of that death. Unless he had caused it himself—always possible, though unlikely—somebody must have let him know before their arrival.

Vulcan nodded. "The poor fellow was so . . . disturbed, he could give me few details at first, but that's only to be expected, after all, considering . . . well, those long years of rivalry, wiped out in an instant. For such a man as poor Whatfield, the shock is bound to have been acute. Nothing, and no one, left, any longer, to loathe!"

"Strong words, Professor," said Trewley.

"No more than the facts," the scientist replied, in crisp tones. "Whatfield was Sylvia Bannister's cousin. They had always been close, I gather—indeed, if it hadn't been for certain . . . family pressures, which may well have contributed to her religious fervour, they would have married, or that's how I understood the case. Whatever the truth of the matter, there was a very strong attachment—a bond unlikely to please most husbands, let alone a man of Holbrook's type. And Whatfield also had a brilliant mind, quite the equal of his rival's, though in an entirely different way. The sort of brooding, quiet mind which unexpectedly produces excellent work. . . . A mind capable, I always suspected, of—of challenging, of threatening Holbrook's preeminence as he himself saw it. . . . He didn't care for anyone or anything which might make him question the rightness of whatever he did, or thought, or said."

Vanity, Trewley decided, was the understatement of the year. Of the century.

"It was this threat, I suspect," went on the professor, "which made Holbrook go into industry instead of remaining here to follow on with postdoctoral research and greater academic recognition. He probably wished, as well, to remove his wife from her cousin's strong influence—that jealous streak again, you see. . . . But poor Whatfield

needed her quite as much as she—or so I suppose—may
have needed him. He went completely to pieces. Lost his
confidence, failed to write up his honours project—
floundered badly in his Finals, poor fellow, and was
awarded an Aegrotat in the end. He had to recuperate for
several months in some nursing home or other before he
could return here after his nervous breakdown. . . . We
made him a Research Assistant, a sort of glorified techni-
cian, you know. It gave his, ah, creative genius full rein by
taking the pressure from him. He certainly couldn't have
coped then with all the worries of a nonacademic
environment—couldn't have coped at all."

Stone thought of some of the academics she'd known,
and wondered. Trewley's thoughts were entirely his own.

"When," continued Vulcan, "Whatfield finally left to, ah,
pursue the commercial side of metallurgy, it came as a
tremendous shock to discover Holbrook also worked at
Allingham Alloys. It wasn't as if they'd kept in touch.
They'd lost all contact, I know, after his cousin's death.
Whatfield would rather have gone elsewhere, he said, if
only he had known in time. But he needed a job, and time
was pressing—and, in the circumstances, he could hardly
have stayed here, poor fellow." Vulcan frowned, and
coughed, and looked as if he wished he had been a little less
forthcoming.

Trewley pounced. "What—circumstances—would those
be, Professor?" If the old chap knew anything about Philip
Whatfield—with Holbrook mysteriously dead, and a long-
standing rivalry between them . . . "Mr. Whatfield blotted his copybook somehow?"

Vulcan was shocked. "Certainly not! He left us with the
highest references—a brilliant man, and much easier to
work with than ever Holbrook had been. We were sorry
indeed to lose him."

Trewley pressed on with quite as much insistence on the
facts as, normally, the scientist would have been delighted
to indulge. Professor Vulcan seemed decidedly uneasy at the

demand for information; the superintendent had to hint at all manner of sinister possibilities before, with a reluctant sigh, he agreed to spill the beans.

"But I fail to see how this could help you in your work—and please don't let poor Whatfield know I told you. I'm sure he would wish it to be as little known as possible, though nowadays these things are much better understood than before, and there need be no disgrace in admitting . . . well, as I told you, he is a highly strung character. Nervy. His breakdown during Finals is only one example—there were other instances . . . but the event which finally drove him from Grantaford was the removal of the department to this new building. The old Metallurgy Department had, as I recall, faulty foundations—over ninety years old—and the form his illness, if we can call it that, took—and can still take, under stress—was a pronounced claustrophobia."

———— Nineteen ————

STONE COULD HAVE kicked herself. Claustrophobia! The open-necked shirt—the open-air interview, even in November—Whatfield's spectacles, tinted so that he wouldn't have to see the world crowding in on him . . . It was obvious, now it had been pointed out to detectives who'd already remarked the man's nervous speech patterns: one minute, diffident and disjointed; the next, an unstoppable flood. . . .

"These rooms have such very low ceilings, you see." Vulcan nodded upwards. "Far lower than in the draughty Victorian hole which housed us for so many years—which was the great attraction of Allingham Alloys for Philip Whatfield, of course. The open plan offices!"

Trewley, like Stone, had been thinking. He tried to hide his growing interest by saying the first thing which came into his head. "I suppose Dr. Holbrook must have been delighted to see Mr. Whatfield again."

Professor Vulcan snorted. "If you imply, Superintendent, that the sudden shock of renewed acquaintance with his, ah, former rival may have prompted Holbrook to do away with himself, then you are, believe me, entirely mistaken. Basil Holbrook had altogether too high an opinion of himself for suicide. Indeed, I would even say that he was the sort of man who, had the occasion been thought to warrant it, would have chosen to remove Whatfield from this earth, rather than himself! The idea that his wife's cousin was the man whose suit might in some ways have been preferable to the lady . . . But don't misunderstand me. It was a happy enough marriage, in its own strange way. Holbrook was devastated after her death—although, of course, there may always have been some element of, ah, guilt. . . ."

Both detectives at once sat up, and listened as hard as they could. Vulcan, however, soon dampened their hopes.

"Oh, it was an accident—a fall downstairs, believed to have occurred while she was hurrying to answer a telephone call Holbrook himself was making to her from twenty miles away, while he attended the Metallurgical Society dinner. A most unfortunate accident . . . but a sensitive man—and in some ways even Holbrook must have had his sensitive side—would feel to some extent to blame. . . . That old religious guilt, perhaps. He became a virtual recluse—lived almost entirely for his work—why, it's four years since the world heard anything of him beyond a couple of papers in the technical literature. There were rumours, naturally, that he was working on something special—and now Whatfield tells me he is to, ah, take up the torch so untimely dropped by his former colleague." The professor's eyes gleamed. "To work on a new alloy, destined to revolutionise the electrical industry. There's irony in that somewhere, isn't there?"

"I suppose there is," said Trewley. "But—suicide, now . . . Holbrook broods all those years about Sylvia preferring to have had Cousin Whatfield if they'd only let her—then Whatfield turns up again out of the blue . . ." *And gets his own back on Holbrook*, he silently concluded. And if Vulcan chose to interpret these hints another way, whose fault was that?

"I repeat, Superintendent, that I can far more readily see Holbrook doing harm to Whatfield than the other way about." Nothing, noted Trewley, about Whatfield's likely feelings toward Holbrook. Was Vulcan protecting the living at the expense of the dead? "For all his personal faults," the professor continued, "Basil Holbrook was a conscientious scientist. Would such a man deliberately choose to cease work at a vital stage of the research? I find it hard to credit. Why, metallurgy became an obsession with him, after his wife's death—and his solicitor has informed me that, by the terms of his Will, Grantaford is to benefit by the foundation of the Basil Holbrook Bursary to further the study of metallurgy in all its aspects. A most dedicated benefaction, I think you'll agree."

"Very generous," said Stone, as Trewley was silent.

"Very . . . expensive," said Trewley, after a pause. "Not that I know much about that sort of thing—but I'd say it was a tidy sum for a bloke in Holbrook's position to be able to hand out. From what I've read, his wages wouldn't be enough, never mind how highly his employers thought of him and his research."

Stone was nodding at his side. "Is it," she enquired, "an annually awarded scholarship, Professor?"

"It is indeed—a more than generous bequest, I agree, Superintendent," with a slight bow in Trewley's direction. "But one should not forget that Holbrook's wife's family is very well-to-do. She inherited a considerable holding in the family business—she was a rich woman in her own right, and on her death it came to him. Since they had no children—and this, too, must have caused some matrimonial distress, for she at least continued a devout Catholic— in what better way could poor Holbrook choose to bequeath his fortune? He must have looked back on his time at Grantaford as especially happy—here he won his wife, and his doctorate, and the growing professional admiration of his colleagues. . . ."

And the enmity, possibly, of one of them?

It was the day after the excursion to Grantaford and London: a crisp, cold morning, with the blue ice-bleached from a steely sky, and the sun as yet too feeble to melt the glass-hard, glittering puddles in the roads. Kerb-parked cars wore newspaper blinkers; feather-fluffing sparrows, trying to clear their throats of the night's icy thickness, watched climbing clouds of breath freeze from their very beaks.

Scowling—not at the view from his office window, but at

the memory of Sergeant Pleate's accusing looks—
Superintendent Trewley spun his chair around, and kicked
his desk with a large, gloomy foot. He sighed.

"So now we've got to talk to that blasted solicitor again.
From my reading of our friend Garland, I'm not so sure it'll
be a worthwhile trip. That man can be as close as an oyster
and as tricky as a cartload of monkeys, when he wants."

"Why not try telling him," suggested Stone, "that you,
um, already know, and simply want him to confirm it? That
sometimes does the trick, sir."

"Know? Don't make me laugh." The bloodhound face
looked even less inclined to laughter than usual. "Whatfield
and Holbrook want the same girl, Holbrook gets her, for
some complicated family reason we don't know . . . and
that sends Whatfield potty. Years later, Sylvia snuffs it, and
hubby inherits the lot. Then Whatfield shows up for work
where Holbrook already is. They still loathe each other,
and . . . and what, for heaven's sake?"

"Come on, sir, there are endless possibilities." Stone
stabbed with the point of a pencil into the blotter on her
desk. She caught his challenging glare. "Well, possibilities.
For a start . . ."

"Yes?" Just one word, but menacing.

"Yes, sir. Sylvia's accident: it killed her, remember. It
sounds innocent enough—but suppose Whatfield didn't
think so." She sighed. "If we'd known about it when we
were in Town, we could have had a go at looking up the
details . . ."

"*And* the terms of her Will." Trewley glowered out of the
window again. "I'd rather cope with a million microfilms
than Garland, if he's feeling in an awkward mood—or even
with that blasted computer, come to that."

"You'll survive, sir." Stone ventured a chuckle. "And
you'll have me for moral support. . . ."

"Fat lot of help you are, when it matters. With all your
fine training, my girl, I'd've thought you could have pulled

a few medical strings to get us in to have a word or two with Kirkwood . . ."

"Intensive Care, sir, means precisely what it says," she returned primly. "There's no time for anything else. They said he wasn't to be disturbed, and they meant it. I can't perform miracles down the telephone—and I honestly don't think," as he eyed her with something approaching a smile at the back of his lugubrious brown eyes, "it's worth ringing again. Nobody improves that much in half an hour."

"Then I give up. Garland it is." He kicked his chair out from the desk, spun himself round, and lumbered to his feet. "Don't sit around all day, Sergeant. By the time that computer's condescended to tell us what we need to know, we could have solved half a dozen murders *and* talked Garland into spilling the beans. . . ."

Mr. Garland, rubbing his hands, greeted this second visit with the same impish interest he had shown before. "A fine day, Superintendent—Sergeant. More questions, I suppose?"

"More questions, Mr. Garland." The superintendent might have been confirming his own death warrant. "And, before you ask, we still haven't got a search warrant, but we hope you'll agree to cooperate. Otherwise, our investigation's going to lose a fair bit of ground while we wait for all the necessary paperwork."

"Aha! Cooperation. . . ." For one moment only, a mulish expression showed on Mr. Garland's face; then he relaxed, and chuckled. "You require, no doubt, further details of Dr. Holbrook's Will, Superintendent. Oh, yes," as a look of surprise showed in his victim's eye. "In matters of murder—there's no need to prevaricate, you see—it is only to be expected that the estate of the deceased should be subjected to the closest scrutiny. *Cui bono?* I have sufficient knowledge of fictional crime for that to be now my watchword!"

Trewley was thrown off balance by having braced himself to defy somebody who, it now seemed, had no intention of being defiant. "Then you'll tell me what I want to know?"

Mr. Garland's eyes gleamed behind his gold-framed lenses. "Insofar as I may be able to assist your enquiries, I shall most certainly do so. An unpleasant affair—not one in which I should wish a client of Gooch and Honeycombe to be involved—but, since it is so, so be it. Ask me your questions, Superintendent—as many as you please!"

Trewley decided to risk it, though it made him uneasy that things seemed to be going more smoothly than he'd ever expected. "I suppose . . . it wouldn't be possible . . . for me to see a copy of Dr. Holbrook's Will, would it?"

Mr. Garland pursed his lips, and pondered. It was clear that he was weighing distaste for the proceedings against his habitual professional discretion. The latter, at last, lost—but only by a nice legal quibble.

"I regret, Superintendent, that I cannot see my way to allowing you access to the actual documents in Mr. Kirkwood's files. During his, ah, absence, that would seem to me discourteous. But"—as Trewley was about to argue the point—"there are also, of course, notes and rough drafts: although the Will was drawn up some four years ago, we keep all such papers for a minimum of ten years before we dispose of them. You never can tell," he enlarged darkly, "when some client or other might not say we have misrepresented his instructions. Or—begging your pardon, my dear Sergeant, but—more usually, hers."

After a short wait, during which Stone—and Trewley—reflected that it would be a brave client who dared to question Mr. Garland, the solicitor returned from his foray to the office of Mr. Kirkwood with the draft of Basil Holbrook's Will in his hand. On poring over this document, the two detectives found that its contents were much as they'd been given to understand. The Bursary to read Metallurgy at Grantaford was the only bequest of note; most of the Will was taken up with the conditions for establishing and maintaining the Trust Fund, and for handling its investments.

"Dr. Holbrook was obviously a good deal better off than we'd realised," said Trewley, handing back the draft to Mr. Garland. The comment was not phrased as a question, but the intent was clear.

Mr. Garland capitulated. "His wife, as I feel sure you know, had predeceased him; and to him, as her sole heir, she left her not inconsiderable future."

"How much?" This was no time for tact: *not inconsiderable* could mean almost anything.

"In, ah, round figures, Mr. Trewley, three-quarters of a million pounds sterling," announced Mr. Garland, peering over his spectacle frames to watch the reaction. He smiled. "Free of tax."

Stone gasped. Trewley gaped. He rubbed his chin, and stared. "Nearly a million quid? But . . . how . . . ?"

"Sylvia Holbrook—the former Sylvia Bannister—was a grandchild of the founder of Bannister's Biscuits. Doubtless you have heard of Bannister's Biscuits?"

"My favourite brand," said the stunned Sergeant Stone, remembering the top drawer of her desk. And then she remembered that odd remark of Professor Vulcan about Sylvia's family not having been on the breadline. No wonder he had been surprised the detectives hadn't picked up his jocular reference to the source of Sylvia's wealth. He must have assumed that they knew, but were too serious-minded to feel amusement during such an earnest discussion.

"Your favourite brand? And mine also," a gratified Mr. Garland informed her, beaming and rubbing his hands. "Well, now. By the time Miss Sylvia had reached years of discretion, the firm had diversified—diversified most satisfactorily." He rubbed his hands again. "Most. From biscuits to other foodstuffs, and thence to the processing side—canning, bottling, packaging. Which processes they also undertook for outside firms. A shrewd business move—a series of such moves." Mr. Garland radiated approval of the shade of the deceased Grandfather Bannister. "Sylvia Holbrook became a very wealthy woman in her own right, even after inheritance tax—and, consequent upon this, Basil Holbrook was, after her death, a very wealthy man."

"I see." And Trewley lapsed once more into a thoughtful silence. Mr. Garland watched politely for a time, then gave a dry little cough. The superintendent blinked. "I don't exactly recall," he said at last, "the exact circumstances of her death. Wasn't it some sort of accident?"

Mr. Garland's eyes narrowed, though he chose not to speculate aloud upon this sudden interest in Sylvia Holbrook's unfortunate demise. "She, ah, fell downstairs—a tragic affair. They were staying in the London house of an absent friend, you know, while Holbrook attended some, ah, stag night of the professional society to which he belonged." The solicitor's distaste for the implied improprieties was plain. "Poor Mrs. Holbrook had been unwell—suffering from one of her not infrequent, ah, bouts of illness. . . ."

"By *not infrequent*," interposed Trewley, as Mr. Garland shuddered to an expressive halt, "you mean frequent, don't you?"

Mr. Garland, about to protest, caught the superintendent's look, and bent his head in acknowledgement of the reproof. "I accept your emendation, Mr. Trewley. Mrs. Holbrook was prone to . . . ah, to certain . . . distressing physical symptoms at, ahem, fairly frequent intervals. Her doctor," and he brightened, "could doubtless furnish you with full details should you deem it necessary to, ah, take the matter further. But it was during the, ah, throes, as it were, of one of these attacks, I understand, that, while her husband was absent at his dinner, she hurried to answer the telephone. And, in her hurry, somehow, she tripped, sustaining injuries in her subsequent fall from which she, ah, died."

Though the central computer hadn't yet made its report,

Trewley was an old-fashioned copper with his own computer in his head. He frowned, and glowered back into the past. "I believe I remember something . . . Accidental death, wasn't it? No sign of a forced entry, the husband out with his pals all evening, no possible motive for anyone else . . . but it happened in another area, so we had nothing to do with it, here in Allingham."

Mr. Garland looked unhappy. "But surely there could be nothing in this sorry affair to have interested you and your colleagues, Superintendent? She went to answer the telephone, tripped, and broke her neck. Dr. Holbrook, I know, held himself very much to blame, because he felt that it had been a call from himself—to the effect that he and a few cronies would be, ah, going on elsewhere, that she was not to expect him to return at the original hour . . . his call must have prompted her to leave her sickbed and thus, indirectly, to succumb to what we may call, ah, a dizzy spell. It is most regrettable that it should have occurred at the top of the stairs, in an unfamiliar house, and that she should have been wearing a long dressing gown. . . ."

"No wonder the poor bloke had a telephone phobia," said Trewley. "I'd forgotten the details"—he crossed mental fingers as he spoke—"until you reminded me . . ."

Mr. Garland's expression was unfathomable. "You appear to have remembered quite a few yourself. All except the blown light bulb—nothing more than a sad coincidence, of course, but it made the stairs even more dark. A sorry accident indeed. . . ."

"Yes. . . . Yes, I remember." Trewley's mind was working furiously. He wondered whether Stone, with her medical knowledge, was thinking along the same lines. Frequent attacks—giddy spells—sickness, most likely . . . Natural symptoms, or not? If not—had they been contrived?

Contrived by someone for some sinister purpose?

Could it have been poison? Arsenic?

Murder?

They must visit Sylvia Holbrook's doctor. Immediately.

Twenty

GROUP PRACTICES AND health centres were forbidden concepts in the surgery of Dr. Stowe and his son: old-fashioned bedside manners were clearly in the order of the day, if not the year, or the decade. There was a motherly receptionist to turn the making of an appointment into a reassuring ritual, rather than a form-filling, timetable-checking mortification.

"Is it Old Dr. Stowe you want to see, or Young Dr. Felix? He's in surgery now, but his father's out on his rounds. . . ."

Careful questioning decided the superintendent and his sidekick that an interview with Young Dr. Felix would serve: and they guessed, rightly, that this youthfully named medico would turn out to be in his mid-forties, and no stripling fresh from medical school.

Dr. Felix Stowe had a fine head of greying hair, and the beginnings of a comfortable corporation, across which he wore a gold-chained watch, safe in its pocket. With it he undoubtedly timed his patient's pulse, and calmed tumultuous or fretful infants by allowing them to play with it. There was nothing brash or newfangled about Young Dr. Felix: you would trust him, it was plain, with your life.

As of course you inevitably did, with any doctor. But here would be no hurried referral to a trendy specialist when matters grew too baffling; no panicking of a patient with jargon-rich second and third opinions—straightforward and soothing, knowing his limitations but even so keeping your confidence: that was Young Dr. Felix.

It was only to be supposed that so wise a personage would at once guess the purpose of this police visitation.

"I told my father only this morning you were a bit late coming to see us. I'm right, aren't I? You've come about Basil Holbrook's suicide?"

"Yes, you are." Obviously, the more sinister rumours hadn't yet reached this far—or did the Stowe practice, in the manner of Gooch and Honeycombe, Solicitors and Commissioners for Oaths, shun any mention of murder until it was absolutely necessary?

"Maybe we should have got in touch," continued Dr. Felix, "but the other patients don't like it, you know. After all, the poor devil's gone, hasn't he—but they're still here! And it unsettles them to think of anyone they know being so thoroughly wretched that he chooses to end his life like that—and it reflects on us, for not having been able to help him. . . . We guessed you'd come along to us when you had to, and not before."

Trewley found himself settling into the chair in much the same comfortable way, he suspected, that an anxious invalid would have his mind made easy. "So, Doctor, you weren't surprised to hear of Holbrook's death?"

"Good lord, no. He'd always been . . ." Young Dr. Felix groped for the apposite term. "On the eccentric side, let's say. The mad boffin type. After his wife died, mind you, he really went over the top in a big way—practically turned into a hermit. Most unhealthy. An abnormal amount of grief, indulging himself for far too long—it was guilt, of course, for thinking he'd helped to cause the accident—er, you know about that, I suppose?"

Trewley nodded. Dr. Felix nodded, too, and gave him a shrewd look, but made no direct comment.

"He was . . . cultivating the episode, you could almost say. Dwelling on his misfortunes to an alarming extent. . . . Most people work it out of their systems naturally, given time, but not Holbrook." Dr. Felix looked disapproving, then remembered the grim reason for his visitors' interest in his former patient, and softened his expression. "Mind you," he went on, "his general state of health in recent months certainly can't have helped. He'd known, you see, that he was on borrowed time for the last fifteen months or so."

With a further softening of his expression, he sighed. "That sort of knowledge would be enough to set anyone normal to, er, brooding on things, let alone a chap like him, who's halfway round the, er, brooding bend already." He smiled grimly. "My father tried a spot of plain speaking on more than one occasion, but Holbrook refused to listen— just went on his own sweet way regardless. Neither of us is the least bit surprised that he should have killed himself."

"You reckon his—his mourning for his wife was a bit much, then?"

"Nobody can wallow in guilt forever, Superintendent— and nor should they! His telephone call that night may have been a contributory factor in her death—in fact, I'd go so far as to say that it was—but he'd no business to be still brooding over it after four years. There's such a thing as perspective, Mr. Trewley. Balance, gained through the passage of time; but Holbrook's . . . general eccentricity turned, over the years, to obsession. There was a melancholy streak in him—he was too prone to dwell on sin and misery. . . . I confess that my father and I became concerned about him, but without his consulting us . . . which he did not—as was his right, of course . . ."

"What d'you reckon caused this . . . melancholy streak? Was it just losing his wife? Or was he like it before? Did he worry about his work? Or his marriage? Or . . . ?" And the superintendent, who had for the moment run out of alternatives, paused invitingly.

"His marriage—ah, yes. Of course, his wife's unhappy mental state can't have made things easy for him—but Holbrook's attitude towards her hardly helped the situation, I have to say. If anything, indeed, it made matters worse."

This was something altogether new, and not what Trewley had intended. He leaned forward, alert. "I don't understand, Doctor. What are you saying about Sylvia Holbrook's . . .

unhappy mental state?" And he recalled suddenly those oblique remarks of Professor Vulcan concerning Sylvia and her cousin, the nervy Philip Whatfield—who, religion and family pressure aside, might have wished to marry her.

Family pressure. Why . . . ?

"Oh dear. I had the distinct impression—I thought you must have known, or I would never . . . But then, the poor soul's dead, and if it will help you in any way . . ."

"I think it might." Trewley waited for some moments, then added the argument he'd tried with others, about disliking mysteries. Dr. Felix smiled, and relaxed. A little.

"In cases like this . . ."

He paused, uncertain, hesitant. Trewley and Stone exchanged glances. Did the doctor, after all, know that there was talk of something more sinister than suicide?

He came to an evident conclusion. "In cases like this," he repeated, "it's the duty of the medical man to assist his constabulary colleagues in any way he can, so . . . Sylvia Holbrook. She was a Bannister, you know, the biscuit people—her father was the old man's youngest son. Married a girl who'd kept rather quiet about her background until it was too late. Something a little bit . . . lacking, shall we say? Acutely nervous—mother killed herself, I believe. And the mother's sister was a similar type, too."

Stone was about to say something, then didn't. Trewley, like his sergeant, recalled that Sylvia had bowed to family pressure not to marry her cousin Philip. Philip Whatfield—son to the identical twin sister of Sylvia's mother?

Felix Stowe carried on with his narrative.

"Like many men of very high intelligence, Holbrook had scant sympathy with what he termed feminine self-indulgence—nerves, phobias, that sort of thing. They couldn't have children—she desperately wanted them, felt herself lacking without them—I remember when we confirmed for her that she never would become a mother . . .

"In the circumstances, it was probably as well that she

couldn't, but she didn't see it that way—and it distressed her very much. And he blamed her, I'm sure, for failing him—his masculine pride, you know, wanting to found a dynasty of scientific geniuses. And it was from that moment that her . . . illness . . . developed. . . ."

"She drank?" hazarded Trewley; he'd known one or two similar cases. Dr. Felix looked horrified at the suggestion.

"Certainly not, Superintendent! She merely . . . retreated, at first, into her home, where she felt safe. Safe from outside pressures, from prying eyes and careless comments which might reflect on her unhappy childless state. She was a devout Roman Catholic—she felt a failure, that she was being punished somehow for something she couldn't begin to understand. . . . And then, she suffered from anorexia, about which we didn't know then as much as we know now, unfortunately, though of course we did our best. But her home life didn't help, and everything . . . combined to make her worse than she need ever have become. There were times when it was impossible for her to leave the house—and it wasn't just the anorexia. . . . There were gastric attacks, that was the later physical manifestation—but they, we realised, must be due to an increasing agoraphobia, which persisted after the anorexia seemed to be going into remission."

The doctor shook his head, and sighed. Stone, who had a healthy appetite, echoed his sigh, regretting the sad, helpless folly of so many of her sex. Trewley felt a trickling chill down his spine. His three teenage daughters were as weight-conscious as his wife, even if, so far, it was only *his* weight they worried about. . . .

"It was," said Dr. Stowe, "purely psychosomatic—as, by their nature, phobias are." He did not know that half his attentive audience had some medical knowledge, but hurried to enlarge on his explanation. "Psychosomatic doesn't mean the sufferer has invented the suffering, that it's all in her mind and she can snap out of it when she chooses—it simply means the *cause* of her sufferings is in her mind. The sufferings are only too physically real. . . . And with the right sort of—of cosseting from a sympathetic person who could be at the same time firm, it should never have become as serious as it did . . . but that was something her husband was unable to do for her. My father and I helped, to some extent, with the anorexia, but there was more to her problems than a simple eating disorder. Agoraphobia is often called the Calamity Syndrome. Poor Sylvia had suffered the most grievous of calamities—the shock realisation that she was unable to fulfil what her natural inclination, and her religion, asked of her was, in the end, simply too much. . . .

"Expert therapy could have helped, even in the later stages, but neither of the Holbrooks would, unfortunately, hear of it. *She* had begun to—to cling to the illness; and her husband wanted to shrug the whole thing off as an aberration which would pass with time. A scientific mind of his calibre should have known enough to check the facts and gain some understanding, but in this matter he was too . . . personally involved. Which is yet another reason he would have felt guilt after her death—realising how he'd treated her . . . his cruelty, thoughtlessness, call it what you will.

"He had her cremated, you know." Dr. Felix looked his visitors firmly in the eye, and for the first time in some minutes managed a smile. "Absolutely no question of anything wrong, I assure you. As you'll know, by law she had to be thoroughly examined by two medical men for the certificate. And of course, as she died away from home, neither of them was from an Allingham practice."

Trewley rubbed his chin. "Sounds as if somebody's asked you about this before, Doctor."

"There were bound to be rumours, particularly when it became known what a rich woman she'd been—they'd lived a very quiet life even before her, um, retreat. Holbrook had no intention of living off his wife's money—said it was hers, she could spend it as she pleased, but he must visibly support them both. Masculine pride again; he was head of the household—I was going to say *of the family*—but of course that lack of a family was part of the trouble. . . . And his view, as far as possible, was always the one she took—in public, at least, or rather what passed for public, in her unhappy terms. Poor woman. Even after her death, his will prevailed over hers. It had been her wish to be buried in the family grave, but he overruled it, to have her cremated. There was rather a fuss about it, from her parents. Against her religion, for one thing."

"I thought Holbrook was a Catholic, too?"

"He was a scientist first, Superintendent. Maintained that it was the only healthy way to dispose of one's remains— well, I think so myself, but I'm hanged if I'd go arguing with my wife's relatives about it. They'd known her, after all, far longer than he had. They must have felt they had a right to know what her wishes would have been—and it's understandable they should feel aggrieved when those wishes were so blatantly ignored."

Trewley sighed. Over the years, he'd had good reason to learn how easy it was for people to feel aggrieved. So much of his work was the result of family argument. . . . "Anyway," he said, "the body was examined and . . . well, passed fit for cremation? There was no hint that the anorexia—the agoraphobia—the nervous attacks, if that's what you'd call 'em—had been . . . contrived?" He was too intent on his theory to consult with Stone, his usual medical adviser. "All the . . . the upset—it really was the result of the poor girl's mental state?"

Dr. Felix regarded him with interest, tinged with some anxiety; but he spoke in level tones. "Any phobic experience, Superintendent, is basically a panic attack. Symptoms of panic include sweating, palpitations, paralysis of movement, faintness, pounding heart, dizziness—enough to upset the toughest tummy!" He did not notice Stone, nodding at Trewley's side. "Sylvia Holbrook," said Dr. Stowe, "had a thoroughly miserable time, and deserved a great deal of sympathy—which she got. But she got it from me, from my father, from the neighbours. Not, more's the pity, from her husband."

"And neighbours gossip." Trewley was thinking aloud. "Suppose a newcomer to the district heard the story, all the gory details of these . . . attacks of hers. Is it possible he could suspect—if he had a . . . an erratic sort of mind— that her husband might have . . . manufactured her illness?"

"I see," said Dr. Felix slowly; and thought, very hard. "Yes, of course, in the old days it was always arsenic in the soup served lovingly by the spouse—and the symptoms, to a layman, could well seem the same, when relayed through a third or fourth or still more distant party. After all, medical men in the past have confused the two . . . think of Seddon, or Armstrong. Yes, I have to agree that it would be possible for someone to believe she'd been poisoned—but I repeat, she was not. She couldn't have been cremated without the death certificate—which was awarded after a proper postmortem. Whereupon she was cremated, Superintendent."

Trewley thought again of the rivalry between Holbrook and Whatfield: Whatfield, who'd lost touch with his cousin after her moody, jealous husband had taken her away from Grantaford, and cut her off from the rest of her family. . . . "Yes, she was cremated," he said. "But at her husband's insistence."

And Dr. Felix Stowe, with a sigh, had to agree.

"No, thanks," said the superintendent, with much firmness. "No biscuits—just a cup of tea'll do me for now."

"They're Bannister's Biscuits," said the temptress, pushing the packet across the desk. "Fresh today—and we don't want *you* getting anorexic, sir."

"Umph. Women." Trewley reached for the packet, and contemplated the name on the label. "Bannister . . . makes you wonder. Sylvia Bannister Holbrook—who died . . ."

"And so did her husband, sir. Somebody conned Bert Gadgett into fixing that valve in Holbrook's gas fire—and whoever it was must have known it would kill him, sooner or later." She sighed. "So—who was it?"

"Short of dressing 'em all up to look like Holbrook, and seeing if Mrs. Gadgett recognises our man, there's not a lot more we can do right now." Trewley scowled. "Except try a little pressure on the likely suspects—so long as you're not going to try calling it suicide any longer."

She shook her head. "Not after what we got out of Dr. Stowe, sir. My money's on Whatfield, I think. He turns up here unexpectedly a couple of months ago—just long enough for him to find out, or at least to *think* he's found out—he's nervous, he'll have an imagination, I bet he jumps far too quickly to conclusions—to find out that Holbrook might well have tried to, um, dispose of Cousin Sylvia with arsenic. I bet there's tons of it lying around the metallurgy lab. And he suspects Holbrook grew tired of waiting for it to work, and did it quickly by rigging that business with the darkened stairs and the telephone call—so he decides to pay him back, by disposing of him."

"September," said Trewley, brooding. "Yes, I'd say that'd be long enough for the blighter to work out a plan for clearing Holbrook out of the way. Probably got brother-in-law Chattisham cheering him on from the sidelines. . . ."

"Let's bring him in, sir." Stone drained her tea, and jumped to her feet. "An identity parade takes too long, and with Heath still unconscious we're stuck here. . . . Central Records are taking forever, and we're just twiddling our thumbs. We could . . . lean on Whatfield, sir. Just very gently, to start with. If he has anything to hide, I don't think his sort can hold out for long. . . ."

Having set their hearts on action, they found it frustrating to be delayed by two sets of traffic lights at road works along the way to Allingham Alloys; they felt they would have had a better chance of arriving in time if they had walked. Trewley rumbled about young What's-his-name, Stone's intimate friend from Traffic, and threatened demotion: but, at last, they were there.

The security guard, recognising a police car, waved them through. Stone parked neatly as close to the main building as she could. Despite their eagerness, the two went through the motions: a call, first, at Reception, who duly passed the message to Julia Springs in R&D. Unruffled as ever, Dr. Kirton's secretary met them as before, and led them to his office; he was on the telephone, she told them, but wouldn't be very long.

"Mr. Woolverstone again?" Trewley hadn't forgotten the managing director's insistence on haste for completing the Squib research. He frowned. If their guess was correct, it wouldn't be in the near future that Allingham Alloys went public with that particular patent as bait. . . .

Dr. Kirton seemed less happy to see the detectives each time they appeared, though he tried to hide his feelings. "More questions? Oh, dear—this is becoming a habit. We, ah, must try to stop meeting like this, Sergeant. . . ."

Stone smiled back at him, with sympathy in her eyes. Trewley tried not to scowl.

"Sorry, sir." He didn't sound it. "But we can't be expected to leave Dr. Holbrook's killer wandering about the place, free to kill again, maybe. Whether it's a man or a woman," he added, to Stone's silent amusement. The sight of Julia Springs must have reminded her colleague that there could still be suspicion attached to the secretary: once the computer had cleared her, that would be another matter, but until then . . .

"We've a job to do," the superintendent continued. "The same as you and all your department—and we're just like you scientists. We want the facts. The truth. It's only a few more questions—but this time we'd like to . . . invite the person concerned down to the station, to help us with our enquiries." He nodded slowly, and lowered his voice, as if sharing some great secret. "A bit more private, you see, with

your researech area being open plan. . . . So, if you'd be
kind enough to let us have a word with Mr. Whatfield—"

"Whatfield? Oh, no! But what about the Squib?" came
the inevitable response from the harassed Head of Research.
"Mr. Trewley—this is dreadful! If you arrest him—"

"I never said we'd be arresting him," interjected the
superintendent swiftly. "Just asking him to help with our
enquiries, that's all. So far," he felt obliged to add. Dr.
Kirton turned pale. Trewley hurried on:

"It's just that we'd prefer, at this stage, asking Mr.
Whatfield a few questions in the, er, privacy of the police
station. . . . So, with your permission"—*or without it,*
those dogged tones seemed to suggest—"we'll pop along
now. . . ."

"I suppose I have no choice," groaned Whatfield's
wretched boss. "But—but oh, dear, what am I to tell Mr.
Woolverstone? How long . . . when will you let him come
back to work, Mr. Trewley?"

And he seemed to find the superintendent's inability to
give an exact reply more distressing than anything else. His
face flushed, his jaw dropped; he slumped heavily in his chair,
unable to move except for shaking his head in an incredulous
rhythm. "Whatfield . . . Squib . . . Holbrook . . . Oh,
dear, Mr. Woolverstone . . ."

"We can find our own way to his office," said Trewley,
with a quick glance at Stone, and a wary eye on the top
drawer of Dr. Kirton's desk. But the sergeant gave him a
reassuring nod, and the scientist made no move towards
his tablets: possibly he'd become inured, now, to further
shock. The arrest—if one had to be made—wouldn't kill
him. . . .

Trewley's hand was already on the doorknob—he and
Stone were edging themselves out of the room—when the
grim silence in the office was broken—suddenly, sharply.

The telephone on Dr. Kirton's desk rang.

Waking from his trance, the scientist reached out his hand

for the instrument. The police officers, politely waiting to bid him farewell, hovered in the doorway.

"Hello?" he said wearily. "Why, yes—yes, he's here." And Kirton held out the telephone receiver to the superintendent. "It's for you, Mr. Trewley—from the hospital. And he says—he says it's urgent."

Twenty-one

THREE LONG, HEAVY strides covered the distance. Trewley almost snatched the telephone from Dr. Kirton, muttered a hasty word of thanks, and was at once absorbed in whatever important message the voice on the other end of the line had thought it worth interrupting proceedings to deliver.

"Trewley. That you, Benson?"

A gabbled, urgent buzz from the earpiece.

"Has he, now!" The superintendent mouthed something unintelligible to Stone, then spoke to the telephone again. "Did he say anything?"

Further, frantic buzzing.

"He said *what*!"

A lengthy, explanatory buzz: during which Stone edged closer, trying to listen. Normally, her superior was happy to go shares in any information he received: but now, in the excitement of the moment, he seemed to find her invisible. All his attention was focussed on the high-pitched, electronic bulletin coming from the hospital.

"And he's prepared to sign a statement?" Suddenly, his sergeant was no longer invisible. Trewley turned to grimace at her, before turning back to the telephone. "And it's all according to Cocker, is it? You didn't clip your old chum round the ear, or take a truncheon to the blighter, or anything like that?"

An indignant buzz.

"Yes. Right." He became deadly serious. "Right. . . . So tell me. Do you believe him?"

An affirmative buzz; imparting also, it seemed, some afterthought whose impact was clearly startling.

"*When*? Say that again, will you!"

Repeated buzzings, elaborate and impassioned.

"I see. Thanks." Trewley seemed all at once drained of energy, the light of action fading from his brown eyes. "We'll check at this end, of course, but—I think . . . Yes, thanks, Benson. Hop along back to the station, will you? Type it all up ready for him to sign—though better send for Hedges first to take your place, just in case he changes his mind. Right?"

He hung up, and stood, for a thoughtful moment, speechless. Neither Kirton nor Stone cared to break the brittle, tense silence, as the superintendent tried to clear the confusion from his mind.

"Bob Heath's come round properly at last," he announced after what had seemed like an age. "And he's made a statement to the bobby on duty by his bed. Benson—a good man. Knows him, in a roundabout way," he added, for Kirton's benefit. "So, maybe it was the Old Pals Act, but at least the lady's finally coughed why he bolted like that when he realised there were coppers on the premises—*and* why he took off when he saw the police car outside his house."

"Well?" Bob's boss leaned forward in his seat. "Why did he rush away in such a careless fashion and leave the picric acid to explode?"

"He says," Trewley said, "it was because Miss Springs let it out we'd come to see you on business to do with Dr. Holbrook."

"You don't mean—"

"I mean Holbrook seems to have come across Heath pinching scrap copper from your dud samples pile, intending to sell the stuff—and it wasn't the first time he'd pinched it." He shrugged. "You told us yourself, Dr. Kirton, that your miscasts and rejects were worth a fair bit. Edward Chattisham said the same. Copper's quite a valuable commodity, by all accounts."

"So it is." Dr. Kirton frowned, wondering why the name of Chattisham should disturb him without apparent reason;

then he recalled the Metallurgical Society dinner, and gave an uncomfortable cough. "Oh dear—yes, of course."

"Heath is strapped for cash," continued Trewley, who felt sorry for his blushing fellow man. "Well, aren't we all? But he had to get married, and his house is knee-deep in kids, with his wife expecting the third, I think he said. He found a handy, ask-no-questions scrap merchant the other side of Allingham, and the rest . . . was only too easy."

Kirton was speechless; Stone at last recovered her startled wits. "But surely, sir—I mean, whatever happened to the security around here? Someone just—just walked out of the place with a fortune in his pockets?"

"Don't worry, Sergeant. It could've been worse—though not much," he added. "But it wasn't in his pockets, it was in the panniers of his motorbike." He found himself chuckling. "No wonder he was so short of the ready. Must've used one hell of a lot of petrol, with all the extra weight of what he'd nicked!"

Kirton was still flustered. "But . . . but how did he do it? The scrap metal skips are always locked, except when we're filling them—and they can only be moved by authorised contractors. Was he somehow arranging for collection by an unauthorised vehicle?"

Trewley chuckled again. "Nothing so fancy. He didn't need it—a scheme like that might've worked for a one-off robbery, but he wanted a regular milking, a permanent supply small enough to go undetected, big enough for the game to be worth the candle. He just knocked the stuff off before it reached the skips, that's all." He nodded to the puzzled Research Head. "Most of your scrap—badly made valves, or whatever—comes from the production end, doesn't it?"

"The factory produces the larger part, yes, though I couldn't say in what quantity. We in R and D produce samples—test designs and various formulas for different alloys, of which many fail to meet our requirements once we've tested them. Which is why we dispose of them. . . . And Heath," concluded Dr. Kirton in an altered tone, "is the only laboratory assistant working with metallographic samples!"

"And there you are." Trewley said nothing more, giving the man time to think it over. Stone had already thought. She cleared her throat.

"Dr. Kirton, didn't the people who bought your scrap in the skips notice that there wasn't as much copper as there used to be—before Heath started to work here? Surely it must have been obvious!"

He shook his head. "Our manufactured quantities vary considerably from week to week, depending on demand: and, in the same way, the quality will vary, too. Short of comparing the contents of the skips with production records, how would anyone know?"

"And," interjected Trewley, "I'll wager the amount from R and D wouldn't have that much of an effect on overall scrap, if it's not so big a share of the total amount. That'll be what he relied on, of course."

Dr. Kirton moaned softly. Stone hurriedly remarked that at least it proved Bob Heath had, well, some potential for organised thought. It might be worth exploiting that potential, at some later date. . . .

The scientist achieved a weak smile before he turned back to the superintendent. "And Basil Holbrook found him out. How?"

"Ran into Heath on his bike Tuesday evening, as he was coming out of work, apparently. Heath said he must've been in a tearing hurry. He was looking where he was going even less than usual, and if that's true we can imagine how much of a hurry he was in—you know what he was like. He shot right across in front of him, Heath says, and you can guess what happened next. And the panniers rattled, or the motorbike felt too heavy when Holbrook helped to pick it up, or something—Heath didn't say . . . but Holbrook spotted the copper scrap. And he said he'd have to report it to you, Dr. Kirton, or maybe to the police—he'd have to think about it—so, when we turned up on Friday morning, it was obvious to Heath what we must have come about."

"But, sir." Stone suddenly found the flaw in all this. "If the accident happened on Tuesday—Tuesday last week—"

"Yes," Trewley said, with a ponderous nod.

"Then it can't have been—I mean, that was Saturday of the week before . . ."

"Yes," repeated the superintendent, in a warning voice. "Unless the lad's lying, that is. He could always be pulling the wool over our eyes even now—but someone must have seen the incident. We can check it out—and I'll wager it checks. . . . Which means, I'm afraid, Dr. Kirton, that never mind everything else—we do still want to talk to Mr. Whatfield. Don't we, Sergeant Stone?"

"Yes," agreed Stone. "Oh yes, sir, we do!"

Dr. Kirton, who had allowed himself to relax as the guilt of Bob Heath in the matter of Dr. Holbrook's death seemed to be proved beyond all question, at the final remark came suddenly to life again. "But—but . . ." he began to protest.

"We'll just ask him to step down to the station with us—for a little chat," said Trewley. "And, if—anything—happens, we'll let you know as soon as possible."

Dr. Kirton closed horrified eyes at the euphemism, and uttered a hollow groan. Things were happening far too fast for him; he heard the office door open and close again behind the two police officers; and, dreading the anticipated explanations to Mr. Woolverstone, he groped across the desk for his telephone, and removed the receiver. Let Miss Springs deal with the problems. He couldn't face any more right now!

Julia Springs was surprised to observe the detectives leaving so abruptly. "I was about to offer you a cup of coffee," she told them. "Will you be coming back? Or do you want me to take you somewhere first?"

"We know the way, thanks," Trewley told her.

"And," said Stone, with a tentative look for her chief,

"with, um, fire drills and so on, we'd better just let you know that Mr. Whatfield will probably be coming down to the police station with us. Do you have to mark him out in a book, or anything?"

"The departmental register," said Julia, reaching it from her desk and managing to stifle her amazement. "Will you be leaving the building right away?"

"Oh—yes, I expect so." Trewley didn't want to wait: of course she'd had to be told, but every second could be important now. If Kirton let anything out . . .

Excusing themselves, they walked rapidly away; Julia's eyes, avid with a curiosity she was too professional to admit, followed them towards the work station which housed that brilliant but nervy successor to Dr. Basil Holbrook, Philip Whatfield.

His head was bent over a heap of files; his pen, in a white-knuckled grip, danced across a sheet of graph paper, leaving scrawled black tracks in its wake. Jotted notes on lined paper in another, even more scrawling hand were marked here and there with Whatfield's comments; there were charts and tables of results, illuminated by a desk lamp bright and all-embracing. Philip Whatfield had created his own world which totally absorbed him, which claimed him for Squib and its research to the exclusion of everything else: he was about to prove that he was as good a man, as competent a scientist, as Basil Holbrook had ever been—and he would not shrink from that proof.

Trewley and Stone had seldom witnessed, even among their colleagues, such wholehearted involvement in a task, such controlled energy of mind and purpose. And what a mind it must be! Devoted to one aim; inspired; intelligent, calculating, cunning.

The mind of a killer?

It almost seemed impertinent to shatter so intensely dedicated a mood. At last, however, Trewley cleared his throat. Mr. Whatfield shook his head, looked up, blinked at the sight of two human figures through his tinted spectacles, and slowly surfaced from whatever depths of concentration he'd been working at. Only slowly did his eyes focus on his visitors; and it was slowly that he spoke words of greeting to them.

"Oh . . . Mr. Trewley—Miss Stone . . . I had no idea . . . I didn't know . . ." He shook his head again, clearing away a few more cobwebs. "Was it—was it me you wanted to see? Only I—I have these notes of Holbrook's to read through, and . . ."

He didn't seem too surprised to see them, Trewley and Stone decided—unless he hadn't yet fully taken in the fact of their arrival. Maybe his flustered greeting had been to give him time to work out how to deceive them—or maybe he was a genuinely single-minded boffin, whose thoughts were still with his research, who could spare only limited attention for visitors and their purpose in seeking him out. . . .

"We'd like you to come down to the station with us for a while, sir, if you wouldn't mind," said Trewley. "We've had a word with Dr. Kirton, and he says he can spare you—and we thought you'd rather go somewhere less public for our talk."

Mr. Whatfield's still-blank gaze began to focus. "Talk? Public? Spare me? What do you mean? Why do you want to—to talk to me?"

The last few words were breathless, and jerky. The grip of his hand on the pen tightened to bony whiteness. With an obvious effort, he forced the clenched fist open; the pen, gleaming with sudden sweat, slithered to the desk, shedding drops of ink as it fell across the paper on which Philip had been writing. He made no attempt to blot it: his hands were shaking now, and he hunched himself down in his chair, folding them between his knees to quiet them.

"Just a few more questions about Dr. Holbrook, that's all," said Trewley. "And we thought—"

"Holbrook?" Mr. Whatfield's head snapped upwards. "But I've already—you don't need me anymore, surely—

unless . . ." His eyes widened, then narrowed. He pushed back his chair from the desk. "No—I don't believe it!" His voice rose by perhaps half an octave, and his breath came even faster than before. "You're—you're arresting me? No, please—no. You're mistaken!"

"We aren't arresting you, sir," said Stone, before Trewley could speak. Her theory that Mr. Whatfield would be susceptible to very little pressure had been proved rather too quickly for her liking. "Honestly, it's just for questioning. We aren't arresting you . . ."

But both she and Philip Whatfield could hear the silent addition from Trewley.

Yet.

"No, sir," said the superintendent aloud. "We're not arresting you, but we do have further questions we'd like to ask. And, well, we've already agreed it's not all that private around here, so . . ."

As he felt the gaze of the two detectives fasten upon him, Philip realized for the first time the awful truth that he was trapped. His face turned pale, his eyes darted from one side of the low-walled work station to the other. Small drops of perspiration beaded his brow; he opened his mouth in a series of shuddering breaths. His hands, snatching themselves free from his knees, writhed helplessly as he stared at the two people blocking his escape, then darted in desperation for the top drawer of his desk.

"Oh, no, you don't!" Trewley was caught by surprise, blundering across to clamp a mighty grip about Whatfield's scrabbling wrist. He prised the scientist's hand from the knob of the drawer, and pressed him back in his seat. "Take it easy, now, we don't want any nonsense. You come along nice and quiet with us—"

"No!" Mr. Whatfield was now a pallid green. "Coming with you? I can't—I won't . . ." And he fell to whimpering, the picture of guilt, his whole body trembling, his eyes darting from side to side in a desperate attempt to find any way out.

Stone darted past her colleague to Whatfield's side of the desk. She took the whimpering man's free wrist in her hand, feeling his pulse. She could hardly distinguish one beat from the next.

"Sir," she said, "he's in a bad way. I think somebody ought to see him."

Trewley glared over the work station walls without letting go his hold on Whatfield's wrist. "A damn sight too many folk can see the poor beggar already," he muttered. "You sure he can't come straight down to the station with us, and be seen to there? Just a nice quick ride in a car, instead of—"

Whatfield gasped, and went rigid. In one frantic, sudden movement, he wrenched himself free of restraint. "A car! You'll shut me away—lock me in a metal box—put me in a cell? I'd rather die! You'll kill me—try to make me confess—the third degree—cluttering, choking me . . ."

His outflung arms knocked Stone off balance, sent Trewley staggering back. The sergeant's ankle gave under her, and she tumbled to the floor; Trewley's bulk steadied him faster, and he lunged forward as Whatfield, leaping from his chair, scrabbled again at his desk.

"None of that nonsense, now. You come along with us, nice and quiet. . . ."

Though Philip's struggles were those of a desperate man, Trewley's strength was the righteous force of one conscious of doing his duty. For all he knew, the man had a weapon in that drawer. In an office full of innocent bystanders . . .

Grimly, he held the scientist back from the desk, trying instead to propel him out of his retreat, into the gangway of the office and away from those innocent, gaping eyes. Stone finished picking herself up from the floor, and moved to help her colleague.

Mr. Whatfield's fists flailed in every direction, but the two police officers were—had to be—inexorable. He realised he was in their power. He uttered a shrill, hysterical shriek—his legs gave way—he slumped heavily forward . . . and, unprepared for so violent a capitulation, Trewley and Stone were unable to hold him.

He fell to the ground, moaning. He closed his eyes, and wrapped his arms about his head as he lay, crumpled, shivering, on the floor . . .

While Trewley and Stone, horrified, looked with sudden sympathy at the man they had been brought to arrest—the brilliant scientist now wretchedly broken before them.

━━━━━━━━ Twenty-two ━━━━━━━━

THE SUPERINTENDENT SPOKE slowly, his face pale. "Diabolically clever, that's what it was. Downright . . . diabolical." They were back at the police station: it was all over. "And I said I'd find it hard to credit anyone plotting revenge for as long as six months!"

"Twenty years," murmured Stone. "To harbour a grudge for twenty years . . ." She gazed into the depths of her mug. She had added a stiff tot of brandy to her tea, insisting that—dietary considerations notwithstanding—her superior should do the same with his own: he had willingly agreed.

Both detectives were still shaken after the scene at Allingham Alloys. They sat in silence for a while, taking comfort from the familiarity of their surroundings, contemplating sadly man's inhumanity to man.

"Twenty years," said Trewley, at last. "Talk about old sins casting new shadows—talk about original sin!"

A dreadful thought struck his sergeant. "If he hadn't tried to be just a little too clever, sir, I think he might have got away with it." She shuddered. "It wouldn't have been easy to prove beyond doubt, with so much left to chance—like the temperature setting on the valve, and having to check it after Bert Gadgett installed it . . . but he only made one real, detectable slip. We'd never have got him if you hadn't spotted the inconsistency, sir—and thank goodness you did!"

"If I'd listened to you properly in the first place . . ." he began.

"If I'd only paid attention to myself," she replied. "It

simply never occurred to me that anyone could be so . . ."

"The scientific mind," he muttered. "We've kept hearing about it. Mad professor types . . . logical steps that only make sense when you've got every bit of the story. . . . We talked to all those people, and we heard all those different things about Basil Holbrook." He sighed. "It's only when you know what a man's like—and when you know something of his past—that you can be sure who's likely to want to kill him . . . or who he's likely to want to kill. And didn't their old professor say that, of the two of them, Holbrook was far more the type to murder Whatfield than the other way around? Dammit, I even thought something of the sort myself, at one point."

He sighed again. "D'you reckon it *would* have killed Whatfield, being shut away in prison?"

"I don't honestly know, sir. I'm sure it wouldn't have done him any good at all, and I'm prepared to believe it could well have sent him completely round the bend. . . ."

"Which is what that devil Holbrook must've wanted, or he'd never have cooked up such an infernal plan. We kept being told how ruthless and vindictive and cold-blooded and calculating he was—as if we didn't know! We should have remembered all the fuss about young Benson that time, and how he tried to cause trouble. . . ."

Remembering, she nodded. "He certainly could be a—a nasty piece of work."

"I'll wager he even guessed it'd be Whatfield, the new bloke, who'd be asked to take over the Squib project— who'd be put under all that pressure. The poor devil would be halfway round the bend even before . . . anything else happened. Like being accused of knocking off his predecessor. . . ."

"He'd known him a long time, sir. He probably banked on the shock of bumping into him again after all these years sending poor Whatfield hotfoot to the doctor for a higher dose of his antidepressants."

Trewley winced. The memory of how he'd dragged

Philip Whatfield away from the medicine he so badly needed was not a happy one. Stone caught his expression.

"We might have saved his life twice over, sir. What's the betting Holbrook had nobbled Whatfield's pills somehow? Once they're back from the analyst . . ."

Trewley grunted. "Talk about belt and braces—though you could be right, girl. Better safe than sorry. Plotting a thing like that—after twenty years brooding! My God, he must have been mad!"

Former student doctor Stone, of the mothballed medical textbooks, shook her head. "I'd rather call him . . . obsessive, sir. How else would you describe someone determined enough to sit and drink himself calmly into a stupor, knowing the chances were he'd never wake up from it because he'd have been gassed?" She managed a shaky smile. "Sorry, sir, I mean suffocated. Holbrook wasn't certifiably mad . . . but his obsession had grown, over the years. He came to see poor Whatfield as the man who'd ruined his life. His grand aspirations had come to nothing, his hopes for a great scientific career in academic circles had gone phut, his marriage had turned out childless, there was always that lurking suspicion his wife would really have preferred her cousin . . . and when the balance was tipped by the mercury, he decided to take his revenge. . . . "

"You've been reading those psychiatry textbooks again," he said. The sudden shadow in her eyes darkened his own. She'd been right: she should have paid more attention to what she'd read in other textbooks, to what she'd told her chief and then, in the flurry of detection, had allowed to slip to the back of her mind. . . .

But he should have remembered, too. He couldn't blame her: she might be a medical expert, but only when compared with him. It had been a close thing. . . .

"Well," he said, "for whatever reason, Holbrook thought he had a case for taking the chance when it turned up. When *Whatfield* turned up, to work at Allingham Alloys. The last time he'd seen the bloke would've been Sylvia's funeral, most likely. Poor Whatfield. He'll have been in a state, I dare say, over losing someone he'd been close to from a kid. And seeing him upset would've reminded Holbrook of being only second best—and all when he was in a pretty emotional state of his own. For whatever reason," he added, grimly.

"Do you think, sir, that he had been poisoning her? I know they never found anything at the postmortem, but he was a scientist. Untraceable poisons aren't just in books—someone has to invent them."

"And he made damned sure to have her cremated." Trewley frowned. "We'll never be able to prove it after so long—but I'll give you odds he did. Ties off the loose ends rather nicely."

She sipped her tea. "He could easily have substituted an old, blown light bulb for a good one on the stairs—and made that late-night phone call on purpose. . . . If he'd grown tired of the anorexia, the agoraphobia—if he wanted the easy way out, and was too impatient for a slow poisoning to finish her off. . . ."

"And don't forget the money motive. Three-quarters of a million quid, my girl, and no kids to share it with." Then he rubbed his chin, and sighed. "Not that it did him much good. He never spent a penny of it. Doing all his own jobs around the house, living almost like a ruddy hermit . . ."

"And endowing a bursary at his old university, to read his pet subject." She smiled. "You'll tell me it's too much psychiatric guessing, I suppose, sir, but . . . even if Holbrook wasn't able to have children to perpetuate the line, his name won't be forgotten in a hurry, will it? Perhaps he thought of it as poetic justice—I don't know. His mind was going, after all."

"The mercury poisoning." Trewley sighed. "We should've twigged earlier, girl—oh, I'm not blaming you. I could have read the books as well as you. . . ."

She raised an eyebrow. "Perhaps. With all due respect, sir,

not *quite* as well. Not without a medical dictionary, anyway."
She closed her eyes as she began to recite, from a memory
sharpened by recent events, some of the effects of chronic
mercury poisoning. "Nephritis, uraemia, erethism . . .
that's personality disturbance to you, sir." She opened her
eyes, and smiled a rueful smile. "Which, as Dr. Black told
us, can show itself in shyness, irritability, tremor, memory
loss, insomnia . . . hallucinations, or delusions. Psycho-
sis, sir. It was driving him out of his mind. . . ."

He frowned. "Egging him on to dispose of Whatfield
when the poor chap appeared in his life again. . . . Gives
me the creeps just thinking about it!"

"Twenty years," said Stone, yet again. "It seems so
horribly long—though we don't know for certain, of
course, whether he was brooding the whole time, or whether
he only started once the mercury took hold of him. . . ."

"Time enough, whether it's six months or twenty years,
when you're brooding on hell—on how to create it for
somebody else. . . ." He sighed. "And time, with everyone's different ways of thinking and talking about it, has
been the key to this whole affair. We should've checked our
dates a bit more carefully, Stone. We had the general
picture, all right, from several different and independent
sources—and we both thought it wasn't what we needed to
be too particular about, at the—oh." He chuckled. "At the
time!"

"Lucky you thought of it when you did, sir. It saved us
from a charge of wrongful arrest."

"A damned close call, though." Trewley's growl could
not hide the anxiety in his voice. "It was diabolical, the
cunning of the man—disguising himself like that, just to
arouse our suspicions when we spotted that business about
the bill the way we hoped we would. Of course the bloke
with that damned valve looked like Holbrook—he *was*
Holbrook! But he muffled up his face, he talked in a phony
voice, he made all those crazy conditions about the day of

the week—and that's why he bumped into Bob Heath last Tuesday. He wasn't watching where he was going. In too much of a hurry to get home and make sure the valve had been fitted—getting the first part of the plot under way!"

"He wanted us to think it was odd, sir, and we certainly fell for it, with you spotting the bill and the VAT business—but suppose Mrs. Mint hadn't brought it along?"

He rubbed his chin. "Heaven knows. It could've been taken as suicide, or accident—I suppose either would have suited Holbrook, if he couldn't finger Whatfield for it—which he damned well did his best to do. He knew we'd find out about Grantaford, and Sylvia, and the Dramatic Society—he borrowed those blasted papers of Chattisham's, and left them where we'd be sure to spot them—he must have known they were brothers-in-law. Oh, he set up the clues, all right, the devious old basket! And we fell for the lot. . . ."

"I wonder, sir. If we'd missed them, do you think he had anything else planned that would still have pointed us in the direction he wanted us to go? Or rather—poor Mr. Whatfield—I mean misdirection. Do you?"

"Again, heaven knows. I wonder, too . . . though I think that, if we'd missed it altogether, well, it was likely the postmortem would show up the cancer, so we'd take it as suicide and wouldn't blame it on anyone else. Even a bloke with a fixation like Holbrook's couldn't expect the blame to fall separately on *two* lots of innocent people!"

"Perhaps his conscience was troubling him." Stone did not sound as if she believed it. "After all, he was dying, sir, even before he chose to . . . to hurry things along—"

"And we were told he was dying, weren't we! No doubt about that diagnosis. Confirmed by two different doctors, it was—and bad luck for Holbrook's . . ." From where in his subconscious, the superintendent had no idea, but the very word presented itself after only a few moments' thought. ". . . for his damned machinations that Black should tell us he'd gone to him *a couple of months ago* with nasty symptoms he'd *only just noticed*—and that Felix Stowe talked about his patient who'd known for *fifteen months or more* that he had terminal cancer!"

Stone sighed her relief and appreciation for the brilliance of the detection, and for the unnerving closeness of the call. "What a ghastly plot! Poor Whatfield arrives at Allingham Alloys—Holbrook sees him, and up boils all the old resentment—plus a new lot, I imagine, with that rave review Grantaford gave to his rival. The, um, academic mind, sir. Professional jealousy as well as mercury delusions. . . ."

He rolled his eyes. "So Holbrook trots off to Dr. Black to lay the groundwork for an initial suicide theory on our part, then plays the giddy goat laying clues all over the place in the hope we'll see through them. Talk about the tortuous mind—I'll wager the man never really had the start of a cold at all. But he let everyone think he had—including Whatfield. And he even made a point of talking to the poor beggar that same afternoon. . . ."

Stone found herself looking over her shoulder. "Do you have the feeling, sir, he could still be around somewhere, brooding?" She shuddered. "You can made rude remarks about feminine intuition if you like, but . . ."

"Brooding on failure, if he's brooding at all," Trewley said, in accents rather less bracing than she might have expected. "He tried his damnedest to drive poor Whatfield into a nervous breakdown—but we're not playing. We aren't going to lock the poor devil in a cell. . . ."

"It would," she said, slowly, "be a form of mental torture for someone like Whatfield to be shut away in prison. Claustrophobics are some of the most law-abiding citizens on this earth, after all. They daren't get caught doing anything wrong—they're terrified of the punishment. . . ."

They were silent again. Trewley felt a ghost walk over his grave. Even the reassurances of the doctor, hastily hospitalising their (or rather Holbrook's) pathetic victim, could not erase the vision of Whatfield's abject terror.

"Yes," he said, breaking the silence at last. "Holbrook relied on the claustrophobia to panic Whatfield into acting oddly—suspiciously . . . because the circumstantial evidence wasn't really all that good. . . ."

Then he chuckled. "You know, girl, this has been one of the craziest cases I've ever had. I've been wrong almost right the way through. Everybody else said it was suicide. I was the only one who kept insisting it was murder!"

"It was attempted murder, anyhow," came the loyal reply. "The attempted death of a human mind, sir—and look at it this way. If it hadn't been for you thinking things over just in time, he might have got away with it. As I still have the feeling he got away with murder once before, when Sylvia died. . . ."

"Stone, you're a good girl . . . in your way." He never liked her to feel too full of herself. "Thanks." With a sudden burst of energy, the superintendent stretched his large frame across from behind his desk, and thumped his sergeant on the shoulder. "Come on—I'll buy you lunch."

"Buy?" She grinned. "You mean—pop out to the pub? Leave the station *again*? Are you sure you know what you're saying, sir? We've only been back in the place for five minutes—and Sergeant Pleate's still on the warpath, remember."

"I'm hardly likely to forget. Neither is Pleate—that man can bear a grudge for months, my girl, but as there's nothing anyone can do about it I'm not going to let it stand in my way. Come on. . . ." His chuckle sounded forced. "But we'll, er, go out the back way. Just in case."

She hid a smile. "We should be safe, sir—unless he's posted sentinels, that is. I'm afraid we might have tried the back-door dodge once too often for safety. You pointed out yourself, sir, that Sergeant Pleate has a good memory."

"Memory be damned! If I don't choose to use the front door again today, that's my privilege. . . ."

And then he realised what he'd just said.
And he shuddered.
Memory be damned.
All twenty years of it . . .

About the Author

Sarah J. Mason was born in England (Bishop's Stortford) and went to university in Scotland (St. Andrews). She then lived for a year in New Zealand (Rotorua) before returning to settle only twelve miles from where she started. She now lives about twenty miles outside London with a tame welding engineer husband and two (reasonably) tame Schipperke dogs. Under the pseudonym Hamilton Crane, she continues the Miss Seeton series created by the late Heron Carvic.